I0592829

About the Author

M. L. Tompsett is an emerging author of action fantasy paranormal romance. This is M. L.'s third book.

She has been creating worlds to escape to since she was a little girl. Years later, she is still enjoying her writing in her imaginative make-believe worlds with interesting characters, finally moving forward to the big wide scary world of digital and print publishing.

Married to her childhood sweetheart, they live in Victoria, Australia and have two fully grown extremely talented in their own way - sons.

Over the years, she has worn different hats, apart from being a full time caring mum and loving wife. She has also been a secretary, a football manager, basketball coach, manager's assistant, mum taxi, business owner, author and a lover of fine chocolate, okay, nearly any type of chocolate, especially milk chocolate covered liquorice. (YUM)

With her first series, out on the digital shelves — the eBook's are also available in print and paperback.

M. L. Tompsett is excited to see something she has been working on for far too long finally become a reality.

Make sure to check her out on her website and blog or social media.

www.mltompsett.com

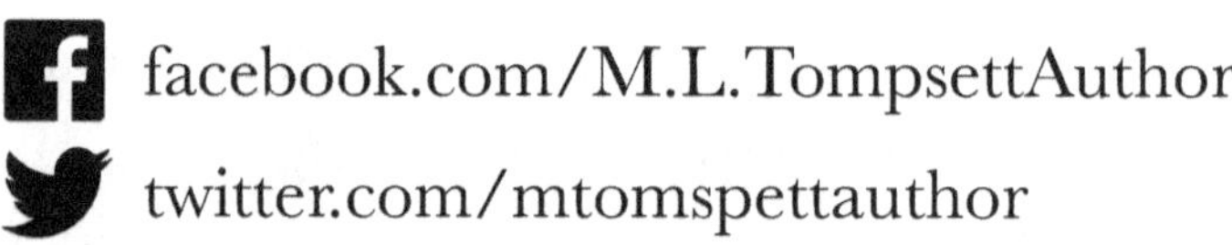

facebook.com/M.L.TompsettAuthor

twitter.com/mtomspettauthor

instagram.com/mltompsett.author

Also by M. L. Tompsett

In the Series

Sex, Lies And Family Secrets

The Guy Next Door - Book one

Dark Surprises - Book two

You Never Know - Book three

It's You - Book four

What You Know - Book five

Sex, Lies And Family Secrets, series. Box set 1-2-3

Other Books

Shifter romance

- Kept in the Dark of Love and Lust

- Kept in the Dark of Lies and Deceit

- TBA shifter billionaire romance

- Paranormal Fantasy eBook *including Witches and Vampires*

YOU NEVER KNOW

Sex, Lies And Family Secrets - Book Three

M. L. TOMPSETT

Tompsett Publishing™

Book Three: **You Never Know** — Sex, Lies And Family Secrets
Copyright © 2018 By M. L. Tompsett™
ISBN: 978-0-9876148-1-0

All rights reserved. No part of this book may be reproduced or transmitted by any person or entity, in any form or by any electronic or mechanical means, including information storage and retrieval systems, without written permission from the author, except for the use of brief quotations in a book review. Any music mentioned, e.g. song titles and/or lyrics contained in this book are the property of the respective songwriters and their copyright owner ·

Cover art designed by **Tompsett Publishing**™ Cover images licensed via Adobe Stock.

This book in the series edition published by **Tompsett Publishing**™ & **M. L. Tompsett Author**™ in Victoria, Australia 2019

Disclaimer: This book is a work of fiction. All characters in this book have no existence outside the imagination of the author and have no relation to anyone bearing the same name or names. Any resemblance to actual individual persons, living or dead, or actual events is purely coincidental. Characters, businesses, places, events and incidents are either the products of the author's imagination or used in a fictitious manner. The town of Darshia doesn't exist but is a fictional location. This book is intended for readers 18 years and older.

New revised edition, 2020. - Larger font - Baskerville.

This book contains - coarse language, adult sexual themes (yes-steamy sex scenes), blood, vampires, witches, young love, violence, nudity, handsome - muscled men. A kick arse independent female - who knows how to shoot and wield a sword, and will do anything to protect the ones she loves. This book is written and edited in Australian/UK English. Which means spelling will be different. If you are offended by any of these themes, this book is not for you.

For my Family always!

To my boys, thank you for allowing me to type and create, including driving you all mad with the world of Alexia and Drake, all things in the world of romance – love you guys.

P.S. - Heads up. Sorry, there will always be more.

This journey has been a long road travelled.

Just think, from the beginning - thanks to a fantastic song by Shakespears Sister, a haunting ballad - named - STAY. My imagination soon created the characters Alexia and Drake and their battle to remain together and a far away kingdom named Darshia. All this drama materialised in my head and here we are, with my first book - THE GUY NEXT DOOR, which continued to Dark Surprises and now to the follow up - You Never Know.

Friends, family and loved ones, you all know who you are, without the generous words of wisdom, encouragement and sounding boards, I would still be typing away and not be publish today. Thank you, for your ears and your reading abilities - and also to you the reader - yes you.

For anyone contemplating, writing for enjoyment, I would encourage you to try it. Grab that pen and paper or computer and have a go. Once you start, you never know where your imagination might take you. You can do anything you put your mind to. Travel to places only you can see, until you introduce them to everyone in your fantastic and creative words. Never allow someone to dictate, 'you can never do something you enjoy.'

Your little typist with a wicked imagination of fiction paranormal fantasy romance.

— M. L. Tompsett

You Never Know

Leaving her family behind, and escaping her future, Alex Smithlyn attempts to live amongst the humans and away from Dark Ones and her destiny.

Years later, Alex is recruited by Dillion Sparks, the head of *The Corporation*. Alex and Branx Rayden work as partners at *The Corporation*, in the city - SFD or the Special Forces Department. Capturing and eliminating the evils of this world, until someone close to our young couple decided Alex is next on the list for extermination.

The past catches up to Alex while using her hidden abilities. She will require her family's help more than ever, to keep her and Branx safe.

As a mysterious man appears, who is he? But, more importantly why did he want to capture Alex? Secrets are revealed, shattering one family's love and trust.

Alex must survive if she is to become the next Queen of Darshia.

Who said the life of a Princess is ever easy?

Secrets to be kept and lies are revealed.

A love, which cannot be broken and only becomes stronger.

Discovering family are not whom they seem, and death is far too easy to follow.

Fighting the enemy even when they are the people you once trusted and believed in.

Protect the ones you love, at all costs.

For tomorrow may never arrive.

— M. L. TOMPSETT

Chapter One
ALEX

"ALLEY, WE SHOULDN'T BE DOING THIS," I whisper.

"We will be fine, Alex. Stop worrying," Alley annoyingly whispers back.

Looking at the massive, closed, solid timber doors, I expected it to fly open at any second. My anxiety increases as my heart races, and knocks against my ribs.

I cannot believe my older sister, Alley, who is only three months away from turning eighteen, can persuade me to sneak up to our mother's office doorway to eavesdrop on our parents' conversation.

A conversation regarding *yours truly*. Yep, little, innocent me. Crap. I hope I am not in trouble. Maybe Alley is right. Our parents might be speaking about me leaving Darshia and travelling to their old hometown to go to school. The hometown where our loving grandparents still live, amongst the humans.

With another shake of my head — *Oh, man. What were we thinking?*

I do not feel comfortable about this. My darling sister loves to sneak around our mother's royal castle. As she keeps reminding me — *'how else are we going to learn what is happening around here? It's not like anyone keeps us updated.'*

I think we just about know all the hidden passageways throughout the castle by now. Apart from what our mother who is the Queen of Darshia, has shown us including the secret Queen chamber. I think Alley and I have come across a few other areas our mother did not know about, and we are not going to mention it to her either.

My irrational rises when I notice the lack of royal security — they are late patrolling the area. The stupid guards should have walked by us by now.

I focus back on the door and continue to use my born witch powers keeping us invisible, along with the aid of the magically charmed necklace my Aunt Lucy assisted me in creating a few months back. Bless her beautiful, cheeky soul.

A unique magical charm necklace to enhance my magical powers. Also at this very minute, preventing our parents or anyone else from detecting us out in the hallway.

When I wear the charm it also has the ability to keep other Paranormal Entities from discovering I am a *Dark One with magical powers.*

Well, I will be a full *Dark One* in less than a year. You can say I am a *Dark One* in training, as well as a witch with some freaky abilities.

In the last few weeks, I mistakenly found myself capable of becoming invisible. Bloody fantastic, when I realised no other *Dark Ones* were able to detect me — even better.

Right, this minute, I am in the process of shielding both my sister and myself. Using my new ability of invisibility to protect the pair of us. Well, I hope for both our sakes we are invisible and at the same time, allowing the two of us the ability to listen to our parents secretly.

Look out world, Alex is here, the next powerful witch in training!

My silent laugh fills my head with an internal head shake. *OMG. How did I allow myself to go along with Alley?* We are going to find ourselves in a big pile of trouble if we are caught.

Now, I am not going to let it slip to Alley, but this is a fantastic experience. Otherwise, I will never hear the end of it as we stand here spying on our parents.

Even our parents do not know I am capable of this invisibility thing and this little piece of information is going to stay that way. I also persuaded Alley, not to mention anything to our other two siblings, Alley's twin and my older brother Damien, and our younger brother Dane.

The only thing, which we can never remove from our minds, is our brother, a very naked Damien. My belly still rolls, at that vision I would rather forget.

We followed him recently, wondering why he was so secretive, sneak off out of the castle and sneaking back inside about two weeks ago. Only to find out, our mysterious brother has found his *soul mate*. Well, so he says anyway.

He snuck out and met up with his latest girlfriend. Alley and I became trapped in the same room with the pair of them. Let me just say, witnessing our brother having sex, might have scarred me for life.

There are just some things you never need to witness, and that is one of them. With a shudder, I force some of the rising bile back down my throat with a hard swallow.

The day our brother lost his virginity to his girlfriend… Blah. Another shudder rakes my body just with the thought of it, and I just hope this girlfriend of Damien's is who she makes out to be. Sadly, I have a bad feeling about her, and Alley agrees with me. There is something about this girl.

We worry because Damien is the first-born Prince of Darshia of the Royal Blue dynasty, not to mention our family is wealthy. This might be the real reason why this girl is seducing Damien, fooling him into thinking there is more to their relationship than just the sex. To me, she is just a money hungry, power-seeking bitch. Thus, the reason why I am keeping my new talents hidden from everyone.

It is bad enough Alley, and I are already starting to develop the thirst for blood. Being *Dark Ones*, we knew the day was coming; we only hoped it would not have started for at least another year. As *Dark Ones* are born human, some can still exhibit *Dark One* qualities before they turn into a full *Dark One* at the age of eighteen.

We spoke with our mother not that long ago, and she said the same thing happened to her at our age, with the craving for our father's blood, on her lips. However, Mum had been under the impression, with Dad encouraging her to try a new delicacy was because our father had been consuming her blood at the time, and this she thought had been the reason and not her turning into a *Dark One*.

Until our mother had fallen pregnant with Alley and Damien just before her eighteenth birthday, Mum never knew *Dark Ones* existed. She thought vampires were some type of myth. But as it turned out, *Dark Ones* are part of our family history, not actual vampires.

Boy, did Mum learn the hard way, and fast, especially when she started sprouting two sharp pointy teeth. Now look at her, the Queen of *Dark Ones* and rules her ancestral family home, which is hidden away from the human realm in a secret place named Darshia. All the while, our mother still looks like she is the age of an eighteen-year-old.

I look back down the corridor, waiting for

our mother's security to show up. This is strange; I would have thought at least one of the security guards would have walked past her door by now. Hmm. I think I might have a little chat with the Head of Security, my mother's trusted friend, Riley.

Feeling an elbow to my side, Alley catches my attention. "Pay attention, Alex. Mum and Dad are talking about you," she hisses, quietly.

Giving her a brief nod, I focus on our parents' voices, hearing our mother speak.

"Drake, you know we have come to an understanding when Alley is twenty-five, she will become the next Queen of Darshia. And if for some unknown reason Alley does not, then Alex will become the next Queen instead. Either way, both girls know one of them will be the next Queen. Until then, I will continue to Rule. We made sure both girls gained all the relevant knowledge and information there is, including negotiations, and not to mention fighting skills in all areas. We have treated both girls with the same respect, and not favouring one over the other."

Alley and I look at one another, smile at the same time, shrug our shoulders, shake our heads, and roll our eyes, without laughing. Good old Mum. We love her to bits, but we would prefer for her to remain Queen a little longer. Usually, it all happens when the princess turns eighteen, but mother put a stop to that and changed the rules. Including all the changes, making Darshia prosper and thrive towards a new modern society and a better future.

Our precious mother would like both Alley and myself to have a better education than she did. As our mother had just barely completed high school before taking over the new role of Queen.

"Yes. Yes, Alexia. We have treated all our children the same," our father replies, "but, why does Alex want to go to our old school? Amongst the humans?"

"Drake, you sound as if you have spent far too much time away from the human lifestyle. Alex would like to have the chance to live away from *Dark Ones* and other Paranormal Entities for a year or two. Personally, I think it will be good for her."

I nod my head in agreement.

"I just don't know, Alexia. What about her safety?"

Alley and I both look at one another and

roll our eyes. Geez. He acts like we are still little kids.

"Drake, we will make sure Alex has a couple of our trusted bodyguards with her. This time, one of them will be female."

"It looks like you have thought of everything," my father says grumpily.

"No Drake. Not everything. I thought I would leave the security and where Alex lives up to you."

Alley's eyes go wide. Uh-oh, our overprotective father is in charge of my security. Great. I won't be able to have any fun.

"What? You think Alex should live in our house, next door to your parent's home," my father says in a shocked voice.

Yes, I might have some fun. I begin to smile.

A small victory, finally, and some freedom — I do an internal happy dance.

My mother replies, "Yes, she should. However, Alex will still require guards and personal bodyguards. And, that Mr Smithlyn, is where you also come in. You have assisted with Riley through the years. You know the training; you know the men and women who have trained. Plus, my parents can act as her guardians for school. As we still look far too young to be having teenagers her age."

Alley gives me the *let's go* look. I shake my head, mouthing, '*Not yet.*'

I turn my ear towards the door to continue listening.

"Okay, Alexia. With all our talking, I think I have calmed down enough. Do you really think Alex, will be okay?"

My mother's voice starts to change a little. *Why is her voice changing pitch?*

"Yes, Drake. Alex will be fine. I feel it will be good for her to live in the human world. She needs it. Her magic is progressing, and her lessons will continue. Alex has her head on her shoulders, Drake. She has read as many books as she could place her hands on; preparing herself as anyone could, regarding her magic."

"Alexia, I just worry. That is all. I will miss her."

"Oh, Drake. We all will miss her. You can easily go and visit Alex, any time. It is not as if she is going overseas. Alex will only be five minutes away via the portal, at our house or we might have her stay with my parents. However, the way Alex is maturing before our eyes, I think our little rebelling daughter will prefer to live in our house."

Relief fills me, knowing my mother is winning the battle to allow me to go to school amongst the humans.

In a quiet voice, Alley whispers to me, "Come on Alex. We better go."

Scrunching my face, I frown at Alley, shooting her a wry look. Giving my head a slight shake, I turn my ear once again towards the door. Now having missed some of their conversations.

"No. I never did find out, but it is time we did. Whatever Ms Lexington is, it is going to be interesting. I think it is time we allow our little girl to grow. You never know, Alex might find her *soul mate*."

Wow. Feeling shocked, I glance to Alley and whisper, "Mum thinks I might find my *soul mate* out in the human world."

With a nod of her head, Alley replies quietly, "Of course you will find your *soul mate*. We have already worked out; he is not here in Darshia."

Alley and I have already looked into all the eligible males in Darshia, and no Darshia male is our *soul mate*. We both know, our *soul mate*'s will be beyond the boundaries of

Darshia and somewhere out in the human realm.

"Looks like I will be leaving Darshia and going to school amongst the humans," I happily say, just about jumping up and down with excitement.

Turning our heads, we start to hear strange noises coming from within my mother's office. I look towards Alley. With our hands covering our mouths, and our eyes nearly bulging out of our heads.

Oh, no. Our parents are kissing.

Well maybe, more than kissing, by the sounds coming from within the office. Both Alley and I start to shake our heads, while our faces screw up with the gross sounds that penetrate our ears.

Ew, yuck. Our parents are having sex. Is there something in the water? First our brother and now our parents. With my body shuddering with horrible visions of a naked Damien, I think it is time to get out of here.

Chapter Two

ALEX

BREATHE ALEX.

Come on girl, you can do this.

Okay, now. Another step, another breath, step again.

Don't forget to speak, walk and think; I can do this, after all, I am a Princess of Darshia, and my mother is walking right beside me.

What was I thinking?

Here I am, walking with my mother and Grandmother, freaking out, in my parent's old human high school. Okay, the new version.

While my parents were students here, the old school was blown up. All I can think of is what happens if any of Mum's former teachers are still here and they recognise her? She still looks the same as she did back then. My mother can be thoughtless at times.

'Alex, I can hear your thoughts. Now stop it. I am safe. There are no old teachers here anymore. Only Ms Lexington is in the office, and she is not human, so she does not count.'

Huh? Ms Lexington? I do not remember Grandmother discussing a Ms Lexington. Great, Mum is listening to my thoughts.

Why does she do that? Ever heard of privacy? This mind talk stuff might be handy, but until I turn into a full *Dark One*, I can only use it to speak to other family members who are full *Dark Ones*. It is not fair, I mentally pout. My mother's voice brings my attention back to the present.

'Alex, maybe if you practised your lessons in mind control, you would be able to protect your mind. As for Ms Lexington, she was the school secretary when I was a student here. She has since married and is the new principal. Also her name is now Blacksford. Mrs Blacksford to you!'

Ah. Now I know whom Mum is speaking of.

'Mum, why are you here? Grandmother and I can handle all this new school stuff.'

'Alex, you are my daughter, it is my duty to be here. I will not sit back while you attend your first day here, amongst the humans. If anyone should ask, I am your cousin. If anyone asks questions, just say, 'I was named after your mother and casually change the subject.'

'Yes, Mother,' I reply in an annoyed tone.

'Don't be smart, Alex, it does not become you.'

Shit. I think I had better start blocking Mum from my thoughts.

'Alex, watch your language. Good luck with blocking me, Ms young one.'

Grrr. Damn. Parents. Hearing Mum's laugh in my head is annoying.

'Alex, watch your tone.'

'*Yes, Mother,*' I grumpily protest.

Just then, I start to feel something different in the air.

Something...

Hmm. I do not know if I want to hold it, eat it, or love it? My mouth begins to water, and my breasts start to feel different, as my nipples begin to turn to hard points. I had hoped with each step I had taken my lacy bra might be the answer to this erotic feeling surrounding my body, causing this feeling of, want, touch and sex.

Whoa there...where did sex come into this? With an internal groan, my nipples feel rock hard and extremely sensitive against the lace fabric surrounding and caressing my tender and aching breasts. What is happening? Somehow, I do not think the lacy friction is enough to cause these strange feelings?

My eyes quickly dart around the hallway and then towards the office area, trying to find the cause of my body's strange behaviour. Could someone be using magic? Nah. My necklace should prevent anyone from casting any magic over me. What is this peculiar feeling then? Until my eager eyes land on a tall, nicely built guy.

With a lift of my eyebrow, I admire the scene in front of me.

Hot damn. And the view from behind is not too bad, if I may say so. All I need is for this male piece of deliciousness to slowly turn around and show me the rest of the merchandise.

Hot double damn.

Drinking in the gorgeous view in front of me, my sister comes to mind. Alley will be spewing missing out on this view, wishing she had come with me instead. I start to laugh in my head at my good fortune.

Missing a step in the process of my mental ramblings, then righting myself instantly before anyone notices. I shake my head, how do I concentrate when all my eyes want to do is drink in this tall, dark, lip-smacking specimen? Wow, if his pants are any indication, Mr Sexy-a-licious arse fills the denim fabric out nicely and his t-shirt, oh my.

The need to fan myself increases, as my internal body heats up and ready to combust into sexual flames. I envy the fabric straining to hold in his hard ripped muscles and broad shoulders if only my warm moist tongue can run around those delicious muscles.

Visions of Mr Sex-a-licious naked and spread out as my own personal banquet. Hmm-mmm. The urge to rub my thighs together increases.

Oh, my...slowly he turns enough for my brain to acknowledge, the sight before me — is an artist dream of sculpture paradise… wow. OMG — a gorgeous male, is standing not far from where we have to go.

If he is a student here, I think I am going to love attending this school, providing I can see him every day. With another swipe over my bottom lip, my moist tongue darts out before my teeth bite into my lip.

Uh-oh. I feel my mother's gaze on me. Bugger, now this is embarrassment plus. Not noticing in time, my mother has just witnessed my reaction to my lip biting, mouth drooling behaviour over a hot stud with ripped muscle physique.

Oh, geez. More than just embarrassing, as I feel my face heating up. When I look back up along the tantalising male body of this sexy stranger, only to find, a pair of smoking hot bedroom eyes staring right back at me. Uh-oh.

Can the ground open up and swallow me now?

Finding I am not able to look away, I continue to drink the vision of the sculptured godliness up. Oh, my, and that smile. I bet Mr Sex-a-licious has all the female population wrapped around his little finger. Hmm, I wonder what his fingers are capable of?

Geez, it is getting hot in here. Did someone turn the heat up? Someone must have, as I sense my body heating up and ready to go up in flames, under the penetrating gaze of his sexy bedroom eyes. Somehow, I would not be permitted to remove my restricting clothing to cool down.

Managing to blink, breaking the heated connection with this sexy stranger.

My thoughts fly to my mother, feeling frustrated. *'Ah, Mum. As you can see, the human boy over there is looking at me. What do I do?'*

Only to hear Mum laugh at my predicament. Crap. Now, what am I going to do? *'Mother, can you help me out here?'*

'Oh, my baby girl. Alright, first thing Alex, try to calm down. Has any other boy back in Darshia,

ever affected you like this before? Because I have never witnessed either you or Alley behave in such a manner.'

'No mother, this guy is the first. Why. What is going on?'

'Hmm. If I did not know any better, I think this human might—'

Before Mum can finish her sentence, a woman with high-heeled shoes and a big bright smile interrupts us. Walking straight up to my mother and engulfing her in a big hug.

What the...? Who is this person? My eyes dart around for the magically hidden, Riley, my mother's personal security guard and friend. Shouldn't he be ripping this person away from my mother right now?

'It is okay, Alex. This woman is Mrs Blacksford, and she is the school Principal,' my mother says with a laugh and tightly hugs the strange woman back.

I start to glance around the hall until I notice the hunky guy again. Oh, my. He is still looking at me. I quickly look away and glance back towards my mother, and hope the gorgeous guy did not notice me staring at him.

I continue to watch Mum and how she casually speaks with the school Principal while showing off her wedding rings. Weird. Why would they be discussing Mums wedding rings of all things?

I casually glance back towards the gorgeous muscle guy. As soon as my eyes meet his, we both smile at one another. Busted. I think my cheeks just turned red. Why do I feel so shy all of a sudden?

Oh, my word. I think I am about to melt into a puddle on the floor. Why am I having such strong feelings for the human? All I want is his body wrapped around mine, keeping me safe, warm and loved.

Confusion hits me square in the face when I realise the direction my thoughts are heading, uh-oh.

Is this love?

Nah — no way.

This lovey-dovey stuff and weird feelings about a boy, is not like me, where are these thoughts coming from?

Chapter Three

ALEX

WHILE DAYDREAMING ABOUT THE HUNK OF sexy maleness or do I just call him Mr Sex-a-licious, whichever name, the scrumptious guy out in the corridor — my mother somehow managed to walk me into the Principal's office. Taking me away from the hard ripped muscle Mr Sex-a-licious before me, leaving me feeling bereft of this person's presence. My body screams in annoyance along with an ache in my chest.

Nooo. I do not want to leave Mr Sex-a-licious, take me back to him.

With a click of the door, my attention is brought back to the present and the strange woman before me. Who is this woman? All

Mum mentioned is this woman is not human. Great information Mum! NOT.

Even I can work that part out for myself, and it had been one of the first things I sensed. She has magic and something else. I will have to think about this. Alrighty then, let's get this show on the road. I can see Grandmother, Mum and what was her name? Oh yeah, Mrs Blacksford are now speaking about me.

Great, not feeling embarrassed at all.

What seemed like half an hour later, or less, I stand and shake Mrs Blacksford's hand. Pulling my hand away; my fingers tingle from her touch; our eyes meet in surprise. Hmm. Interesting…

This stranger, who just happens to be my new school Principal, definitely has some form of magic. I will have to discuss this with my Aunt Lucy and get her opinion on the situation.

With her eyes still focused on mine, Mrs Blacksford says, "It has been a pleasure meeting you today, Alex. I hope you will like our school. Your mother has shown me your school files, including your school reports."

With a pause, Mrs Blacksford turns her head back to my mother before facing me with a smile. "Usually, you would be placed in grade eleven, but as your grades and attitude far exceed that of the average year eleven student, and the written test you completed and excelled in answering, I am allowing you to start the year off with our seniors who are completing their final year. Congratulations Alex. You are now a grade twelve student."

Slowly, I nod in agreement. Wow. I think I am in shock, me a year twelve student. With reality starting to hit me and Mrs Blacksford words penetrating into my slow brain… Oh, my. I am officially a senior. Me. No more being a year behind Alley and Damien; instead, I will be completing school at the same time.

Wow, feeling pretty good about myself while I start a celebratory dance in my head. Who knew attending a human school would hold such benefits for me?

Go me. Go Alex. Go Me. Go…

Feeling everyone's eyes on me, oops. Great, I have just been caught wool-gathering, to a happy dance. With a guilty smile and a shrug of my shoulders, I wait to see if Mum will fill me in on the missing information I have just missed. Nah, nothing. Great thanks, Mum.

I quickly reply, "Wow. Thank you. It has been a pleasure meeting you, Mrs Blacksford. I only hope I can be an asset to your school. Now, for my subjects…"

I trail off and look towards Mum, hoping she will answer the missing information.

Within minutes, we are walking out of the Principal's office and towards the front desk. The dull pain in my chest, I noticed earlier seems to be easing off, which is a relief; I wonder what had set it off. Surely, that gorgeous boy had nothing to do with it, especially when he seemed to be human.

With a new sensation rushing through my system, my heart rate begins to speed up. What is going on? Looking up and around me, until my eyes focus back on the scrumptious male.

Oh, my goddess. That male of hunkville, Mr Sex-a-licious himself is still standing at the front office.

I wonder who he is?

I'm so focused on the hunkville in front of me, I did not hear Principal Blacksford begin to speak. By the time I acknowledge Principle Blacksford, her voice becomes background noise, and my focus remains on the sexy guy.

The scrumptious lickable panty-wetting specimen in front of me.

Shit. What did Mrs Blacksford just say?

Oh crap, she is introducing us to the hunkville. Oh, no I just missed this sexy hunkville's name.

'Mum,' I scream out with my mind, hoping my mother has heard my plea and will fill in the blanks for me.

'Alex, settle down and take a breath, will you. The young man's name is Branx. Branx Rayden and he is a senior here at the school.'

'Really?'

I continue to drink this delicious specimen in, causing my body to behave strangely. I just hope no one has noticed my nipples standing erect because they feel like they are going to rip through my bra any second.

With another sexy, megawatt, panty-melting smile from Branx, causing my heart to flutter and my lower belly to tingle... my brain refuses to function.

Focus — Alex.

Yep, I am going to like being here, with Branx to keep me company.

Yes, indeed.

With my lips lifting up into a big smile, I am going to enjoy attending this new school.

Chapter Four

WELL, HELLO AND HOLY SHIT.

With the movement behind my zipper, it did not take long for my dick to become alert. Somehow, it knows when the perfect female wanders into his territory. *'Whoa boy, we have to learn her name first.'*

I absorb her features, her beauty, everything I can see, I instantly memorise each and every one of them.

Who is this beautiful girl walking towards me? I will have to get her number. I think this girl is the woman of my dreams and the one I will one day marry.

Oh, shit. Did I just think — *Marriage?* With a shake of my head, *what am I thinking?*

This sexy girl is playing havoc with my hormones and brain.

Alrighty, I'd better find out why I am here at the office because I do not have time to waste. Especially now when there is new blood arriving at the school.

Crap, my ex is going to be pissed. Jezzy was hoping for the two of us to either get back together again or hook up after school. Why did I give in and start having sex with her last term? The female is trying to stick to me like glue. Geez balls, if I did not know any better, I would think she is trying to get herself pregnant and trap me into marrying her or something.

Thanks, to all that is holy, I had enough common sense always to use condoms and disposed of them myself. No way in hell, would I ever tie myself to that girl. Jezzy is driving me crazy with her attitude and drama shit. Why can't she just grow up and act like a mature female? Whichever way it is, Jezzy is way out of luck. Especially when this brand new beauty has arrived before me, whoever she is, she will be mine.

Looking back at Mrs Lolki, sitting back behind her reception desk, I give her my trademark smile. The poor woman has never been able to resist my smile or charm.

The woman should be ashamed of herself, though. I have seen the way she looks at me, undressing me with her eyes. Oh, yes, this woman has had many fantasies featuring me. I can sense her thoughts most of the time when I am near her and frankly, it is disturbing and disgusting. Even my dick is trying to hide and, that is saying something.

With my hand I casually pull on my t-shirt, making sure to cover myself blocking her view. I just have to make sure I never go behind that reception desk by myself with the disturbed woman.

Hiding my disgust, I continue to smile, while I wait for the woman to get over her gross sex dream, and finally speak with me.

Hearing a shuddered sigh leave her old woman lips, and with a skin-crawling purr, Mrs Lolki finally says, "Why, hello young, Branx. Thank you for coming this morning."

Ah, really. I think by the flushed look on Mrs Lolki's heavily made up and wrinkled face, she is the one who has just come. Eww. Giving my head an internal shake, as I just spewed a little in my mouth.

"The Principal will be here in a moment.

We have a new student starting today, and Mrs Blacksford would like you to show the student around the school."

Hmm. I wonder if the beauty behind me is the new student. If it is, Mrs Blacksford has just made my day and most likely my year. Okay, let's play dumb — first question.

"Mrs Lolki, are we receiving another male student to play on our football team this year," I say with as much innocence.

With a shake of her head, Mrs Lolki replies, "Sadly, no."

With another internal body shudder ripping through me; lucky it will not be another male student, safe from Mrs Lolki's demented sick thoughts. Imagine if she tried to make her perverted dreams and fantasies real… Oh no. I can feel the vomit rise along my throat, I force myself to swallow it back down and exaggerate my lips to form a smile.

"But first, I will need you to look at this schedule, Branx; it belongs to the new student. You will be required to show her the ropes, as they say. She is in most of your classes, which is why Mrs Blacksford selected you, as well as your polite manners towards the other students, of course."

Yes, of course, *I am always polite*. I think while I do a mental eye roll.

Oh, man. I need to get out of here. This woman is starting to make my skin crawl. Placing the printed schedule on top of the counter, I quickly study the list, the only class different to mine is for sport. It looks like our new student is into martial arts. Hmm. Interesting.

At least we will both be having sport at the same time, just different activities. Hmm. I wonder if I can change my football class to martial arts instead, I was thinking of dropping football anyway; thus escaping Jezzy and the other cheerleaders.

It's not like I will be playing football when I am in college, I am determined to be like the men who work with my mother. Working in law enforcement, but a special type of enforcement taking down those strange and hideous creatures like men. With the martial arts class requesting new students, this will give me the perfect excuse to practice my skills and stay close to the unique beauty. Brilliant.

"Ah, Mrs Lolki," I slowly reach for the printed schedule, even though I keep my eyes focused on Mrs Lolki, "I am glad you brought up the topic of subjects. You see, I was on my way to see you regarding my P.E. class."

With a lift of her eyebrow, Mrs Lolki worriedly asks, "Oh. Is everything, alright?"

With my smile forced into place, I reply, "Yes. It is just…if there might be a possibility to change to another activity, say for example the martial arts class. You see, my loving mother has been on my back, wanting me to change my football class to something more…beneficial this year."

Keeping her focus on my flexing muscles; to confuse her enough to change my class subject without any questions, if only Mrs Lolki knew, how quickly she can be manipulated.

With her gleaming beady eyes drinking my muscled physique in once again, making my body start to do another internal shudder, until her eyes land on my face, giving me her scary smile. Well, scary to me, most likely lovely to other people.

"Hmm. You would like to change to what…martial arts, you say." Mrs Lolki's eyes rove over my shoulders and chest.

"Hm, is this what you want to do, Branx?"

Grrrr. I force my smile to remain on my face, by the sounds of Mrs Lolki's voice, is she trying to sound sexy, her voice will never pull off a sexy purr. The only thing it is capable of pulling off is the impression of fingernails down a chalkboard. Oh, boy, another internal shudder rakes my body.

Come on Branx, keep the pretence up, you nearly have her.

Keep smiling.

"Yes, ma'am. My mother and I would be pleased if you can arrange the switch before classes start today," I say with a smile.

With a bigger smile, Mrs Lolki replies, "I don't see why not. With you attending, this will make the numbers of students even. Yes, I think this will work. Okay, just give me a minute to bring up your file, and I will change you over right now."

Wow. Now that was far too easy. Mrs Lolki begins to pronounces my full name, I do not think she realises she is speaking out loud, "Mr. B. R. A. N. X. R. A. Y. D. E. N. Branx Rayden."

"Thank you, Mrs Lolki. That is terrific."

I wait a minute or so before turning around, while Mrs Lolki continues to tap away over the keys of the keyboard, listening to each annoying press of the plastic. I lean against the reception counter, feeling the hard bite of it press into my hip. It is not long before that strange sensation starts once again in the middle of my chest.

With my thoughts wondering what is happening to me, I glance up, and the beautiful girl who was here earlier is back. I wonder who she is? Hmm.

I start to daydream about her when Mrs Lolki's voice breaks into my fantasy, "Ah, here is the new student now. Hmm. I thought we were only to have one new student, not two?"

Two? With a quick turn of my head my eyes glance at the two other women, well one of them might be another student, she seems young enough, even though I did notice she is sporting wedding rings. She's not bad looking, even though it looks like she is taken, something about her — I shake my head. Nah, she is not my type.

I continue my visual of the three until my eyes meet with the most beautiful set of brown eyes I have ever seen.

Looking into a set of cinnamon eyes, is that blue? My brain slowly registers she has a blue ring around the amazing shade of cinnamon brown. Hmm, interesting. However, then, as I survey the other girl and the older woman, I notice they all have the same colour blue sitting around their eyes. Ha, must be a family trait or something.

Looking back on the beautiful girl again our eyes meet, as we smile at one another a surge of lust fills me.

Oh, geez balls, my dick is waking up again. He is becoming a little embarrassing as he starts to stand to attention and knocking against my zipper.

My beautiful visual disappears by a dark figure, I blink and squeeze my eyes a couple of times and refocus only to realise Mrs Blacksford is approaching me with her friendly smiling face, and her trademark high heels, click-clacking along the hard flooring.

"Branx, thank you for meeting us here. Mrs Lolki, hopefully, has informed you why I require your assistance." Mrs Blacksford eyes dart from Mrs Lolki and back to mine, trying to gauge if I am up on the task they have set for me.

Lifting my eyebrow, I smile at her and give a slight nod. My eyes then move and land on the captivating beauty before me.

Holy shit, I think I am not the only one who is feeling the effect of the chemistry between us, especially when I try to stay focused on Ms beautiful eyes glowing face.

Even though I can see Ms beauty's tits in my field vision and holy shit, her nipples have turned hard. Oh geez balls, my dick is wanting out, now. Thank fuck I managed to pull my t-shirt free of my jeans earlier, to cover it.

Whoa, boy. Feeling him pulse and push against my zipper, the warm metal starting to bite into my eager flesh. *'Don't forget we still do not know who she is, and we still do not know this beauty's name.'*

Chapter Five

WITH MY HAND REACHING OUT, I OFFER TO shake the small, beautiful hand of Alex. Seriously. Who would give their daughter the male name of Alex? The strange thing is, the name does suit her, in some peculiar way.

Now… For the touching and handshaking, as I look up at the beautiful face in front of me.

Before I know it, I am held hostage by her beautiful eyes, trapped within her unique depths; everything else disappears around us. The powerful hold this girl now has over me, for the first time in my life, I want to remain trapped right here with her, as if we are the only two people here in the corridor.

A sensation of little erotic electric currents zipping between our fingers and hands startles me. Oh, geez balls what a feeling and we have not even touched completely yet. The sensation increases to a slight surge of power between our hands, just as our skin begins to touch.

Oh, wow. I do not know if I will be able to stand here for much longer and hide my growing erection. An erection which is willing to break through the denim of my jeans and bust through the zip it is straining against to reach her. I wonder if Alex can also feeling these erotic sensations because I am having trouble staying upright.

A throat clears beside me, reminding my brain we are standing here in front of other people watching us. Oh, wow, whatever this feeling, I want more of it. Just then, I notice the other girl, what was her name? Alexia. The married cousin, and here for moral support to Alex on her first day at a new school.

I notice the twitch of Alexia's lips as her eyes make their way down to my bulging pants. Oh, my geez balls. Talk about embarrassing. I just hope the grandmother does not notice. Shit, my eyes dart towards the grandmother — Mrs Steele, and sure enough, her eyes grow wide at my predicament. Oh, shit.

No. Not embarrassing at all, I think sarcastically.

Shit.

With our hands firmly embraced in one another, mixed sensations of desire, want, need, and trust, zip through our touch. I do not know, if I ever want to release her hand, again.

Then the most gentle voice I have ever heard fills my ears, nearly sending me to my knees to worship the ground she walks on.

Holy shit, what is happening to me? I have never behaved like this before. If my mother were here, she would flip and ground me for a month.

Shit. Shit. Shit.

Get a grip on yourself Branx, time to be a man and grow a pair of hard balls and stop allowing Mr Dick to run our lives.

"Hello, Branx. It is a pleasure to meet you."

I think my brain has stopped. I hope I don't have drool running down my chin, because of this girl… Wow. "You must be busy already; there is no pressure. I do not want to take up your time, unnecessarily… If you are not able to show me around, I should be okay."

Oh, my geez ball. I think I have fallen in love and gone to heaven. That voice, those eyes.

Shit, she is waiting for a reply. Come on Branx get a grip man. I better answer before this beautiful morsel thinks I am a complete moron.

Presenting her with another megawatt smile, I reply, "Oh no, Alex. The pleasure is all mine. And I am happy to show you around. As it appears, we have all the same subjects. So I am afraid to inform you, you are stuck with me for a while. Well, until you feel comfortable around the school, that is," now I do sound like a moron.

I wonder if she has noticed we have not released one another's hands yet.

A loud noise sounds around us. Hearing the warning bell, that is our cue to leave and head for our first class. Damn it. Now I will have to release her hand. I have to make sure the other guys receive the hint to back off. Alex is mine, and I do not share.

Chapter Six
ALEX

WOW…WHAT AN EXPERIENCE. M**Y** FIRST WEEK has turned out to be great amongst all these humans. I had been apprehensive at first being surrounded by so many humans in one place. However, with Branx by my side, I am adjusting quite well. I was amazed to discover other Entities here at the school, detecting a few Paranormal Entities amongst my senior year level a little unnerving, not realising just how many of these creatures really do live amongst humans undetected.

Each time I would walk past one of them in the corridors, we would give one another a slight nod in acknowledgement and then keep moving. I wonder what Entity I come across to them?

Originally my Aunt Lucy encouraged me to wear one of her many quartz Chakra stone pendants, full of her special magic — instead I had decided on something a little more permanent.

Thank goodness for my Aunt Lucy, who was able to assist me with my tattoo of a rune on the inside my wrist — A little symbol of a leaf.

Using a spell, we cast and performed both a charm and ward spell in one. A magical ward to protect me from anyone from detecting the type of Entity I really am, all they would know is I am not human.

Fingers crossed, the other part of the spell we cast is for the protection against evil, including demons, and nasty type things. When we created the magical spell for the rune, we also combined with the ink my blood to create a powerful ward inside the rune.

When I start to close my locker, I feel the presence of a nasty piece of trash, coming up behind me. This chick has been nothing but trouble for me all week.

With a quick sidestep and a flick of my wrist, my locker door slam shut, catching the girl in the face. The same girl who is sending out nasty, evil vibes towards me.

So far, she seems human, but whoever the hell she is, she is a real bitch. Word around the school, she used to go steady with Branx, but he ended things with her last term, just before the school holidays. However, this chick Jezzy does not want their relationship to end, pity she refused the memo regarding Branx and me.

With a loud whack, Jezzy hits my locker door. Ha. She was not expecting me to move so quickly. The stupid bitch thought she would be able to slam my body into the metal lockers. What is her problem?

Just as I start to move and spin around, I let out an oomph as my body slams into a hard muscle chest. Strong arms are instantly surrounding me keeping me from falling. As I look up, my breath catches in my throat as I look straight into a set of sexy bedroom eyes.

Branx.

My insides are instantly turning to mush, and my knees turn to jelly. We both smile at one another before I realise Branx is speaking to me when I feel the brush of his lips against my earlobe.

"Are you all right?" Branx whispers, sending goosebumps along my body.

When my mind finally catches up, blinking a couple of times to clear my head, I finally reply, "I think so; this girl nearly collided with me, narrowly avoiding hitting me with her body. Lucky I moved when I did."

With another smile, Branx replies, "Lucky you did, you could have been hurt. Are you ready for our next class?"

Branx has been right by my side all week. I have noticed him giving his friends the warning *'back off'* look when he thinks I am not watching. He seems to be protective of me, especially when other guys become too close to me. The other guys do not interest me. With Branx attending all my classes and sitting next to me, he acts as if we are a long-term couple.

I am not quite sure what is happening between us, but every time we are apart from one another, I feel lost and empty. The only time we separate is when I go back to my family's house, next door to my loving grandparent's home.

Just as I am about to answer, we both turn to the screeching of a banshee. Oh, I mean

Jezzy. With other kids rushing up to her, I see Branx lift his chin and casually glances at the screaming biotch.

I hear a sigh leave his lips, before he says in an annoyed tone, "Really Jezzy; you have been told not to run around the corridors. You run, you fall and look what happened, you ran straight into the lockers. You are lucky your silly antics didn't hurt anyone else. Grow up."

With that, Branx turns the pair of us and leads us in the direction of our next class, as the screaming continues and the hatred of Jezzy fills the air.

I better start taking extra precautions when it comes to this human. Shit. Jezzy is going to cause major trouble for me, all because she is jealous Branx is spending time with me.

Branx leans towards my ear sending chills through my body and says, "Don't worry about her, Alex. She needs to grow up. If Jezzy gives you any more trouble, just let me know, and I will be your knight in shining armour."

Oh wow. If anything I have learnt from my older siblings it's that I have to stand on my own two feet. Speaking of my protection, I have to keep reminding my guards; I am okay. I quickly glance over at them, we nod as Branx, and I pass right by. They came mighty close to tackling that biotch to the ground. Having two of them following me around is a little unnerving here in the human realm, but hey, I am adjusting.

At least my guards are using the magical charm hiding and masking their presence to all but me while I am attending school. As long as I continue to wear my magically enhanced necklace, I will be able to see them.

To annoy my parents; I had Aunt Lucy assist me with a rune tattoo, an extra rune blood ward, a matching smaller leaf placed on the side of my ring finger to the larger one on the underside of my wrist days before leaving Darshia.

Some days, I find having twice the protection helps. I have the feeling it has come in handy, detecting other Entities who themselves wear some form of protection ward. Technically, it should also help me see my guards, at the moment, I think I'd prefer to rely on my necklace, for now, feeling a little hesitant to rely on a single rune for multiple abilities. I am not going to take any chances with my life while out here in the human realm.

Walking to the gym, Branx escorts me to the girls changing room door. Branx smiles and squeezes my hand and says, "If you need me, just call. I'll be here."

Within ten minutes, I have my gym locker locked with my belongings secured away, with an extra ward spell I placed on it, for good measure. I am not going to allow anyone to mess with me. I am a Princess of *Dark Ones*, and no one will treat me with disrespect. Especially that little biotch Jezzy.

As I start to walk out into the gym foyer, wearing my workout clothes, I head over to the two doorways side by side for classes. It is not long until I notice the class instructor dressed in his black martial arts — Kung Fu uniform, standing in the doorway of another room, taking notice of the sign above the door indicating *indoor activities*, which must be where the martial arts class is going to be held.

My very first lesson in this class, I only hope I am good enough to pass, and I do not want to hurt any of these humans. I have to keep reminding myself I am stronger than all of them.

With just a few feet progress towards the entrance, my senses pick up a commanding presence in the building.

Shit.

What is my mother doing here and oh no, also sensing my dad is here as well. Double shit. I try to walk as normal as possible, Branx quickly walks beside me as we make our way into the large, padded floor classroom.

'Alex, watch your language, young lady. Your mother and I will be assisting your instructor today. He is an old friend of ours and knows about Dark Ones. So do not worry about us.'

'Oh Daddy, really? And whom am I meant to pass you off as? Or are you going to say you married my cousin? Yes, people already know, Mother is my cousin around the school.'

'We will go with that; I married your cousin. Now, who is that boy you walked into the gym with? Should I be having a 'certain' talk with this young man?'

'You wouldn't dare, Daddy. Please do not embarrass me.'

'Relax, sweetheart. Your mother and I are here to assist your school. You do remember, your mother and I used to teach this stuff when we were your age. Self-defence classes were our part-time job at the time.'

'Yeah, yeah. I remember you explaining all this to Alley, Damien, Dane and I. Can you please not embarrass me? Can we start with our lessons? Please.'

With a loud voice, the instructor of our martial arts class starts to address the students and requests for everyone to pair up, at the same time he informs us of his name.

Mr Pletishe, a slender man with a muscled, toned body and a graceful nature and movement with each step he takes. He is also shorter than my dad and nearly shorter to Mum, which means even I might be taller than him. The smaller he is, the more likely he will place me on my arse. Great, this is going to be an interesting lesson.

"All right class, quickly now, we do not have much time. I would like to introduce to you my assistants for the day. Alexia and Drake, everyone makes sure to give them your full attention. They will be demonstrating to the class today the lessons you will be learning over the next couple of weeks. Drake, please prepare yourself. Alexia, you may begin."

"Wow, Alex. Isn't that your cousin?" Branx whispers near my ear, which sends goosebumps up my arms.

"Shhh. Yes, it is, and Drake is her husband. You better pay attention," I whisper back.

"Hello everyone, as Mr Pletishe explained. My name is Alexia and Drake here is not just my assistant but also my husband," my mother says and smiles while looking at each of the students. "Now we will require a volunteer."

Mum's eyes roamed over the class until her smiling face lands on me. With a shake of my head, warning Mum not to pick me, my mother did not care though. I knew it; they are going to make an example of me in front of my classmates.

Terrific. Just bloody terrific.

"Alex, I think you should be able to handle what we have planned, can you come over here please."

With a sigh, I slowly begin to move forward.

I know what they are up to. And I am not

going to like it. At least I know how to protect myself and fight. However, up against my parents — Oh, crap. This is not going to be pretty, and I will end up with bruises.

Shaking out my hands, arms, legs and feet, I prepare for what they are about to unleash on me.

They are going to get it for embarrassing me like this.

Chapter Seven

BRANX

HOLY SHIT.

I nearly swallow my tongue when I caught a glimpse of Alex walking out of the change rooms — that body of hers...wow. Whatever this chemistry is between us, Alex will be my girlfriend, if not a lover. But whatever it is, we will be long-term, and long-term will lead down the path to marriage, kids and family, the whole nine yards.

Oh, shit. Am I out of my mind or am I finally maturing? Because this girl has my heart and soul on fire and I need her to keep me alive.

Catching up with Alex, I walk beside her as we make our way through the foyer of the gym to our first session. Walking straight into the padded floor room, I scan around the large room, where the martial class takes place. So, this will be my new classroom for the year, a padded floor to throw ourselves around on. Hmm. I can think of a few other things we can do on this floor, and it has nothing to do with my new class of martial arts.

What the school does not know is I have a brown belt in this sport and several skills in another hand-to-hand combat also. My mother has made sure I know how to protect myself. Some of her work colleagues usually have me tag along with them when they see their instructors for further training, so I literally learned the moves and practised the sessions with them since I was a kid.

Even my friends do not know I can fight like this. I have always kept it secret and hidden from all my school friends, especially with my mother reminding me, I have to have some personal secrets.

Listening to our new instructor, Mr Pletishe introduces himself to the class, when I glance at the girl I had seen on the first day of school with Alex, I wonder what she is doing here. What was her name? Al...

something, Alex's cousin, that's right — Alexia. This girl's name is Alexia, and she is married, and by the way, she keeps eyeing off the other new guy beside her, either she is interested in him, or he is her husband.

"Wow, Alex, isn't that your cousin?" I say right near her ear, as my nose inhales a fragrance I am not able to name, but has my mouth watering for more.

"Shhh. Yes, it is, and Drake is her husband. You better pay attention," Alex whispers.

Ah. So the big guy's name is Drake. Hmm. Interesting. I have caught him giving me the deadly stare a few times now. I wonder what his problem is?

"Hello everyone, as Mr Pletishe explained, my name is Alexia and Drake here is not just my assistant but also my husband." Alexia, explains to everyone, especially the three girls I had seen drooling over Drake when we first entered the room. Drake is off limits. Laughing inside my head, it does not take a genius to see the disappointment in the girls' eyes.

"Now we will require a volunteer."

Alexia's eyes roamed around the room eyeing each student, until her smiling face lands on Alex. Why do I have the feeling this is not going to be good?

"Alex, I think you should be able to handle what we have planned, can you come over here please?"

With a sigh and a shake of her head, Alex slowly takes a step forward and glances between Alexia and Drake.

Is it just me or is there some significant tension in the air between these three? Hmm. This is going to be interesting.

Go, baby, you can do it.

Chapter Eight
ALEX

OH, MUM AND DAD ARE GOING TO GO DOWN for this, embarrassing me this way.

'Alex, stop your whining. Just pretend this is one of our regular workouts. I am going to speak to the class while your father is going to charge at you. So be ready, you can use whatever move you like, but do not go overboard. Please do not forget; we are in front of the humans not Dark Ones, behave.'

With an eye roll, I do not say a word. I look towards my dad, watching, calculating what he is about to do. No way in hell am I going to let him beat me. Well, beat me by much anyway.

I centre my body and adjust to moving about on the padded flooring, keeping in mind not to curl my toes under me, that is the last thing I need, a broken toe. I change my standing position, and I begin to bounce on the balls of my feet. While I focus on the task ahead, making sure to loosen up my muscles.

Taking in a deep breath, I quickly glance around the room, all the guys and one girl seem to be focused on me, while the rest are watching Dad, a few of them, eew, seem to be drooling over the fact, my father ripped off his t-shirt and displaying his muscled male physique. *Oh, geez.*

With an eye roll, I cannot believe Dad would try a stupid stunt like the one he just did in front of Mum in a room full of hormonal females. With a quick glance towards Mum, I can already see, she is annoyed with Dad.

Realising Dad only removed his top to prevent me from grabbing it and allowing a handhold to use to my advantage. Well, two can play that game.

With a swift movement, I remove my t-shirt revealing my bright coloured sports top. Thank goodness, I decided to wear it today, instead of a regular bra. With my toned stomach muscles twitching, I notice a few of the guys taking even more notice of my body.

Geez, you would think, they have not seen a female with muscles before. When I glance over to Branx, I can see, he too is annoyed, just like my mother. Hmm. I thought he would have enjoyed seeing my naked skin...

Okay, then, I had better start to concentrate, on my opponent. Feeling ready, and with a flick of my fingers, I encourage Dad to proceed. We slowly begin to circle around our area, taking in each one of my father's steps with caution, when I can see he is performing his usual pre-workout style of fighting, I slowly take a relaxing breath in.

I bet Dad is providing me with a false sense of security, noticing his next step is slightly different, my body goes on high alert; my father is starting his tell-tale signs he is about to charge.

Barely hearing my mother voice as she continues to speak to the class, I have to keep her voice blocked out of my head, keeping my focus on Dad. After all, he is my opponent.

I know enough about my parents to expect the unexpected from the two of them because they keep reminding not just myself, but also that of my siblings — *the enemy is not going to play and fight by the rules*. They will use whatever advantage over you as they can. If that means two against one, so be it.

I make sure to keep my senses open just in case my parents' swap and change tactics — I hate it when I am right.

With movement out the corner of my eye, my mother comes at me hard instead. *Oh. Shit.*

Quick, move. I tell myself.

Mum narrowly skirts contact with my side.

Quickly pivoting, I dodge another attack from Mum on my left side, making sure to jump and flip landing back on my feet this time facing my dad.

I roll just in time to avoid one of Dad's counter attacks he always performs, manoeuvering to my feet, jumping back over his body, and landing a hit to his head. Oops. Now that is new, I have never made contact like that before.

Just as I land, I am already pivoting on my toes with my arm and hand coming up to block another attack from Dad, first with one of his hands then followed by the other.

We keep up our movements slowly building in pace and strength. I do not know if Dad is trying to tire me out, but if we keep moving this hard and fast, I am going to be exhausted before I know it.

Thankfully, Mum continues her discussion with the class and leaves Dad and me to our little performance, reminding me of our weekly practice sessions back at the castle.

After another minute or so of demonstrating some of our high combat moves, probably are a little too advance for this class to attempt, at least my new classmates will be kept entertained.

I keep on my toes as I duck and weave, feeling a wind sail past my head. What is Dad up to, as he continues to come at me harder, making me move faster and quicker. With my energy starting to wane, Dad manages to land a couple of his hits, slamming against my body, causing me to stager a step back. Shit that one hurt.

I continue to try focusing on Dad while I breathe in through my nose, through the pain... What the... What does Dad think he is doing? He will hurt me if he is not careful.

With my senses on high alert, I focus solely on my dad. I quickly spin, making contact with his body. Knocking my father a step back, I kick high with my right leg, another high fast spin. Only for Dad not to know, I am turning, my left leg and knee are making its way towards his chest, which should knock him onto his butt, providing he does not block me first.

Making contact, I feel the sting vibrate through my leg, as I land back on my feet. I look back at Dad and wow. I finally got him, I finally sent my dad down, with him falling and landing hard on the mat. My little internal victory dance is short-lived, for I stopped my focus on where Mum had been standing.

With a painful yelp, I hit the floor. My legs have been taken out from underneath me, the wind knocked out of my lungs and landing on my left arm awkwardly. Usually, I would roll and be standing straight away ready to protect myself and fighting back, not this time. With my energy low, and my body in pain, the only thing coming to my mind is ow that hurt. With the wind knocked out of me, the room starts to spin. Uh-oh.

Struggling to take a breath, with pain

radiating up my side and especially my left wrist, I know full well I am going to have a big bruise on my hip.

Oh, crap. My eyes grow wide when I realised I stuffed up big time.

Failing to get up and out of the way from the unexpected attack from both Mum and Dad, I soon find myself, not able to prevent my parents from making contact with my body.

With white noise filling my ears, and the sensation of the room continually spinning around me, I know this is not good. Realisation soon hits me; I am about to pass out.

Oh, shit no.

Dark dots start to appear before me just before everything starts to turn black.

WITH A CALMNESS SURROUNDING ME AND A familiar scent filling my nostrils, I slowly open my eyelids and find a pair of sexy bedroom eyes staring right into my own. Worry and concern etched on Branx's face. I continue to watch his lips move, and yet there is no sound leaving his mouth, I... do not hear a single syllable he is speaking. Without moving my head, I look around for my parents, until I find my dad is back on the mat and my mother is hovering over him. Oh, that is not good.

I continue to glance around the room, until I see our class instructor, escorting the rest of the class students out of the room. Once again the room starts to sway, uh-oh. I do not feel right. My eyes close and I feel as if I should be sleeping. Bugger, my wrist is sore. What happened?

Focusing on remaining conscious, I try to open my eyes once more.

Struggling to keep my eyes open, the first thing I focus on is the sexy Branx. Our eyes meet, and I start to smile. With a frown on his face, he glances up and over to my parents. He nods and looks back down to me.

"Hey baby, you going to stay with me this time?" Huh? Did Branx just call me baby? 'Baby,' while in front of my parents. Oh, boy. He is a brave man, but then he does not know they are my parents.

"Hey, Branx. What is going on?" I slowly ask, sounding sluggish and weak.

"Um, Alex, do you remember demonstrating with your cousins. Well anyway, somehow, you were hurt, and they did not stop. And um... I kind of...”

Uh-oh. What just happened, what did I miss?

“Branx. What did you kind of, what?”

“I stopped your cousins from continuing their assault on you.”

“Ah. Thank you, Branx.” I cautiously glance over to my parents. And notice my dad is slowly rising to his feet, while my mother remains right by his side.

I try to move and sit up, only to fall back against Branx. Ow, that hurts. My side is painful, and my wrist is killing me.

Shit, don’t tell me my arm might be broken. Damn it. No.

Looking back towards my parents I say through our mind link, *‘Mum, Dad, I think my wrist is damaged. It feels as if it may be broken.’*

Just with those words alone, my parents instantly look straight at me and then to my wrist. With guilt written on their faces, they soon realise, I do not just have a bruised ego.

Hearing my mother’s voice in my head as she kneels down beside me, *‘Ah, crap on a stick. I am so sorry, baby girl. We should not have been so aggressive. You usually train better than this back at the castle. We had expected you to get up. We sometimes forgot you are still human.'*

With one hand sweeping along my hair and the other one hovering over my aching arm, I know what she is going to do. As kids Alley, Damien and I would always get into mischief and end up with a lot of cuts and scrapes, by accident, our mother was able to feed us some of her blood, healing us instantly.

'Oh, mother, not in front of the human. Don't do it in front of Branx,' my mind pleads with Mum.

'Baby girl, I am so sorry. We have hurt you. Sometimes your father and I forget you are not a fully turned Dark One; you still have human limitations. I will never forgive myself for your injuries. Your father and I will heal you, and we will take you home.'

'Mother, why was Dad on the ground, surely I did not do that to him?'

'No. It was not you, Alex. It was your young man, Branx. He jumped in to protect you. He knew you were hurt before your father or I knew. He is extremely talented. I would not be surprised if he is more than just human.'

'What?'

Chapter Nine

BRANX

WHAT IN THE HELL IS WRONG WITH THESE people?

Why have they not sent for an ambulance? Noticing the last of the students being escorted out of the classroom by our instructor, I wonder how gullible my fellow classmates are to think it was part of the performance and not real.

I cannot believe Alexia and Drake went on attacking my beautiful Alex. How did I know she was injured? Somehow, I knew she was badly hurt; I had to do something, they could have killed her.

This couple is strange in a way; I cannot put my finger on it.

Looking down at Alex, she seems to be slipping back and forth from consciousness. I look up at her cousin Alexia; I can see the guilt and shame across her face. She knows what she did is terrible; I can see she is struggling with something. I want these people to help my girl, not stand around gawking at her.

All I know is I want Alex with every fibre of my being. It is like she has cast a spell over me.

"Branx, we need you to leave. We will look after Alex and make sure she arrives home safely."

Hearing Drake, I do not know, if I want to hit him or tell him to get lost. No way in hell am I leaving Alex by herself with these two crazies.

The look on my face should have indicated how pissed I am as I look back up towards Drake and Alexia, I reply, "Sorry guys, where Alex goes, I go. I am not leaving her alone with you two, after what you did to her."

"Branx, Alex knows how sorry we are. Alex is a better fighter than this; we do not know what happened. However, we need to take her to the hospital, and we do not have your parents' permission to take you with us from the school grounds."

Say what? Staring daggers at Drake, I do not care for bloody school rules. I start to shake my head at the thought of parting from Alex. With a big NO, am I not leaving Alex, and that is final.

Hang on; Drake just said, '*Alex knows they are sorry.*' How? When I have not heard them speaking with her something is going on here. Something strange.

"Look, Drake," I try to keep my voice as calm as possible and tone down my death glare. "I am not leaving Alex. I do not care if you are related. I am not leaving her alone with the pair of you, after that stunt you both pulled on her today. What were you thinking?"

I feel my aggression building, and I remind myself to stay calm for Alex's sake.

She is my main priority.

"Branx, sorry we cannot wait around here for you to play bodyguard. We are not about to hurt Alex any more than she already is. Now, move so that we can leave."

"Look, Drake and Alexia, I am staying with Alex. If you have a problem with that, then take it up with her parents. Once they find out what you did to their daughter, do you really think they will allow you to go anywhere near her again?"

Drake and Alexia glance at one another, with a strange look. Again, what is with their looks? It is like they have their own conversations with one another and no one else is invited.

Whichever way it goes, I am not leaving Alex.

Just then, Drake turns to me and gives me a weird look. Shit. I do not know to be pissed or extremely nervous right now, as I ball up my fist to prevent myself from getting up and hitting the guy.

"Branx do you care for Alex?"

My eyebrow slowly moves up my forehead in disbelief. If I did not care for Alex, I would not be here ."Yes. Yes, I do. What has that got anything to do with Alex receiving medical attention?"

"Branx, we are going to pick Alex up now and take her to a waiting car, just outside. We will be travelling to a special location, and you cannot come with us."

The nerve of these two, as if I would leave!

"Like hell. I am staying with Alex, and

you will not stop me," I say through gritted teeth. "Either you allow me to come, or I will phone for an ambulance. You know...what you should have done already by now."

Watching Drake and Alexia both do that look thing with one another and a shake or nod of their heads, their eyes finally turn back to Alex and me.

"Branx, okay. You can come with us. However, I hope you do not disappoint us because where we are about to go, is top secret and extremely confidential."

What the...what in the world is Drake going on about? Confidential and top secret. What is with the cloak and dagger stuff? I suppose there is only one way to find out.

"Drake, I think you have wasted enough time. Alex requires medical attention, now. So I would advise you to start moving."

My eyes glance over to Alexia, with her head tilted slightly to the side, the look she is giving me, is as if she is studying me.

What and who are these people?

With that, I very carefully lift Alex in my arms and start walking towards the exit, when I look down towards her gorgeous face — shit, Alex is unconscious. Concern fills me, and I shake my head in annoyance; my girl must be in a lot of pain for her to pass out again, these two morons better know what to do.

Glancing over my shoulder, I notice both Alexia and Drake strangely staring at me. Taking a breath in, I say, "You guys coming or what?"

Chapter Ten

ALEX

I START TO WAKE UP, TO FIND MYSELF BACK IN my bedroom at the family castle. For me, that is nothing unusual, but why am I here? I search my mind until a vague memory of getting hurt at school starts to form.

Oh, Goddess, my arm was injured and my side…without overthinking, I begin to wiggle my fingers before I lift my arm to test it, before gingerly touching my side, only to find both my arm and my side are pain-free — relief fills me.

I take a deep breath in when my sense of smell indicates Branx's scent thick in the air.

How in the world is the scent of Branx in Darshia?

I start to contemplate why, I can detect Branx's scent, when I start to stretch and roll over, only to discover a body lying beside me.

Oh, shit.

My body stills as my heart rate increases with the knowledge someone is here. *Who in the hell is in my room and my bed?*

Reaching for my necklace, I start to cast a spell, when the body beside me starts to move, revealing a pair of sexy bedroom eyes.

Holy shit. Branx is in my bed!

"Hey," I say, not sure what is really going on, as I glance towards the bedroom door expecting my parents to barge in at any second.

"Hey, yourself. How are you feeling? How is your arm?"

With a slight smile, I look back to Branx as I reply, "Good." I wiggle my fingers to prove my point, "No more pain."

"That is good. The doctor was in here earlier. This place is interesting."

I glance around my bedroom trying to see it from Branx's point of view until I face him once again.

"Um. Branx, don't take this the wrong way, but what are you doing here, in my bed especially here in my family home?"

"Ah, yes. The family home," Branx says as he looks around my room before glancing towards the window. "Well, after I knocked your father on his arse in the gym." Ah shit. Branx knows. OMG. "Yes, Alex, I know, Drake and Alexia are your parents, not your cousins. I refused to leave your side. I said to them, '*I do not trust either of them with your safety,*' after the stunt they pulled back at school. They had seriously hurt you."

Boy did my parents ever, and I can't believe they would hurt me like that. I wonder what they have told Branx?

"Um, Branx. What exactly have my parents explained to you?"

Watching his gaze move back to mine, I notice when the hard look in them softens and a slight smile forms on his lips.

"Alex, I know, I am in a weird place named Darshia. Your mother is the Queen. Oh, and according to the doctor, you and I are *soul mates*."

I inhale sharply.

Whoa, slow down and back up a second, did Branx just say, what I think he just said?

Are we *soul mates?*

Holy shit.

I gulp.

"Ah, Branx. Did my parents happen to say anything else about us?"

"What... that they are Vampires or was that *Dark Ones*? Also, you have the choice to turn into one, and live to be extra old and still look young."

My eyes grow wide as I nod my head. "Ah, yes, that would be what I had been thinking," I whisper.

"Then yes, Alex. I know you are what is known as a *Dark One*. I even met your sister. She said for me to give you a message."

Oh, crap. I start to groan. What has my sister said now?

With a smile in his eyes, Branx says, "Tell Alex she is a bitch for obtaining one first." Smiling and with a shrug of his shoulders. "Whatever that might mean?"

With an eye roll and an internal laugh, I shake my head. Trust Alley to say that to Branx's face. Biotch. Just then, I thought of something. If I am all better, I bet Mum must have given me some of her blood, to heal me. I quickly glance at Branx.

"So, did you um, see me drinking blood or anything?" I nervously ask as my teeth snag my bottom lip.

With Branx this close to me, I can feel his

body heat through my sheet, and if I am not mistaken, I am not wearing all that much either. Oh crap. I hope I am not naked under here. I glance back up and see Branx nod his head while his eyes focus on my mouth, especially my bottom lip.

I watch as Branx moves his head closer to mine, his mouth hovering over mine.

"I am going to kiss you now, Alex. If you do not want me to, say something quick."

Without replying, I move my head enough to brush my lips against his. I feel Branx's warm, soft lips against mine just as fireworks take off in my brain. Without any thought, I start to move my lips and deepen the kiss. Oh my, I am kissing a boy in my bedroom on my bed, and my head wants to expand and explode from all the joy and toe-curling feelings moving throughout my body, while the fireworks are going off around in my mind lighting up my thoughts, making all brand new memories.

I automatically reach up, allowing my fingers to slide through Branx's soft short hair as I bring his head closer to mine. Feeling the weight of Branx's body move over mine... and his, O.M.G is that... Oh wow, is that his erection, digging into my leg? The urge to rub my thighs hard together increases, if only I can ease the friction, I am feeling.

Instead, my heated core rubs itself against the thick fabric of Branx jeans, the hard length of him extends and increases in size. With each movement we make, each rub and body caress, I can feel the heat within me build.

Not really knowing what my body needs, or what I require, all I know, Branx will be able to extinguish the heat between us before we both go up in flames.

My body continues to move in time with Branx, and my hips rise to meet his body in the old erotic dance between two lovers. Hearing a groan from Branx, is he in pain, what did I do? Did I hurt him somehow? Branx pulls his warm moist lips away from mine. *No. Don't go...* My mind whimpers.

Ah. The impression of moist lips ghost over my jaw and along my neck, until the sensation of teeth scraping along my tantalising flesh, sends erotic chills through my body. Now, this is better, ooh, I like that.

I feel Branx teeth nip and slide along my throat, causing my nipples to turn hard as diamond points, as my back arches off the bed. The only thoughts in my head are the new fantastic sensations overpowering my body, as my hard tips scratch against Branx chest, creating a delicious friction within me.

My fingers reach back up sliding through the soft strands of hair, until I pull his head back enough, exposing his succulent, delicious vein, for me to devour. Detecting his fast pulse against my lips, its tattooed beat, calling me, enticing me to move closer.

My own teeth slide along his flesh, feeling goosebumps appear along his flesh, the ache in my mouth the only warning my incisors are about to descend.

Caught up in fiery passion; it is not until I am savouring the best ambrosia to cross my lips and tongue, is when I realise I am drinking Branx delicious blood.

Holy shit! I am drinking someone else's blood! I don't know to stop drinking, or keep going? I hear Branx moan his pleasure, as he says, "Keep going baby; your mouth feels so good. Take more… Drink more…"

With a thrust of his hips, Branx entices my body, soul, and me. With my legs widening and my own hips lifting, my legs wrap around his waist, with my heel pressing into his muscled butt, encouraging him to push his body into mine.

I continue to drink, swallowing mouthful after mouthful of the most delicious blood to ever touch my lips. A moment or two later, a niggling feeling begins to indicate I have drunk enough. With a swipe of my tongue, I seal the two puncture holes and watch as they instantly heal over.

Our kissing continued, as our tongues twist and battled for dominance in one another's mouths. Branx deepened our kiss causing the fireworks to go off again, behind my eyes as his body continued to caress mine in an erotic dance of love.

Feeling so confused by my body's needs, all I know I want Branx, no I need him closer, naked skin touching, caressing closer. With another groan leaving my tender, moist lips, Branx brushes his hot wet lips along my jaw until he pulls his eager mouth away from my wanton body.

"Oh, Alex, I need you so much," with a sigh, Branx whispers near my mouth. "But, this is not the right time to go any further. As hard as it is to pull away from you right now, if I don't, we might regret it. And that is something I do not want you to feel, ever. I want our first time together to be perfect. Not some rushed quick hormonal fix. Please understand I want to make love to you so badly. I feel in my heart; you are my life. With each beat of my heart, it only continues beating for you. And my lungs, you are the air I need to breathe. Do you understand what I am trying to say?"

By this stage, the haze of our kisses is starting to wear off; my lips still tingle from Branx's touch. My mind a little fuzzy, trying to contemplate Branx's words, were we about to have… *WHAT?* My mind screeches.

Did he just say, we were about to have — *SEX?*

Sex in my bed. Sex.

I struggle to swallow, with a loud gulp.

Oh, shit.

I give myself a mental shake, to clear the fuzz in my mind. I cannot believe things had progressed that far so quickly.

OMG. Thank the goddess, Branx managed to come to his senses, because mine left the building.

Chapter Eleven

ALEX

AFTER SEPARATING MYSELF FROM THE WARM, muscled, sexy body of Branx, I managed to shower and dress. Leaving the safety of my bedroom, well maybe the temptation of my bed, Branx agreed to be escorted around the castle.

Showing Branx around some of the castle was an exciting experience, along with avoiding and dodging security, especially when I pointed out some of the high walkways the staff use to avoid being seen in their day-to-day activities.

Branx was amazed when I started to reveal several hidden passaged ways. Our fun ended when Branx and I were slipping out of one of the secret tunnels when we literally walked into Alley and Damien. Grrr siblings.

"So Branx, what do you think of our little home?" Alley asks in her annoying voice when she is up to something, and her eyes are lighting up with mischief, meaning she will most likely try to embarrass me in front of Branx.

"It seems very big. It's fantastic. I was just thinking, as a kid, this place would have been the best to play games in and explore."

I give Alley a knowing look. Oh, yes. This castle has been a kid's paradise to play and hide in. Alley smiles back to me, and this place had been the best.

Damien pulls that face when he is about to say something he should not. "Tell me, Branx. Our parents informed us you are the *soul mate* of our sister, here. I should warn you; you should run now before Alex can weave her web."

With a swift hit to both sides of his head, both Alley and I hit our brother Damien.

"Ow. What was that for?" Damien quickly tries to dodge another smack to the head from Alley.

Before Alley or I can yell at our annoying brother, Branx speaks up in an annoyed tone, "Dude, if you knew what this feeling of being a *soul mate* truly is about, you would never say those words to me."

I know my brother is teasing, but maybe, he does not know what the feeling is. Hmm, interesting. My eyes look to Alley, and hers meet mine in a knowing look before I turn and speak to Damien.

"Damien, I know you are joking with Branx, but we thought you had found your *soul mate*. You should know what this feeling is. If you did, your *soul mate* would not be far from your side right now," I say, knowing his new girlfriend is not his real *soul mate*. Now I know what the feeling is, I know for a fact, this new girl in Damien's life is only using him.

Now, Damien just had to realise that.

With his forehead scrunching up in thought, I think we might have Damien thinking about his girlfriend. Who we are positive is an annoying money hungry female out for anything she can get her grubby little hands on and who is not the *soul mate* to my brother.

"So Damien, this girlfriend of yours, do

you think she might be a girlfriend only?" Alley quietly asks, knowing full well to tread carefully when it comes to Damien and his love interests.

Damien's eyes look up at me, then to Branx. "Branx, what do you exactly feel regarding my sister. And please I do not want to know any sex stuff. Or I will vomit all over you," he says with a playful shudder.

With a laugh, Branx gives me his megawatt smile with a wink followed by a gentle, but quick, kiss on my lips. "I think I need to speak with your brother privately. I'll be back in a minute," Branx quietly says near my mouth.

With that, Branx slaps Damien on the back, and the pair of them start to walk off, busy chatting away down the corridor and out of sight.

"Oh, shit Alex, does Branx know anything about Damien and his girlfriend, or that we have seen them having sex?"

"Shhhhh. Lower your voice, Alley," I hiss. "No. I have not said anything to Branx. When I finally woke up in my room and found Branx laying beside me in my bed, talking was not something either one of us had on our minds. Well yes, we did talk, but just the obvious stuff like, what he was doing in Darshia, he knows Mum and Dad are not my cousins, but really my parents. We are *soul mates*, oh, and we are Dark Ones. After that, we were kind of busy." I blush, remembering the hot scorching kissing on my bed.

"Wow. So you got to play tonsil hockey. What is Branx like? Hmm, come on tell me. All I keep seeing is our brother, and I want to bleach my mind. Blahhh."

"Alley, all I will say is, my *soul mate* is the best kisser I have ever had. He is a gentleman also."

Refusing to look Alley in the eye, no way am I going to tell anyone I also drank from Branx neck.

"What do you mean a gentleman? Why? What happened?"

"Well," my eyes glance around the two of us, making sure we are still alone. "The kissing kind of got out of control and if it was not for Branx stopping when we did, we might, might have...you know." Turning back around, facing Alley, ah crap my face has turned hot, "Gone a lot further."

"Oh my God, Alex. You nearly had sex with Branx. Holy shit. Way to go, girl," Alley screeches.

"Ssshhhhh," I hiss again, as my eyes quickly scan the area. I do not need the castle staff to know about my sex life.

Just five minutes later, I sense Branx before I see him. When my brother and Branx turn the corner down the corridor, my eyes meet a pair of sexy bedroom eyes. Oh, man is that love I can see in Branx's eyes? But then come to think of it, he did say as much back in my bedroom with his declaration to me. What did he say — *I feel in my heart, you are my life? With each beat of my heart, it only continues beating for you. And my lungs, you are the air I need to breathe.'*

Oh, my. I think that might be love.

What about me, though? I am not sure what I am feeling about Branx just yet, but one thing I do know, I have deep feelings already, a deep inner sense for someone I have only just met. On the other hand, I do not want to live my life without him. My body, heart and soul ache each time we are separated, how will I be able to live away from him? I do not think I will be able to do it.

Hmm. Maybe I am in love with Branx Rayden, after all.

Oh, wow. After all, this might be a forever

kind of love, and we are newly discovered *soul mates*, and as new *soul mates*, we have much to learn about one another, with our new love growing and our bond forming, this is only the beginning.

Chapter Twelve

PART TWO

Five Years Later

ALEX

With thoughts and fond memories of the day we first met and by the time the first week came to a close all those years ago at school and my first time consuming the delicious blood from Branx vein, I can completely agree with my first assessment. I do not want to live my life without Branx. I love him with all my heart and soul.

"Come on, Branx," I whisper. "Come on, baby, wake up," I plead, feeling drained with exhaustion. Words my mother had repeated to me over the years comes to mind as I look at my beloved. "Never. Never, give up," I murmur. I keep focusing on his face if there is any sign he is listening to me. "Never. Never give up, Branx. Come back to me, I love you."

Damn it, still no response. Why can't I sense Branx's thoughts? It's like he's not there. His head seems empty, no thoughts, memories or dreams — nothing. What am I going to do if he doesn't wake up? This man is my life, how will I live without him? A single tear makes it way down my damp cheek.

Still holding his warm hand, I start to remember our secret wedding back in Darshia. A small intimate wedding followed by our *Joining Ceremony*. Deciding I will wait a few more years before becoming a full *Dark One*; I really did not want Branx to look like he married a teenager when he is still ageing. Has it only been twelve months since I turned completely into a full *Dark One*? With it, my magic and *Dark One* abilities strengthened and yet I had been powerless and failed to prevent Branx from nearly being killed.

"Branx. Baby, please wake up. I have something special to tell you. Come on honey; I need you to wake up and come back to me. Remember I love you, Baby," I plead as warm tears make their way down my face.

The soft noise of the door slowly opening behind me, has my head turning over my shoulder, to see who is intruding on my grief-pity party.

With relief, I see it is only the nurse, with her pixie-like face with short dark cropped hair. With a shortish slim body, wearing her blue scrubs and funny looking shoes, she did her usual thing, going over all the screens and bags of liquid and marking off his progress on the charts of her hourly observations on my severely injured husband.

With all the leads and tubes going to and from his body, at least with the monitors I know he is alive, and his heart is once again beating strong. As for his mind...his brain has gone on holiday for all I know. I am not able to reach him, and this has me worried.

"Is there any change?" I asked her, noticing her name tag 'Maxine' this time around.

The nurse glanced up from the machine to me, taking in my appearance, her smile soon disappearing. With a sad look on her face, Maxine replied, "No, there's no change." With a small shake of her head, the nurse looks down and continues writing more information in another section of Branx's medical chart, before looking back up towards me.

"Look you really should go home or something and get some rest, maybe some food or even a shower to freshen yourself up at least. You have been here for the last..." Looking down at her watch Maxine's eyes take in the time, before glancing back over to me, "Twenty-three hours; someone will call you if there is any change."

Looking back at Branx, I repeat my usual answer, "Maybe later, after Branx wakes up."

Sensing Maxine moving towards me, I glance up as Maxine writes something else on Branx medical chart and places the clipboard into its holder at the end of the bed.

Maxine started speaking to me again, only this time in a professional mannered voice, "Look, don't take this the wrong way, I think you should think about going home and taking a shower and changing your clothes, I can smell you from the other side of the bed."

Wow. Now that is rude, what a bitch. If I had the spare energy, I would stand up and bitch slap her for those comments.

Looking up at her, I am more than a little shocked and ticked off by her response.

Taking a breath in and reminding myself to act like the adult my mother expects me to be, I stopped and thought about the nurse's comments. Before long I came to a conclusion, I probably do smell whiffy.

Feeling a little ashamed of myself. After all, I had passed up the chance to wear a set of clean hospital scrubs when I first arrived here at the hospital, especially when the staff noticed me in blood-soaked clothes, with whatever else coating me at the time and come to think of it my clothing is starting to feel a little stiff. So it might be time to go home and shower and crawl into some clean clothing.

"Okay," I murmur. "I'll go for a little while, but if there is any change with Branx, and I mean any change at all, good or bad, I want to be notified on my mobile or my home number ASAP okay?"

I reached in my jacket pocket and pulled

out the little notepad and a pen, which one of my work colleagues from the SFD or the Special Forces Department, had given me just as I had started to climb into the back of the ambulance with Branx.

A notepad to write down anything I might have missed from the previous information I have already provided regarding the capture and torture of Branx and myself. Thankfully one of my work colleagues had came back to the hospital with my handbag containing my keys, purse and phone.

Quickly scribbling down my contact details for Maxine, easing my conscious knowing the nurse will be able to phone me directly. I gently tear the page from the notepad and hand it to her with a forced smile. "Don't forget to phone me if there is any change at all."

Leaning forward, I place a gentle kiss on Branx's forehead, still sensing nothing, I straighten up and walk out of the room and head for the main entrance of the hospital.

Grabbing a taxi home has given me some time to think about the details of this horrible case and what my so-called mother-in-law is doing about it. I cannot stand the bitch. I never have. Branx has always kept reminding me to remain civil to the woman, with his words of, *'She is the only mother I have.'* Whichever way it goes, I do not like or trust the woman.

I know the woman is some form of Paranormal Entity, so is Branx for that matter. Only for Branx's infamous mother, Brodlyne has kept the truth about his father from him. Including what type of Entity Branx is, if it had not been for my family, Branx would be none the wiser.

Even though he sensed Paranormal Entities since he was a teenager, and had thought some of his early abilities was something ordinary for everyday teenagers until Branx learned online what he can do is not normal, but unique. From that day forth he has kept all his abilities hidden, making sure no one found out about them, including Brodlyne.

The woman, or the *Bitch from Helz* as I call her in my head, has never liked me, in all the years Branx and I have been together. Only she does not know Branx, and I are *soul mates*.

All *Bitch from Helz* knows is that her son and I live together, and she is under the impression we are engaged, even though we are legally married back when I turned eighteen. A lovely service just before the *Mating and Joining Ceremony*, we had a small gathering of witnesses, very intimate and romantic until the actual *Soul Mate Ceremony* started.

Geez, I soon found out what my mother had tried to warn me about. At least the ceremony has changed slightly since my parents went through theirs. Thankfully, I did not have to follow in my mother's shoes and conceive. If I had been about to step into the role of the Queen, as my mum did, then things would have been different.

The following day my wonderful parents allowed Branx and I to remain living in their house, next door to my loving grandparents. Branx and I attended university for two years, and from there, straight into our law enforcement course and placement.

Thanks to the part-time jobs we had back then, Mum, Dad and my Grandparents taught us the financial side of investments, which lead to a large, healthy nest egg, allowing us to purchase our very own apartment in the city where we currently work. Mind you; I do not have to work for a living, as I am incredibly wealthy thanks to my parents, Aunt Alivia and Grandmother Mary.

Where we work, in our division in the city, the employees are Paranormal Entities of some variety. Because of my charmed necklace and the matching warding rune tattoos, everyone thinks I am more human, with some unique talents and skills, not knowing I am indeed a *Dark One* and a powerful, talented witch.

Branx and I work as partners in the SFD, or the Special Forces Department, in the City branch. Basically, we solve crimes, catching the bad guys. Extreme bad guys, which are BPE or Bad Paranormal Entities went rogue. Also, the *Bitch from Helz* is our boss, even though I deal more with her boss, Dillion Sparks, which pisses, Ms high and mighty — Brodlyne, off.

Dillion is a shifter with vampire blood running through his veins, he knows I am a *Dark One* princess, and has been sworn to secrecy regarding my identity. It's amazing what can happen when one meets my beautiful mother when she is in protective parent mode. *'Never mess with a mom.'*

The difference between a vampire and a *Dark One* — with a *Dark One*, we are born, we also have the choice to complete the turning process once we turn eighteen. Or we can go through the Turning Ceremony at a later age, with or without their *soul mate*. Alternatively, if a *Dark One* decides not to become a full *Dark One*, they can remain human. Live an average human lifespan, and some of them do happen to have some *Dark One* traits and abilities.

Or in my case, I waited a few years before turning into a full *Dark One*. As my husband is not a *Dark One*, he will continue to age. Therefore I did not wish to remain resembling a teenager, while he looked like a sexy man.

I know, my nan, Amelia, has some *Dark One* abilities and she chose to remain human when she turned eighteen.

Now, for a vampire, they are turned, usually against their will. There are some, who consume the blood of a vampire, and even *Dark One* blood — and slowly turn into a vampire over a set amount of time. These people do not do so well in sunlight, as their skin becomes super sensitive. Unless you happen to be some form of Paranormal Entity previously, then you might skip the vulnerability to the sun, but still, have some wicked abilities.

Vampires that I am aware of are evil. Mostly evil as they have turned rogue because they cannot handle the blood hunger. And if they have someone who is evil convert them, the higher the chance in which the poor person will be evil themselves.

I have heard of the odd one or two vampires who have managed to be good, Paranormal Entities. I should know, I have been working with a few.

With a shake of my head in disgust, I think about the stupidity of the case we are working on.

Branx and I were following a group of ten rogue vamps and shifters on the outskirts of the city. These criminals had been raping and murdering their victims, leaving the battered or ripped apart bodies for the humans to find. It did not matter if the unfortunate victim was male or female.

All Branx and I wanted to do was track them down and deal with them. Usually, this meant exterminating them, because if we managed to bring them in, some rich, social ladder climbing BPE, would somehow manage to have these psychopathic killers back out on the street.

Chapter Thirteen

ALEX

THE TRIP HOME FROM THE HOSPITAL IS STILL A little hazy, and I don't remember arriving home and walking into my dark, lonely apartment.

As if I am set on autopilot, somehow, I managed to plug my mobile phone into its charger, followed by heading straight for my bedroom.

Not bothering to grab any clothing, I stripped off, dumping all my dirty, bloody mess on the tiles on the bathroom floor. Using the toilet first, I relieve my aching bladder, not realising it had been a while since I have been to a loo.

I stand in front of the sink drying my hands and avoid looking in the mirror. Instead, I ran my tongue over my teeth and begin to shudder feeling them disgustingly furry.

After brushing my teeth, my mouth feels human again without the feral breath to go with the pungent stale taste. With clean teeth, I grab a couple of clean towels for my much-awaited shower.

Once the hot water begins to slide down my body, I start to add fragrant soap foam to my body and cleanse my sensitive flesh. It does not take me long to scrub my hair and body clean of the filth my body has collected over the past few days.

After my shower, I carefully dry my moist skin, feeling each ache along my body, before applying moisturiser.

I know I have to look in the mirror and I am dreading what I am going to discover. My breath caught when I scan my body in the full-length mirror. Oh goddess I am covered in hideous bruising. Turning my body from left to right seeing bruising on my ribs, front, back, legs and arms.

At least I do not feel it, for the bruising to

still be there since last night, or was that the day before? I must have received some seriously hard hits.

However, over the years I have had worse, it is all part of the work which we do. The only difference is, I would have healed long before now if I had been consuming Branx's blood. With him being so severely injured, I ended up feeding him my blood instead, to keep him alive. If my mother were here, she would kick my arse for not feeding and neglecting to keep my strength up.

Glancing over my reflection, I rub my bloated belly tenderly. No, my rounding belly, noticing for the first time, my flat muscled tone stomach is now gone and replaced with this budding, pregnant belly. A small baby bump! Feeling my eyes mist up, I wish Branx was here to witness our little miracle.

Walking back to my wardrobe, I pulled out a set of fresh clothes. Something comfortable enough to wear at the hospital. Afterwards, I picked up my hairbrush and began to brush my long damp brown hair, before placing it in a high ponytail at the back my head, and then added a little makeup to my eyes and put on some lipstick.

Branx comes to my mind; he has always loved the shape and feel of my lips. The way he would look into my eyes and keep reminding me how much he loves them and me. As for my eyes, they are similar to those of my mother and her family, our family trait and heritage with the blue circle outlining our brown to indicate we are part of the Royal Blue dynasty of Darshia.

My mother adores Branx, well the whole family loves him. Damien and Dane, enjoy having an extra male around, especially when my family are well known for only producing girls. And here is my beautiful mother breaking the mould and producing both boys and girls with my father.

When Branx improves and can leave the hospital, I think it is time I introduce him to the Darshia way of life and how to sit back and relax with the rest of my family in our secret paradise getaway. Well, my parents and siblings can stay away and leave Branx and me alone, that is.

When I attended school in the human realm, even though I love all my family, I just needed something else. I think deep down I had been searching for my *soul mate*. I found I was missing something in my life. When I met Branx, I felt like I was home. Finally, the feeling of belonging and my soul felt complete.

It is not long, and I have all the smelly and dirty clothing from the floor and hamper in the new washer and dryer we picked up three months ago. This machine has saved our clothes several times since it arrived, thank goodness for the drying feature, is all I can say.

I hear the washer start its cycle, I turn and start walking back to the kitchen. I empty and replace the water in the kettle with clean, fresh water and flick the power switch on to boil the water to make a cup of tea. I move my head out of the way, as I open the overhead cupboard for my favourite mug.

Needing milk, I move to the fridge and open its door and stare into an empty fridge. Ah shit. We were meant to go food shopping two days ago, or was that three days ago? Being held hostage prevented either one of us from going to the grocery store.

Making my way slowly towards the pantry hoping we have something to eat, my toes try to curl against the coldness of the stone flooring. Thinking I should go and pull on a pair of socks, before searching for some Long Life Milk. My belly lets out a loud groan and grumbles for me to feed it. I think socks and my toes can wait. *There better be some food hidden away in the pantry.*

Hmm. Noticing a brightly coloured packet on a high shelf, yes, I am in luck as the sight started to cause my mouth to water at the delicious treat. Reaching for a carton of Long Life Milk and a brightly coloured packet of sweet biscuits, I am grateful there is some type of packet food in our apartment. I need something to savour while drinking my hot beverage with milk. Thank goodness for long life shelf food. I opened the packet of chocolate biscuits and placed them in the bickie jar; it's not long before I had eaten three delicious biscuits and emptied my cup of tea.

Hmmm. Yum.

A little sated, while savouring the taste of melted chocolate on my lips, I stand up, to make myself another cup of tea. Still, on my feet, I manage to drink about half of it when the red blinking light of the answering machine catches my attention. With my cup in hand, I sit back down on the stool, facing the dreaded device.

Hitting the play button and finding no messages from the hospital, I suppose no news can be good news. It does not take me long to go through all the voice messages. Unfortunately, three of the messages are from Branx's mother, bugger. Half listening to the first one, she informed us, she has just landed at the airport, and she is on her way.

The second message from her is she is stuck in traffic which was an hour ago and the third message, questioning why I am not answering my phone? Gee, I think I have to turn my mobile phone on to do that... Bugger, looking at the time, she must have phoned while I was in the shower.

With reality slowly dawning on me, my hands turn into tight fists by my sides. The bitch is on her way here, right now, I have to try and focus on calming myself down. I don't know if I will be able to calm down enough knowing Brodlyne is nearly here. I will have to face her, something I do not want to do right now and have to answer all her annoying fifty-million questions.

I stand back up and fill the kettle with more water, and it does not take long to boil for another cup of tea. I placed my butt down on the kitchen stool and lift my hot tea to my lips, the doorbell and phone both began to ring. Startled, I nearly spilled the hot drink on my hand. Well, that is timing, whenever you want to sit down and relax with a cup of tea, someone always interrupts. I wonder if it the same person? Placing my cup down, I suppose there is only one way to find out.

Glancing at a small screen mounted on the wall near where I am sitting I can soon see who is standing at my door. With an internal cringe, I can sense and now see the *Bitch from Helz* standing at my front door. Great, the mother-in-law from hell has arrived, or the boss from hell, whichever way, I wonder how Brodlyne will present herself to me. Do I want to open the door and let her in? Nah...

With another shrill of its ringer reminding me the phone is still ringing, I quickly run to the wall phone and noticing an unknown number on its display screen — I wonder if it might be the hospital? Picking the cordless phone up, I make my way towards the thick timber front door.

Just as one hand turns the door handle, the other hand's thumb hits the call button on the phone, I open my mouth and answer the caller.

"Hello."

Pulling the door open, I look and meet Brodlyne's glare. With her slim, five-foot six-inch body, long blonde straight hair, green eyes and a pale young complexion — Brodlyne is standing impatiently on the front doorstep.

Stiff shit is all that comes to mind when I can see the building attitude across Brodlyne's face. Trying to be polite, I smiled at her and waved the annoying woman into the apartment.

As I listen to the voice on the other end of the phone — I do not know if it is a relief or panic starting to kick in when I hear Maxine's voice on the phone, "Branx's vitals have changed, and he is starting to stir, he might be coming to. I thought you would like to know."

Releasing my held breath with a whoosh, not realising I had been holding it, my shoulders slump with a sigh, and my brain adjusts to the news. Branx is going to be okay.

"Thanks for letting me know, Maxine. I'll be leaving soon. His mother has just arrived; I will inform her of what you just said and thanks again for letting me know," I excitedly say. Relief is filling my heart until I looked back at Brodlyne.

As I hit the end-key to finish the call on the phone, Brodlyne started her fifty-million questions. *Here we go* I thought!

The peace and quiet did not last long.

Chapter Fourteen

ALEX

"**W**HAT HAPPENED? WHERE HAVE YOU BEEN? Who was that on the phone and where are you going? How is my son? How could you let this happened to him, Alex? Have you caught who did this to him?"

After that first bunch of questions, I just looked at her and switched off, before I said something which I might regret later. I did say might regret…

With Branx's words echoing in my head — *'Be nice! Brodlyne is the only family and parent that I have, she loves me and wants to protect me.'* — Yeah right! She is a control freak and a bitch.

I interrupt her, with my hand just about in her face, and went on to say, "I have to get back to the hospital, so I need to put some things together for Branx. I will be back in a moment to answer some of your questions."

Turning, I walk towards my bedroom to organise a small bag for Branx, making sure to grab his travel toiletries, a change of clothing, pyjamas, and a few things for me, in case I stay at the hospital, with him.

It does not take long to notice Brodlyne hot on my heels following me to my bedroom. Will this woman ever give me a break, I think — *Nah, she hates me far too much. She is driving me insane.* Abruptly stopping, I turn around and face her.

"Look Brodlyne, I do not have much time, go turn the kettle on and make yourself a cup of tea, and I'll be back in a moment. Once I have everything packed and ready I will join you in the kitchen and try to answer your questions before I leave."

This woman is pushing her luck as she started to protest. Not giving her a chance, she has no choice but back off when I walked away, closing the door in her face behind me.

A few minutes later, with socks and shoes covering my feet, I walk out of the bedroom with hopefully everything which we will need and headed towards the kitchen. I take in deep slow breaths and try to focus on what I will have to say to Brodlyne as well as keeping my cool.

As I walked into the kitchen, I looked over at Brodlyne to see her anxious face. I placed the overnight bag on the bench next to my handbag and went over to my cup of tea.

I sit down on the kitchen stool and start to fill her in about the phone call from Maxine. "That was the hospital, his vitals have finally started to change, and he is starting to stir, which might mean all going well, he might be regaining consciousness soon."

With a sigh, Brodlyne appeared a little better with the latest update, but I knew that would not last long, as she would want all the details about the case and how he ended up in hospital.

I start to count in my head as the last of my cooling tea slide down my throat, placing my empty teacup back on the bench. Bugger it; I think I will have another one. I need to be drinking more fluid. Getting up I walked to the kettle, finding it is still hot, I proceed to make a fresh cup and continue counting, fifty, fifty-one, fifty-two...

"Alex, what happened?" Here we go. Geez, I made it all the way to fifty-two seconds. "How could this happen to Branx? What's happening with the case now?"

Taking my eyes off my teacup, I thought about my answer before speaking and turning my head to look at her.

"Brodlyne, up until just over an hour ago, I had stayed with him since he arrived at the hospital. As for the case, I really do not know what is happening with it at this point." I pause to take a sip my tea, feeling the aromatic blend of hot goodness slide down my throat. "A couple of your local agents, last I knew were taking over the case, as someone had to do it, with the current agents out of action. As for the criminals who had been holding us prisoner," I lift my head and glance towards her, "well, they are all dead. As for what happened to Branx and his injuries which he received, I will fill you in tomorrow."

Taking another mouthful of tea, I allow it to soothe my throat before continuing. "I need to get back to the hospital. If you want to join me, you can. Otherwise, you know where the guest bedroom is, make yourself at home, but there is no food in the fridge." Finishing the last of my biscuit and swiping a melted smudge of chocolate from my lips, I say, "We have not been shopping since last week before we were captured." With a shrug of my shoulders, "…Sorry."

With an embarrassed smile, I look down at my cup of tea. Taking another mouthful of tea, only to find my mug nearly empty. Damn. *Okay, time to move away from this She-Devil, I feel my stress levels alleviating in her presence.*

I reach over and unplugged my mobile phone from its charger, grabbed my car keys, picked up the overnight bag and placed my items in the side compartment in the bag before getting up from my kitchen stool.

With my teacup back in my hand I start to take another sip of tea when I saw I have already finished my drink, realisation hitting me this is the most I have consumed in two or is that three days?

I walk towards the dishwasher, ready to place our dirty cups in it, only to take a step back from the odour from within. Gross. With the soap dispenser full and the dirty cups placed on the sliding rack, I quickly close its door and hit the wash button. Hopefully, this will wash the dishes, but also the dishwasher and remove that foul stench.

I give a quick glance around me before picking up the overnight bag, just as I start to turn to go towards the front door Brodlyne starts to talk, "Alex, wait a minute, please." *Here we go*, I thought. "I will go with you to the hospital; I would like to see my son. Thank you for getting him to the hospital. The doctors had informed me, if it been any longer, he would have died."

I noticed her moving towards me. I felt unsure what I should do. Do I need to protect myself, as she places her outstretched arms around me, embracing me tightly — she's, literally freaking me out.

"Thank you, Alex, for bringing my boy home alive."

I thought if she knew what happened before the ambulance arrived, she might not be so quick to thank me.

Chapter Fifteen

ALEX

DRIVING TO THE HOSPITAL THROUGH THE dimly lit quiet streets, it does not take long for my thoughts to wander back when I sat Branx down all those years ago and thoroughly explained about my family heritage. Explaining to him, I am not just a *Dark One*, but I am also a *Witch*. My parents had thought it would be best for me to inform him about other Paranormal Entities, seems they decided not to mention my other talents of being a powerful witch in training.

Apart from close family and a few friends, are the only ones who genuinely know about my magic and Alley, is the single soul who truly knows my full magical talents, well nearly all my talents. The more I learn and practice my magic, the better I will understand and achieve great things and protect the ones I love.

My mother and Aunt Lucy know I am incredibly talented, especially with more than half of my magical powers being transferred to me while my mother was still pregnant with me. These magical powers were transferred from our Great Aunt Alivia, who was my Grandma Ma's youngest daughter.

Alivia's father came from a long line of powerful witches. It is a tragedy how the dark witches killed Alivia's father and Alivia's baby son, in front of her, torturing her for far too long. Thanks to my mother, she was able to seek justice and revenge for Alivia, destroying the dark witches and placing a stop to their barbaric ways.

Just before Alivia died, she somehow managed to pass her magic powers through my pregnant mother to me, making sure her family powers continue through our family line for many generations to come.

With a fond smile, I remember when Branx bit me in the early days when we were first together. On this occasion, Branx had managed to bite my shoulder, drawing blood.

It was an accident; he did not mean to bite me so hard. Instead of him being repulsed by the sight of my blood, he leaned forward and with his tongue swiped across the open wound, tasting my blood for the first time.

After his first taste, he enjoyed the erotic taste so much he suckled the wound on my shoulder harder, consuming my enticing blood with each mouthful.

For my first time experiencing someone drinking straight from me; having Branx drinking my blood, actually made me orgasm. My need for blood had started to grow into hunger cravings when I was around him. Ever since then, I have craved for his blood. It is a good thing he is my *soul mate*.

With Branx close to death, thanks to those BPE, I managed to keep him alive long enough to get him to a hospital. If it were not for my blood, he would have died on the first night we were captured. I know I have to be careful, giving him my blood in large quantities as it can start a chain reaction, turning him into a *Vampire/Dark One*, it is uncommon, but not unheard of.

Three days before our capture in this horrendous case, I had seen the doctor, because, I felt different, my belly felt different, my breasts had increased in size, which usually happened when leading up to a period, but my periods had not occurred in three months. Come to think of it; I have not had a period for maybe six months. As far as I know, I thought my contraception implant would prevent me from falling pregnant.

When I think back to it, several months ago I started to notice a change in Branx, with his paranormal abilities increasing for some unexplained reason. Also, about a month ago I began to notice a difference in my own body, not thinking much about it, until a week and a half ago when I finally contacted Dr Brean requesting a full set of tests performed. I had all types of scenarios travelling through my mind, thinking it might be related to Branx and his increased abilities.

A few days before we were captured, I finally managed to organise the trip to pathology for the blood work to be taken. The following day Doctor Brean contacted me and informed me I need to come into his office. The morning of the day Branx and I were captured; I travelled to Darshia and visited with Doctor Brean at his private clinic. Thinking there must be something medically wrong with me, I became extremely concerned when Doctor Brean ordered an ultrasound to be performed there and then.

The big shock to me, was when I realised what I had been looking at on the screen. Witnessing my baby for the very first time had been more than a surprise to my system, even a bigger shock finding out I am nearly at five months into the pregnancy.

With all this new information, it certainly explained quite a few things to me, especially the increased need for Branx blood. It soon became apparent I would need to stop working on cases which would lead me into physical fights with others; no way was I going to place our new baby daughter's life in danger. I knew if I felt in danger, my magic and *Dark One* abilities would appear and try to protect myself, which of course would reveal whom and what I was.

Within minutes arriving back at The Corporation, in the city, Branx and I received a message on the whereabouts of the group of BPE. Thinking this follow up should not take very long, I left my hand bag in my desk draw and decided I would be able to inform Branx of the tests and scan results that evening.

Unfortunately, we had been set up and

captured before I had the chance to inform him of the pregnancy. With the BPE out for blood, continuously attacking us, they made the mistake of hurting and torturing us, the idiots made sure to inform us we were there to die. Thankfully, using my magical abilities, I was able to protect my baby from being injured.

The BPE boasted I would not be leaving the building alive, and Branx had been taken away to be questioned. I knew then, and there I had to break free from my bindings, especially when I started to hear those creatures viciously torturing my *soul mate*.

Using all the power I could muster, I soon released myself and turned the tables on the BPE. Killing each one of the horrible crazed BPE, finally exterminating the vermin where they stood.

By the time I reached the last two, I was already too late to prevent them from tearing into Branx, ripping his flesh apart. Witnessing the last of the torturous deep slashes performed against an unconscious Branx, the two BPE thought they would enjoy their time torturing me before they kill me.

The talkative pair bragged about how they are going to become rich and live the high life after killing me. The pair had gone on to say how they had been hired to capture me and bring my dead body to some mystery benefactor for money; these idiots had been paid to kill me, not Branx. The morons made the biggest mistake of tearing into him. In the end, the Bad Paranormal Entities gone rogue paid with their lives.

Chapter Sixteen

ALEX

FINDING A LONG-TERM CAR PARK NEARLY became impossible, feeling bloody frustrated, all I can see so far is every car spot taken. No, wonder why people prefer to travel by taxi. With my stress levels rising, I do not need this hassle, especially having Brodlyne sitting in my car beside me. I bet she is enjoying the annoyance and stressed mood I am in.

At least pulling into McDonald's before arriving at the hospital and grabbing some junk food, had been satisfying in itself, to see the shocked look on Brodlyne's face, with the refusal of my offer to feed her. What else was I going to do for food? I have to eat something. At least what they pass off as food is quick and simple and I hope it will relax me enough to fill some of my hunger.

I drink my orange juice first, followed by devouring my burger, McMuffin, fries and the apple pie. With extra care not to burn my mouth on the delicious hot filling, my mouth continues to water from the tasty apple treat. I can still taste a hint of the apple and its sweet, gooey sauce. Remembering the hospital cafeteria should be closed at this time of night, I also ordered an extra-large white tea, two more apple pies and a thick chocolate shake, to consume up in his room.

Eventually finding a vacant car space, we make our way to the fifth floor of the hospital, with my cardboard drink tray in my hand and my senses on high alert. With my magic energy levels low and not wanting to alert Brodlyne of my magical abilities, I attempt to release a small amount of my magic energy to detect any BPE nearby.

With none discovered I am relieved, my fighting skills will most likely be on the sluggish side. I need blood and rest to build myself back up and with Branx out of action and Brodlyne sticking to my side; I doubt I will be consuming any blood tonight. How will I get rid of this woman for ten minutes or so? I need to be drinking blood, not just for myself, but also for the life of the baby I am carrying.

Why does this woman, annoy me so much? There has always been something about her I have never trusted.

With the odour of the hospital filling my nostrils, my belly is debating to start somersaults — bile starts to rise, encouraging me to want to throw up. I am not too fond of hospitals.

I still cannot believe *I am pregnant!* I need Branx to wake up so I can finally reveal the news before someone else notices my body changing. I think I will be giving notice to Brodlyne and her boss first thing in the morning. If what the BPE had told me, my life is still in danger and in times like these, I will feel a whole lot safer back in Darshia surrounded by my family.

Chapter Seventeen

ALEX

I PUSH THE HOSPITAL ROOM DOOR OPEN, revealing an unconscious Branx, pale and lifeless with wires and tubes connected from different sounding machines to him. The sound of Brodlyne's gasp beside me reminds me she is still here, maybe she might believe me about her son's condition, I did try to warn her back in the car.

Out of the corner of my eye, I notice Brodlyne giving me that evil glinty look again. Why does she do that when she thinks I am not looking? Before I can comment, she rushes forward, nudging me out of the way.

"Oh, my poor boy. What did those

animals do to you?" Brodlyne says a little too loudly.

"Shh. Keep it down Brodlyne," I hiss back at her, as my eyes turn to look out the doorway, for the avenging nurses or security to come barging in here. "There are other patients nearby, and I do not want hospital security coming in here and encouraging us to leave. Be quiet."

Turning back towards Branx — my eyes have trouble witnessing what is happening before me. OMG. Is the woman trying to kill my husband? Brodlyne has just flung herself on top of his injured body.

Shock. That is what it is — I am in shock. She is covering my husband's body with hers and is most likely opening some of his internal injuries. I try to use my voice several times — no sound comes out.

I try again with determination. "Brodlyne, get the fuck off him before you cause some serious damage. What are you bloody thinking doing something so stupid?" my words screech out loud, through my parted lips.

With a tilt of her head, Brodlyne stares me in the eye and smiles. "Thank you, Alex, for bringing me to the hospital. I can take care of things from here. You may leave, now."

I blink my eyes several times, breaking eye contact. *What the fuck? I do not think so.*

I lift my chin and square my shoulders as I walk to the other side of the hospital bed, I place the cardboard drink tray with my drinks and food down on the empty hospital portable table and look back at Brodlyne.

Oh, my goddess, if I did not already know this She-Devil is my husband's mother, I would think this crazy woman is a lover or something... hmm, something does not feel right.

I take a step closer to the bed and lean forward to place a gentle kiss on my husband's lips. Just when I start to pull away, I feel his lips twitch under my own.

With my mind, I reach out to his. *'Honey, can you hear me? I love you. Please wake up soon. I have something important to tell you.'*

I try again and press my lips to his, within seconds I start to feel Branx's lips move, he is responding to my kiss. Relief and joy fill me, my husband is finally coming back to me.

'Hey Baby. I love you, too. Now kiss me,' Branx says through our mind link. He does not have to tell me twice to kiss him.

With our lips moving as one, I start to feel, Branx's tongue slide into my mouth. Hearing a groan come from the back of mine and Branx's throat.

'Honey I have been waiting for too long to hear you in my head once again. Welcome back, baby.'

'It is nice to be back, speaking with you like this. Now, what news do you want to tell me?'

Hearing a throat being cleared in a not very ladylike fashion, is not the way I wanted to stop our kiss. Damn, Brodlyne. Oh yes, I still need to reply to her lovely words.

'One moment, Honey, I still have to answer your mother.'

I cannot stand Brodlyne, especially being interrupted, with her looking straight us, watching us, nearly has my stomach turning once again.

Turning my head I look her in the eye, my

eyebrow rising as I reply to her so-called dismissal, "Brodlyne, I will not be leaving Branx anytime soon. So forget about it. While here in the hospital or at my home, you are not my boss. So, do not tell me what to do or threaten me."

Brodlyne lips turn into an angry snarl. "Do not talk to me in such a way, Alex. Or I will have you removed from this hospital. I will have you fired from your job so fast; your little head will spin. Branx is mine; how you are still alive, I do not know. You should be the one in a hospital bed, not my precious boy. This is your entire fault, Branx nearly died. You should be dead."

Warning bells start flashing through my mind. Something is very wrong here. I think she has just said far too much. This bitch is hinting she knew something. Why do I suddenly have the feeling Brodlyne is behind the setup, behind the hiring of those BPE. She has never hidden the fact she does not and has never liked me being with Branx. She had hinted once he was meant to be betrothed to one of her long-time friend's daughters.

Branx has made it extremely clear it was never placed in writing, and the girl they speak of also does not want to be married to Branx. The girl already knows Branx, and I are married. She had been relieved as she was in love with someone else. So it was a win, win.

Chapter Eighteen

ALEX

A GROGGY SOUNDING NOISE, HAS BOTH Brodlyne and me turning towards the bed. Oh, thank goodness. Branx is finally making himself known he is starting to wake.

"Welcome back, Honey," I quickly say, "how are you feeling?" My hand gently folds over the top of Branx's, giving his warm flesh a slight squeeze.

Brodlyne eases off the bed and stands, allowing him some much-needed room. Sensing his body and the amount of pain Branx is experiencing and the moment when he realises he is in worse shape than he first thought and I can see the agony in his eyes.

I internally shake my head with concern,

with his mother here Branx also has to contend with Brodlyne and me arguing. I know Branx hates it when his mother and I fight. However, this time, surely he would have heard his mother make the remarks regarding wanting me dead.

When Branx realises I know how much pain he is in, he quickly tries to convince me otherwise, "Hey Baby. Just a bit of pain. How are you? Should you be up and about?" Branx asks with uncertainty in coating his voice.

Avoiding his question for a few more seconds, I reach for a glass of water from his side table. Without asking, I bring it up to his mouth, with the straw against his parched lips. Automatically Branx takes a tentative sip, swallowing the liquid carefully down, and nods his head in thanks.

"I should be okay. Anyway, you are more important to me right now," Trying to push the issue; I am worried about him more than myself.

"Alex, you were also hurt, I saw them attacking you. Tell the truth, or I will buzz for the nurse and demand for you to be placed in a bed, right here with me," Branx says with a twitch of his lips.

Shaking my head, I can see the worry and concern in his eyes.

"Branx I have some bruising, but nothing for you to concern yourself with. You, on the other hand, had some major damage. You are extremely fortunate to be alive."

Brodlyne is missing the attention and quickly interrupts, "Branx darling, how are you, my...son? Should I call the nurse, what do you need? I will make sure the nurse supplies you with whatever you require... I—"

Branx cuts off his mother's ramblings, "Mother, what a surprise."

With a quick flick of his eyes, Branx focuses on his mother, standing on the other side of the bed. As he looks his mother over, I can see he is thinking of something. Something not very nice. Yes, Branx had been listening earlier to the conversation Brodlyne, and I had been having.

Good in a way, because I do not want any secrets, but wrong on the other hand, I know, this will be hurting Branx and breaking his heart if this is all true and Brodlyne is behind the setup. Oh, geez, I still have to inform Branx of the information I discovered before

I finished off the last of the BPE and finally sought help.

With tears filling her eyes, Brodlyne tries to place her arms around Branx once more, nudging me out of her way.

"What is it, my son? Why are you looking at me like that? Should I go and call the nurse? Are you in pain?"

"Mother, please, move away from me, I cannot handle anyone touching me at the moment. It hurts too much."

Instantly Brodlyne stands back up. "Oh, my Branx. I am so, so sorry. You should never have been taken or hurt."

Branx quickly glances at me, then back at his mother.

Feeling Branx at my mind shields, I allow him in, *'Baby, why do I have the feeling my loving mother is somehow involved in the attack.'*

'Hmm. Maybe, because we had been set up and the BPE had confessed being paid to capture us. Oh, and also they were meant to kill me. The annoying thing is, they never revealed who was behind the setup, or who was paying them to capture us.'

Branx turns his concerned eyes back to me.

I offer Branx another sip of water, before placing the glass back on the small table.

'What? What do you mean it was a setup? Also, why would anyone want to kill you?'

'Honey, please calm down. I give his hand another squeeze, and I hope Branx will calm down before he sets off the hospital machines. *You have only just woken up. You have been unconscious for over twenty-six hours. I have not been able to give you any more of my blood, since arriving here at the hospital. I am sorry.'*

'Sorry, Sorry for what? By the looks of you, baby, you are the one in need of blood. Have you had any at all?'

With a slight shake of my head. Branx let out a curse under his lips, *'Bloody hell, Alex. Are you trying to make yourself sick?'*

'No Branx. There has been far too many staff hanging around. Plus you have been too injured. I am not about to take your blood when you are so

badly hurt. I can wait,' my mind voice pleads with him.

Branx is my priority right now.

'Alex, I will get rid of my mother for a while, and you will have your fill of blood.'

'No Branx. Maybe tomorrow.'

'No Alex. I can see it and sense it. You require my blood. Why do I have the feeling there is something different about you? When we had been captured, I noticed there was something different about your blood. Come to think of it; your blood has been different for a few months now…'

Shit. Don't tell me my blood is already changing with the pregnancy.

'I do have something significant to tell you. But not with your mother hanging around though, as it is very personal what I need to share with you.'

'Sounds interesting, can you give me a hint?'

'Branx, you will have to wait.'

'Come on baby tell me.'

With a shake of my head and a smile to my lips, I reply, *'No Branx. Look, I will go and speak with the nurses and let them know you are awake. The doctor will most likely want to see you. Plus, it will give you time to speak to your bloody mother.'*

'Okay, baby. Go. I can see how you are avoiding answering the question. Go and bring back a pretty nurse.'

With a smile, I reply, *'Branx, you have a catheter so I would not try to start an erection if I was you.'*

'What?'

Leaning down, I placed my lips gently against Branx's.

'I'll be back in a minute. Question your mother. Something is not right here, especially about her.'

With that, I straightened up, winked at Branx and headed towards the door. Turning my head back over my shoulder, I say to the bitch, I mean the mother-in-law, "Brodlyne, I am going to have a chat with the nurses and also inform them Branx is awake. I will be back in a few minutes."

If she was so concerned for her son, she should have informed one of the nursing staff when Branx became conscious. No, she had to see what I would say to Branx. I am pleased with my Dark One abilities and the use of our mind link allowing us privacy when we speak to one another.

Chapter Nineteen

ALEX

WALKING BESIDE NURSE MAXINE, WE continue discussing Branx and the tests the doctor will perform. Only to stop in our tracks at the doorway, when we both see and hear Brodlyne arguing with an agitated Branx.

We can hear the last of their sentences, I do not have to know the full conversation to realise they were discussing me and with the look on Branx's face, he is getting ready to blow his top.

What in the world is she doing, upsetting him when he just woke up? As I said before, she is a real *Bitch from Helz.*

"Mother, I want you to leave."

With an evil eye turned on me, Brodlyne snarls, "No. That woman is not staying here another minute. I'll make sure the hospital knows not to allow her anywhere near you."

Hearing a hitch in Branx's voice, I don't think he realised just how much Brodlyne hates me. "Mother ...leave, now. Before I have security remove you."

Brodlyne turns, her eyes pleading towards her son, "Branx, please. You do not know what you are saying."

"Mother, *get out!*"

"No."

A sad look crosses his face as he says, "If you *love me*, Mother, *leave now*," with determination across his face, Branx continues, "because if you do not leave right now, this will be the last time you will see me."

"Darling. You do not know what you are saying."

Annoyance and bitterness fill Branx's face. "That is it. You have treated me as a child for the last time. Nurse, I want hospital security to remove this woman. While I am a patient here, she is not to come anywhere near me. Do you understand?"

Nurse Maxine walks casually up to Brodlyne, as the nurse slips her hand into her hospital scrubs pocket. Oh wow, I think she just pressed her security alert buzzer.

"Ma'am. My patient has requested you to leave. I would advise you to go now, because hospital security is now on their way here to this room, to escort you from the hospital premises."

When I look to Brodlyne's eyes, there was so much hatred within her, sending a shiver down my spine. Oh, shit, if looks could kill.

"You'll pay for this," Brodlyne hisses, "I will make sure you'll never go near my Branx again." With that, she turned towards him. "I'll be back, and you'll see I am right. I will be announcing your engagement with Angela. The two of you will be married within the month." Feeling the presence of two people moving up behind me, I turn to see the hospital security enter the room.

"Ah, Mother. That will never happen, especially when both Angela and I are already married to other people. We have been for quite some time." With that, Branx smiled his wicked smile and winked at me.

With a shake to her head, Brodlyne murmurs, "What do you mean, you are already married?" With shock written over her paling face, "Since when?"

"All I am going to say, I have been married to Alex for many years. You do not need to know anything else."

Noticing when reality catches up to her, I quickly raise my hands to cover my ears as Brodlyne's face contorts in rage as she began to loudly screech.

"WHAT?"

As her ear-splitting attack continues, and spittle fly out of her pristine mouth, she screams, "No. Branx no. What have you done?" My ears continue to ring from her verbal assault, filling the hospital room, "No. You can't be. No. You're mine."

With that last note, Branx nods his head at the two hospital security personnel who had entered his room, acknowledging they can now escort the screaming woman away.

Chapter Twenty
ALEX

"**O**h, Honey. You do realise Brodlyne is going to be nothing but trouble for now on, don't you?" I say to a smiling Branx.

He turns his head towards Nurse Maxine and requests for her to give us a few minutes of privacy. With a quick nod of her head, she turns and quietly walks out of the room, closing the door behind her.

With a strange tone to his voice, he says, "Alex." The look in his eyes slowly changes to serious. "Baby, come here and lay with me."

Nodding my head, I carefully lay down trying to avoid all the medical leads, tubes and wires. I carefully curl myself up against him, relief filling my soul, being able to feel Branx against my body once more.

After several minutes of arguing, he finally gives in and consumes some of my blood; wanting my blood to help and aid in his recovery before I consume my intake of blood from his vein.

With my head sharing the pillow beside him, I tilt my head enough to look into his caring and sexy eyes; I love him so much. As he says, "Baby, I love you. If we have to give up our jobs, so be it."

Sighing, I inhale a slow deep breath, before replying, "Branx, I have a feeling we will be travelling to Darshia when you leave the hospital." He nods his head in understanding.

With relief, I continue, "Well — One: for you to fully recover." Using my fingers, I count out the reasons, "Two: my life is in danger if what the BPE had informed me is true, someone out there wants me dead, and they are paying for someone to do it. And Three," Pausing, oh boy, how am I going to say the next part? "Three: I am resigning."

"What? Why?"

"Why is because you need to heal from your injuries. Plus, Alley is going to marry the guy our parents had agreed years ago to become her fiancé. We both know she had given up finding her *soul mate* until they met at their engagement party. Plus she has to think about my gorgeous little niece, Alphilia."

"Alex, what has my injuries and your sister have to do with you wanting to quit your job. You enjoy our life, don't you?" Branx carefully asks.

"Oh, Honey. I love working side by side with you every day and catching the bad guys. However, we both have to be realistic. With Alley moving away from Darshia next year, the role of the Queen then falls upon my shoulders. Both Alley and I have always known, one of us will be the next Queen of Darshia."

Taking in another breath, I look Branx in the eye, and I hope he is not about to freak out on me, as I say, "Plus, my loving husband, we are going to have a baby."

Waiting for my words to register, and yep there it is as I watch his eyes grow wide, then a huge smile forms on his face.

"I knew it. I knew there was something different from your blood. I could not place my finger on it." An ecstatic Branx leans his head forward and plasters his lips against mine. "We are going to have a baby, really? How? When?" Branx says against my lips.

The increase of pressure and the slide of Branx tongue turns our next kiss into a power filled lingering erotic kiss, making my toes tingle.

After another minute or so while our lips become better aquatinted once more, I slowly pull away from those empowering lips of his, forcing air into my depleted lungs. My thoughts start to come back to me, knowing there is a question I am meant to answer.

Oh, yes. When?

"The day we were captured is the day I found out for sure. I even had a pile of tests, including a scan," I say a little too eagerly, the excitement in my voice growing with each happy word spoken about the day of the scan and witnessing the miracle growing inside me. "I have seen our baby, Branx. Our daughter. We are going to have a little girl. Our very own daughter." Seeing the pride in his eyes as his lips turn into a beautiful smile, with the knowledge he is going to be a father, I can see he is excited.

"We are having a girl. Wow. I hope she has your beautiful eyes." Watching his facial expressions change, I can see he is thinking back to the day we were captured. "Alex is that where you went? You said you had an appointment back in Darshia. Was this the appointment?"

"Yes, I…I had to make sure. I knew there was something different happening. I just had to find out what. And what a big *what* it turned out to be," I smile at my loving husband. "I haven't told my parents yet, but they will know as soon as I see them in person. They will be able to detect it. Well, my mother will anyway."

Branx wraps his arms around me, a little more tightly and place a gentle kiss on my forehead. I say, "My father said, in the *Dark One* community, a father can mind speak, with his child. I do not know if that would work in our case, as you are not a *Dark One*, you can only try."

Reaching down, I quickly lift my top and undo my pants, exposing my warm naked flesh. Carefully Branx gently places his hand on my lower belly. The warmth of his fingers, brush across my sensitive skin feeling the growing protection of love and security over my body, his large, strong hand touching perfectly against my little bump, covering our sleeping daughter.

"Oh, my Alex. …I don't know how did I not notice this little miracle?" His eyes wide with pride, watching his hand glide slowly over the small rise which is now our daughter. "I can feel your belly is different. How did I not realise your body has been changing?" After a few more gentle strokes, feeling the heat of his hand against my skin, he rests his palm against my belly.

With my mind, I breach into Branx head. Taken back, I gasp with the multitude of his thoughts. Oh, wow. Branx is happy about the baby. Excited to be able to feel our child from within.

Our sleeping baby girl is soon awake, and Branx is able to link his mind with our child's. It does not take long before they manage to communicate a few words to one another. Looking back at his face, he is now sporting misty eyes as a lone tear slowly makes its way down his cheek. The pride and joy of being a father and speaking to his child, making him one proud and excited husband and now a father. Okay, I am going to blame the pregnancy hormones on this one, as I soon find myself with tears of joy rolling down my cheeks.

Chapter Twenty-One

WITH THE DOCTOR FINALLY GONE, AND ALL the wires and tubing removed, Branx eventually left his bed with a big smile plastered on his face. I think that little bit of my blood has helped him tremendously.

He slowly shuffles his way towards the bathroom, with the assistance of two nurses; he is determined to clean himself up. Well, brush his teeth, for one. Plus, he would prefer to pee in a toilet than a hospital bottle, especially after having the uncomfortable experience of the catheter being slowly removed. Ouch. Yep, Branx is ready to soak under the warm water spray in the shower, as long as he is sitting down on one of those shower chairs.

Giving him some time to himself, I make my way just down the corridor, deciding I better phone my parents and update them on what is happening. I am thankful Darshia has kept up to date with its technology, enabling internet and mobile coverage in both realms. My parents are going to hit the roof when I explain what has happened in the last forty-eight plus hours.

"Hello, Alex. It has been awhile. Is everything okay?" Hearing my mother's voice brings my tears back with a vengeance.

"Oh, Mumma. Where do I start?" I try to swallow the lump forming in my throat.

"How about at the start, Baby girl. What has you so emotional?"

I push my back against the white sterile wall, and straightening my back, lifting my chin and form a smile on my face and say, "Well, you and Daddy are going to be grandparents again."

"What? Since when?" Hearing my mother yell out for my father to come over to the phone so he can listen to our phone call as well. Listening to my excited mother inform her husband their daughter is going to have a baby.

Next thing I know, my father's voice is speaking down the phone line, "Alex, baby. Is everything okay? How are you? How far are you?"

Not allowing me to answer, Mum starts with her questions also. They must have placed the phone on loudspeaker. Cutting them both off before they can build up too much steam and prevent me from getting another word in.

"Mum, Dad. I am mostly fine. I have decided to retire from my job. Also, I need your help."

"What is going on Alex? Where is Branx?" my mother questions.

"Well... That is another reason why I am phoning."

"Alex, is Branx alive?"

"Yes, Mum. Now... However, twenty-four hours ago he was far too close to death."

"What?" Both my parents yell at the same time, "Why are you only phoning us now? What happened?"

"Well, Branx and I have been busy working on a case, dealing with the BPE. Anyway, as we found out, far too late, it had all been a setup. Someone paid the BPE to capture us, well me anyway. I have a hit on my head. Someone wants me dead."

"Over my *Dark One* body," my father yells.

How I love my parents.

"Hang on a minute. Alex explain what happened, you are missing a lot of information here." Yep, and there is my mother. She is not the Queen for nothing. Her brain is already working out what is required to be done, and she needs the facts to do it.

Dragging another haggard breath into my sore lungs, I go on to say, "Well, about three days or so ago, I found out I am pregnant. However, before I had a chance to inform Branx, we had a tip-off on our latest case we have been working so hard on. With no time to spare, we left and went to investigate, only to be captured, tortured and Branx nearly killed. As for me, well, I managed to protect myself as much as possible, when up against multiple attackers. I managed to kill my way through the BPE, using my witch powers."

"Oh, crap on a stick, Alex. What you must have gone through. We could have lost you, lost you all."

"I managed to get some answers from one of the BPE before I killed him. It was a setup.

They were paid, and someone wants me dead. I made sure all the BPE had been exterminated and started to give my blood to Branx before I called for help. By this stage, we had been there for about twenty-four to twenty-six hours."

Hearing my parents words of shock through the phone, including a few swear words when my parents realise how close Branx and I came to death. Trying to keep my emotions under control, I continue, "Help arrived, including my fellow work associates to look after the scene, and I travelled to the hospital with Branx in the ambulance, until I went home about five hours ago, showered and changed into some clean clothing. That is when Branx's mother showed up. I drove back to the hospital with Brodlyne in tow, after I received a phone call informing me his vitals had started to change, indicating he might be waking up."

"Oh, my poor, baby. You should have called us. We would have driven you to the hospital and saved you from travelling alone with Brodlyne."

"Yeah, well I managed to drive my car," I say a little too sarcastically. "Anyway, after arriving at the hospital and Branx regained consciousness, Brodlyne and Branx ended up having a big fight, and he had security escort her from the premises."

"Oh, my poor babies. What is happening now?" my mother asked.

"Well the nurses are assisting Branx into the bathroom, and I thought I better phone you guys. We need to come home, Mum. I need to be in Darshia for awhile."

"Yes. Come. Look, Alex, I will send Riley and some of his men to the hospital. You are no longer to remain without protection."

"Okay. Thank you, Mum and Dad. The doctor said I could take him home tomorrow, providing he has complete bed rest under medical supervision. We will have to go to our apartment first. How about, tomorrow afternoon, we will head for Darshia with the guys."

"Only if you are sure, Alex. I will have Riley send at least two guards to protect you there at the hospital. In the morning, he will be there in a palace car to pick you both up, say about 8.00 a.m. That way, you do not have to drive, and if anyone tries to place a tracker on your car, they are not going to be able to follow you."

"Okay, Mum. That sounds good. Look I

better go. I need to see my husband in all his naked glory. Plus, I need to see what injuries he still has."

"Alright love. You look after yourself. Say hello to Branx from us, and we will see you tomorrow."

My shoulders drop with relief knowing we will be going home. "Bye, Mum. Bye, Daddy. Love you both."

"Love you, baby girl," my parents say at the same time.

Chapter Twenty-Two

ALEX

As hard as it is to leave Branx, I allow my husband the time to himself to shower and will enable him to see the extent of the damage to his body.

Branx doesn't need me to hover over him. I know the damage caused to his body. I know what he is like, he prefers to have five minutes to himself, to decompress. He needs to come to terms what happened to himself, to us.

Sensing that he's finished washing, I knew the second he had stood up. He wanted to stand under the water, that is when I knew it is time to enter. Quietly entering through the door, facing the two nurses, I lift my finger to my lips to indicate to keep quiet.

When I started to remove my shoes and clothing, the two nurses smiled at me, quickly realising what I have in mind. With my clothing removed, both nurses start to move out of my way, allowing me the chance to assist my husband with his shower. With a nod of their heads, they casually left the bathroom.

With his washcloth and shower soap in my hands, I soon have the rich lather forming and ready to place against Branx back.

I slowly slide the plastic shower curtain to the side, allowing me a full view of my gorgeous, naked, and very wet husband. Stepping under the spray behind Branx, I start to gently wash my husband's back, paying extra attention to clean around all the waterproof medical dressings.

I try to be brave as I scan his back, all his injuries — I shudder at the horrific scene before me. If I had only used my powers sooner all those hours ago, Branx might not have been so close to death by the time we escaped; I could have lost him because of my delay.

"If you are going to wash my back, I suggest you go a bit lower. I have an itch only you can scratch," hearing Branx speak returns my focus back to him in the little bathroom.

With my mind, I instantly hear his interesting thoughts. He knows it is me, the cheeky husband. Out loud I reply, "Hmm. I would love to, but then my husband might not like me scratching the itch of a naked wet man. What do you think I should do?" I try to keep my voice serious, even though my lips keep twitching into a smile.

"Well, I for one would love to have a sexy sounding woman rub all over my naked body, especially the woman I love."

Feeling his love through our connection, sensing the emotional and physical need Branx has for me. My heart aches for this man; I love him so much. I came far too close to losing him.

With that, I move up behind Branx and wrap my arms around him, pressing my cheek into his wet naked back.

"I love you, Branx. Never forget that."

Feeling him start to move, I release my hold as he slowly turns around, facing me with a big gorgeous smile.

"And, I love you, my beautiful wife." I watch his gorgeous bedroom eyes fill with lust as they travel down my wet, naked body and back up again, just before his vision changes to one of concern, looking me in the eyes, he says, "Now I know you need blood, so take it, while we are alone."

With my mind, I reach out to see where the nurses are, only to realise they have left, going back to their other nurse duties. Hmm. Smart women.

With my magical powers, I lock the bathroom door with a snick of the lock and making the shower chair move behind Branx, so he can sit down while I devour his much-needed blood.

Hearing the chair move behind him, Branx carefully sits himself down and pulling me down onto his lap, tilting his head to the side, exposing his delicious bare neck for the taking.

Without waiting to be told twice, my incisors drop, my mouth opens wide as my teeth glide into his succulent flesh, allowing his warm, enticing blood to fill my mouth and slide down my parched throat, quenching my needs. Encouraging my incisors up, I continue to drink from the twin open wounds. Oh my goodness, I need this so much.

My moist lips gain suction with each delicious pull of Branx's nectar, hearing him moan in pleasure and pulling me closer to his body. Several mouthfuls of his enriched blood later, my eyes snap open when the realisation hits me — my life energy had almost depleted, I was in more danger than I realised.

I continue to swallow mouthful after mouthful of delicious hot blood until I sense I have taken enough blood for now and moved my hand near my mouth. It is time to give Branx some more of my *Dark One* blood, I turn my head and open my vein for Branx and placing my dripping wrist in front of his face.

Without being told, he soon grabs it within his hands. I watch my loving husband place my wrist to his open mouth and feel his warm lips against my flesh allowing him to devour more of my blood to heal his injuries. My sexual appetite increases, with each pull of my blood and every time Branx drinks from my body, he stirs a sexual hunger within me only he can feed and tame.

Turning my head I soon have my mouth back over Branx's neck, I pull on his throbbing vein, instantly filling my mouth and swallowing the much-needed nectar. Trying to be careful not to overindulge, I devour another four more mouthfuls of the delicious ambrosia before quickly sealing the puncture wounds with a swipe of my tongue.

With a groan from my parted lips, I can feel one of his hands making its way between my heated thighs. Sliding between my slippery folds, causing twin erotic sensations to rush through my being, and with every pull from my vein has me on the edge of an orgasm.

With each mouthful of my *Dark One* blood, Branx causes my core to weep and tighten beneath me. As he increases pressure on my swollen, sensitive clit, my handsome husband is making good use of his talented hand.

Right this second, I would prefer to be straddling him, impaling myself upon his hard, silky, solid length, riding him and making sure the both of us orgasm multiples times, until the sun rises, instead of sitting across his naked lap on a showering chair. With a few more well-placed touches, his fingers play my body to the beat of our love, and my core is ready to explode.

With my orgasm fast approaching, the ache in my gums starts, before my incisors drop once again. Turning my head, once more, my teeth slide back through the tender flesh of his neck. Hearing him groan in pleasure, I continue to drink deeply, consuming each delicious mouthful of his ambrosia, feeling the warmth of his blood slide down my sated throat, just as a powerful orgasm shatters all my brain cells and turns my body boneless.

Chapter Twenty-Three

ALEX

Once Branx and I have consumed our share of blood, we complete his shower together, making sure to dress him in loose, comfortable pyjamas. Thanks to the nursing staff, they brought in a tray of hospital food for the both of us to eat. While we ate, I filled Branx in on everything I have found out so far, including the phone call with my parents.

By this stage, he started looking a little better with more colour in his cheeks and feeling stronger. Well, after all, he did have a top-up of my blood, which always helps to give him an energy boost.

With the doctor arriving half an hour later to access Branx, the doctor is amazed at how well he is recovering since regaining consciousness. Before leaving the room, the doctor informed us he would be back to re-evaluate him; if Branx keeps improving, he will be allowed to leave the hospital earlier.

Lying beside Branx, we managed to sleep for over two and a half hours before the doctor returned. After a full assessment rechecking all wounds and changing the dressings, the doctor concludes, if Branx can have full-time medical care at home, he should be okay to leave the hospital.

I promise the doctor, Branx will be well taken care of. The doctor signed off Branx discharge papers and released him into my care. With our bags packed and the two Darshia guards arriving as promised by my parents, we are set to go.

I have a terrible feeling we are going to need Johnson and Greens' fighting skills before long, and I have only met these two Darshia guards a couple of times. They are good at what they do. Otherwise, Riley would not have allowed them to protect me. Sensing deep down, Brodlyne is planning something to get back at me; she wants me out of the way and out of her son's life. Maybe we should head straight to Darshia.

Just as we are approaching my car in the undercover car park, my senses go on full alert only seconds before I notice five dark hooded figures approach us from behind the parked vehicles near my car.

Shit, if I had been at full strength, I would have detected the darkly hooded men, long before now.

Before I can say anything, Johnson passes Branx a handgun and Greens places one of our fighting swords in one of my hands and a handgun in the other. Before I can take another step forward, Greens and I are fighting for our lives, against the five dark creatures, just by their body shape alone, I detect they are all male.

Using my gun and sword, I manage to kill two of the darkly clothed creatures before hearing a gun blast from behind me. I look over my shoulder towards Branx. Noticing he just shot one dark figure, before pulling the trigger and shooting another in the head. I start to turn when I notice several more creatures appear from the shadows. Damn. These creatures are increasing in numbers; we are going to be in trouble if we are not careful.

Surveying the carpark with no humans in

the vicinity, I quickly evaluate the situation. Our lives are far too valuable to hide my abilities; if I do not do something soon, we might find ourselves dead. With three dead creatures on the ground by Branx, two on the ground by Johnson, two by my feet and four at Greens feet, we are dangerously outnumbered as I watch more creatures surround us.

With my abilities coming forth, I start to move faster as a *Dark One*, wielding my magic at the same time. With my witch magic in full force, I start to freeze several of the evil dark creatures in front of me. With my sword rising, swinging, and slicing out around my body, the sharp sword in my hand does quick work connecting through my targets and slicing through their fabric and flesh. The pungent odour of their blood taints the air, causing my belly to roll with nausea.

Taking out three of the creatures, while using my handgun to shoot another two. Dodging, ducking and jumping out of the road of another three of these things, just barely managing to either shoot with my silver bullets or strike them with the sword. Sensing something coming up behind me I managed to freeze another evil, dark creature, as it tried to sneak up behind me, with its knife ready to thrust into my back.

Instead, it is frozen in time, I spin around and with my bloodied covered sword, managing in one fast and hard, clean slice, remove its head from its grotesque body. The look of shock on its face just before the evil creature's head hits the ground with a clunk, quickly followed by its massive body, and the handholding knife noisily clatters to the concrete.

Free of evil creatures, I glance around until I find my husband. Spotting Branx is in trouble and surrounded by far too many dangerous creatures, I take off, moving fast towards him. Releasing my power, and blasting another two more of these evil beings at the same time shooting another one with my handgun. Whatever they are, these creatures still fall down dead when they are stabbed, beheaded, shot or blasted with my witch magical power.

Standing beside Branx, I notice he is bleeding once again. Shit, this is not good. Quickly passing Branx my handgun, and dropping the sword at my feet, freeing my hands, I don't muck around. I zap, freeze, crash, lift and drop the creatures around us.

Using any spell quickly coming to mind, concentrating so hard, I do not realise I had closed my eyes until a few moments later; I feel Branx, place his hand on my shoulder.

"Baby, it's over, we have killed them all. There is no more of them left to kill."

With that, my eyes catch up to the carnage surrounding us, and I shake my head from side to side. I swallow the moisture in my mouth, feeling the increased pressure forming in the back of my throat. I try to gulp down again, hoping to dislodge the lump forming and rising.

Bloody hell, whoever wants me dead is determined. Branx retrieves my mobile phone from my handbag, quickly dials our work colleagues to have them clean up this mess before the humans stumble across all this blood.

With his eyes remaining on me, whomever Branx is speaking with will now know we survived the ordeal. Which may not be a good thing given we do not know who is responsible for the assassination attempts on my life.

Making up my mind, I decided we are heading straight for Darshia now, not tomorrow. I am not going to take any more chances with the life of Branx or my unborn daughter. Now, to inform the guys to the change of plans and have Greens drive my car back to our apartment complex. I want whoever is following and trying to kill me to think I am in our apartment tonight.

Chapter Twenty-Four

ALEX

WALKING INTO MY OLD BEDROOM IN THE castle, the heavy burden pressing down against my shoulders is slowly lifting with Branx by my side.

Having my childhood doctor arrive to perform a medical examination to both Branx and myself is a little frustrating.

"Alex, you require rest. Your blood pressure is a little low, once Branx has rested and eaten, you are to consume more of his blood. You should have consumed more by now, young lady. You are not looking after yourself. Also, yes I noticed the bruising. I will send for the mobile ultrasound machine, and I want to make sure your little girl is healthy and not harmed in any way after all your fighting."

With concern is lacing each word, I ask, "My daughter is okay, isn't she?"

Damn it. I only wanted to keep my unborn daughter and Branx safe.

"Alex, you are low on your *soul mates* blood. You have been hurt. You also have been fighting and using your magic. You tell me, should I be worried or not?"

Looking down to the floor and avoiding the doctor's eyes, I reply, "Okay. I see your point, Doctor Brean. I will rest for tonight and drink plenty of blood when I can."

"Alex, do not avoid answering the question. I will be back with the ultrasound machine after you eat. I will do a follow up in the morning."

"Yes, Doctor Brean," I mumble.

After showering again, we are finally sitting down eating a healthy meal, rich in meat and iron. It was lovely to be able to sit with my husband and not worry about someone trying to kill me for once. Without discussing work, or the topic of his mother, we decide to head to bed for a well-earned sleep.

Once I knew Branx had fallen asleep, I quietly got back up out of bed, walked out of my bedroom, and waited in my adjoining lounge area. The doctor arrived with a portable ultrasound machine and a fold up medical table, a minute or so later. Doctor Brean soon has me lying down on the portable table, squirting the cold gel on my exposed belly, causing goosebumps to form.

Within seconds I hear and see my baby on the small screen. From all the times I went with Alley to her pregnancy scans; I like to think I know what I am looking at on the dark screen. With tears in my eyes, I am relieved when Doctor Brean says the baby is healthy and has a strong heartbeat. The only thing he is a little concerned with is the placenta, and how it is sitting in my uterus. Not understanding what he is trying to inform me, I start to worry.

"Alex, until you have had plenty of rest and blood, I would prefer you to stay in bed for at least twenty-four hours. I will be back in an hour or two, to perform another scan. Then again in the morning. Now go back to bed and rest, and drink your husband's blood. Both you and the baby need it."

Waking with my husband kissing along my naked flesh is one way to start my day, waking up to find his head between my thighs, and spreading them wide is something I will always cherish.

Feeling the swipe of his warm, moist tongue through my sensitive folds, causes my back to arch and my hands to grip my sheets. Branx continues to masterfully manoeuvre his tongue over my little bundle of nerves turning it instantly hard and erect, making my body weep for joy. My hips continue to rock against his enticing lips with each glide and sweep of his talented tongue and suction of his mouth.

Oh, how I love his talented mouth and nimble fingers.

My hips continue to lift and roll to the sensual delights of the sexual haven, known as Branx's talented mouth, encouraging my fast approaching orgasm to reach its peak.

My brain barely recognises the sliding and thrusting of his fingers sparing with his eager tongue, spreading my moist passion and increasing my need. Just when my body starts to shake and my internal muscles squeeze and pulse, Branx quickly slides up between my heated thighs and thrusts his powerful hips filling my wet pulsing channel with his velvety solid length causing my orgasm to explode, shattering my body.

A scream escapes from my trembling lips as stars burst behind my closed eyelids sending me into a spiral of sexual utopia bliss. My sensitive folds gripping his wide girth like a vice until my body can adjust to his large size and my internal muscles start to relax once the aftershocks and rippling contractions of the powerful orgasm he can evoke within me begin to settle down.

Once my internal muscles relax enough, Branx starts the slow slide of his hips and with each slow thrust forward. He manages to touch all my favourite places and to cause my inner muscles to tighten around his length, again.

Feeling my incisors drop, I turn my head enough for my mouth to brush against Branx bare neck, my sharp teeth glide along his succulent flesh until I feel his throbbing vein below the surface of his moist skin.

Within seconds, my teeth slide into Branx tantalising flesh, allowing his delicious heated blood to flow into my mouth and slide down my parched throat, filling my hungry belly and giving me strength. Branx groans with each pull of his blood, encouraging me to take more.

With my incisors lifted, I take advantage of my sexy lover and his blood, taking more of his ambrosia. Picking up speed, Branx begins to thrust faster and harder, filling my body — just how I like it.

With several well placed hard thrusts and the swivel of his hips, Branx reaches his climax in a loud fashion, setting off another strong orgasm within me. My pulsing channel milk's Branx with each slide of his talented hips, as I scream his name over and over in a sexual high, an erotic overload only Branx can provide.

With my body sated and content, I barely managed to turn my mouth enough to swipe my tongue over the open incisions, allowing them to heal instantly. After using all his energy, Branx lands exhausted against my body and pinning me to the bed.

Feeling Branx turn his head enough to press his lips against my shoulder. "Morning, my beautiful wife," Branx breathlessly says. With his body plastered to mine, and feeling his racing heart pounding against his muscled chest. He asks, "How are you feeling today?"

Is he kidding me? Being woken from a deep sleep and straight into a hot fiery orgasm sending my body boneless and he expects me to answer his question, I don't think my mouth is willing to function. I try to attempt to form the words, only to find my mouth fails. Instead, all I can manage is the sounds, "Uh-huh."

Able to feel his smile against my moist flesh and hearing a small laugh, Branx tries to move only to find, he still does not have the strength to do so. With his face back in the crook of my neck, I feel each panted warm breath against my naked flesh. Hearing a satisfied groan; glad to see I am not the only one who is incapable of moving, feeling the heavy weight of Branx as he remains between my spread thighs and against my relaxed sweaty body.

Chapter Twenty-Five

ALEX

BY THE TIME BRANX AND I FINALLY FIND THE strength to leave our bed, I had my fill of his delicious blood for the second time, since waking. We showered and had a big hearty breakfast with plenty of fresh orange juice. By this stage, the doctor arrived and performed another ultrasound, this time Branx seeing our daughter for the first time. With so much joy, he grabbed my phone and snapped a few pictures of the screen belonging to the portable ultrasound machine, pics of the grainy image of our little girl.

Doctor Brean explained to Branx what everything was on the screen. Just as he is about to inform me regarding the results of the placenta, my parents and sister arrive just in time to see the baby and are shocked to find out I am over the nineteen-week gestation period. Once everyone had their fill of baby news my loving family finally left Branx and me in peace. Doctor Brean went on to say he is still not happy regarding the placenta, ordering me back to bed for plenty of bed rest and Branx back to bed, allowing his internal and external injuries to finish healing. The doctor's last piece of parting news, "Be careful of sex. No strenuous over the top bouts of physical sex." *Ha. As if we would do that... Oops.*

So here we are sitting up in bed, drinking morning tea, well maybe afternoon tea, and watching movies, on my wall mounted, widescreen digital television.

"Alex, are you really going to resign from The Corporation?"

"Yes, Branx. I am not going to be able to work and look after our daughter at the same time. At least here in Darshia, I will have access to the best nannies, especially when I become Queen. I will be using this time to learn from my mother and meeting more of our *Dark One* associates and the other Paranormal Entities."

"So you have thought this through then. You are going to be the next Queen of Darshia?"

"Branx, you have known all along there was a big chance I might be taking over from my mother, as Alley's new fiancé will become King of his realm. Which means my sister will be leaving Darhia. Thus leaving me in the position of becoming Queen." Trying to study Branx's face, I should just read his thoughts. It will be a lot easier that way and less time-consuming.

"Branx, you do realise we have to speak about your mother. I am going to have a couple of my loyal experts assigned to do a thorough background check on her. I am sorry, but there is just something not right. Your mother wants me dead, and I want to know the real reason why that is the case."

With his facial features changing, I knew I just overstepped my boundaries and read his mind. Too late now.

"Alex, my mother is off limits for your so-called investigations. I trust my mother. At the moment I do not like her very much, but she is the woman who raised me."

Okay. Now, this is awkward. How do I

inform Branx I have already begun an investigation including a DNA testing?

Hmm. Let me think. Changing the subject might be wise.

"Branx, as the doctor suggested, I should rest, and I will do what Doctor Brean requested. I will remain here in my bed and avoid the investigation for now. How does that sound?"

"Hmm. Why do I have the feeling you have just sidestepped the situation?"

"Because you have a wonderful mind," I say with a smile. "Anyway, we should go to the tropical side of Darshia."

"Tropical side? Since when does Darshia have a tropical anything?"

"Since the beginning of its time. The tropical side is a secluded area, with sun, sand and warm clear crystal water. It is like a holiday destination. This area is only allocated to the Royalty of Darshia, all those years ago, since my parents discovered the abandoned area back when they had been young. They soon saw its potential and organised for it to be repaired and updated, we have been using it ever since as a family getaway."

"If it is so good, why have you not taken me there after all these years?"

"Well, Mr you have to know everything. If someone else in the family was using it, or if I have the chance to travel to one of the fabulous human beaches, then I would go to one of the hundreds of thousands of beach getaways around the world."

"Hmm. I still feel you are hiding something?"

"Look, Branx. I have organised something with the assistance of my parents. They will be taking us up there, for a few days of relaxation. As I said, it is secluded. No one will bother us there. Plus there is no phone or internet either."

"So, your parents will be with us?"

"Well, no. Not technically."

"What do you mean, not technically?"

"We will be in one part of the holiday area in our own cabin and my parents will be in another. They will drop us off with our bags; make sure everything is okay before travelling to their part of Paradise. We will not see them again until the day we leave."

"So does that mean we also have to cook for ourselves?"

"Yes, Branx. If we want to eat, we will

have to prepare and cook food, unless we request the cooks to prepare food here and we heat and serve when we are there." Now that might be an idea. "....Hmm."

"What."

"I think, I might request for the food to be prepared. Then that way we can relax more."

"Well yes. That does sound like a better plan to me."

Relief hits me knowing I managed to avoid the topic of his mother. Now, to avoid any and all discussions of the woman.

Branx leans in closer to my mouth and brushes his warm moist lips against mine, sending waves of erotic sensations through my body. Hmm. I was about to say something... Branx and his body, making my brain turn to mush if I am not careful. Now, what was I going to say? That's it... leave, parents, rest, paradise.

"Okay. Leave it to me. I'll inform my parents, and they can take care of the rest."

Chapter Twenty-Six

ALEX

SPENDING TWELVE GLORIOUS MUCH NEEDED days away, instead of three, lazing in the tropical sunshine and the warm crystal-clear waters — heavenly. By the end of our twelve days getaway, Doctor Brean performed follow-up medical tests to both Branx and me.

For once, Doctor Brean was happy with the results, especially with the placenta now healthy and sitting in the correct position. With my pregnancy back on track and both Branx and myself again at full strength, Doctor Brean gave his medical permission to allow both of us to leave Darshia.

Coming back to reality and finding our

mobile phones overloaded with missed phone calls, emails and messages downright annoying. One person who has overloaded his cellphone and message bank — Brodlyne. Great the *Bitch from Helz* wants to see Branx in her office at the precinct in the city. Well, she can bloody well wait. Branx and I have some other more important tasks to handle first.

By the following morning, we leave Darshia with our typed resignations in hand; Branx and I decided to go and visit our main boss, Dillion Sparks, up at the main precinct in the city first. As he is the boss of Brodlyne and he also knows about my *Dark One* heritage, it will be wise to see him first, notifying him of our intentions of retiring.

Knocking against the solid timber door with the shiny gold nameplate, stating the bosses name — Dillion Sparks, my senses warning me, this will most likely be the last time I will be doing this, standing in this corridor, in front of this door at The Corporation. With an internal headshake to clear my mind, my eyes look towards Branx. Noticing concern in his eyes, I try to produce a brief smile, to inform him, I am okay. Without looking into his mind, Branx, most likely thinks my concern is regarding the meeting with Dillion, especially when we had decided to speak with Dillion separately.

It has been a long time since I walked in here as a young woman, ready to take on the world. I had been relieved when Dillion somehow knew Branx, and I were *soul mates* and decided it would be best if we work together.

Back then, Branx and I had been ecstatic and relieved to working side by side. Brodlyne, on the other hand, had been pissed. She wanted me away from him; she has always shown her true colours to me. Making it very clear, she does not like me. I am glad that Dillion was able to overrule her, keeping Branx and me together in our workplace.

After all, he knew I could communicate with Branx via my mind. If Branx is injured, I would be able to administer my blood to him. Dillion would say to us, *'if only he had more agents with the abilities Branx and I have'*.

"Come on in Alex; make sure to bring Branx in with you."

Looking over my shoulder, I notice Branx stop in his tracks, after hearing Dillion's voice yell out. Wow, Dillion being a shifter and only a selected few know he has vampire blood running through his veins; he has some freaky skills and abilities. Mr Dillion Sparks is good at what he does; at times, I would swear he has some variety of mystical Entity in him. With Branx back by my side, I start to open the door pushing the heavy timber enough for Branx and me to enter.

After quick hugs and handshakes, Dillion indicates for Branx and me to sit down. "Sit down guys. Now tell me. What has you in the city today? I said you could take another week off work."

Glancing to my right, I meet Branx's eyes. With a brief nod of his head, and after taking a breath in, I turn and face Dillion, giving him a radiant smile.

"Uh-oh. You only give me that smile when something important is happening."

This man knows me too well.

"You are right. We are here to hand in our resignations, starting immediately."

With his smiling face turns to shock. "What... Why?"

Before Dillion has a chance to continue, I cut him off.

"I just wanted to say thank you for

allowing Branx and I to work together all these years. However, it is time for us to move to Darshia, on a more permanent basis. My mother has decided to celebrate my twenty-fifth birthday with me being the main attraction in the new Queen ceremony."

"Wow. So you will be becoming the next Queen of Darshia?"

"Yes. My sister will be marrying and moving to her new husband's kingdom, leaving me to become the next Queen of Darshia."

"Well congratulations, Alex. We will miss you around here. However, I have the feeling there is something else..."

Nodding my head, I go on and say, "Yes, there is something else. We are expecting our first child. Even if I were not becoming Queen, I still would have retired. I am not going to place this child's life in danger again."

"Again... How far are you?"

"I am five months pregnant."

"What? Oh, Alex, I am so sorry, if I had only known. You'd never have been sent out that day."

"Look Dillion. What is done is done. I

have to make sure I look after myself for the rest of the pregnancy."

"Yes, yes. You make sure you do that. Just make sure to send me an invite for the big celebrations for becoming the next Queen."

"We will. Thank you, Dillion."

Both Branx and I pass Dillion our written resignations. "We better go and pack up our belongings from our office and empty our desks. Jett and Lexi have always wanted our office."

Thinking of our co-workers and close friends, Lexi and Jett have been our work colleagues for many years; they are one of the Corporations best working couples, especially working undercover. When I first met them, I had detected both Lexi and Jett were not fully human. Fourteen months ago, we nearly lost both Lexi and Jett in an explosion. Rogue Vampires or RV had captured them both; Jett had been turned while Lexi somehow managed to survive her brutal ordeal — barely.

Long story short, Jett went on the run as an RV, became one of most wanted BPE. Lexi was found to be pregnant, nearly went to full term, before giving birth to a healthy baby boy. Somehow Lexi and Jett, got back together, married and are playing happy little family and still working for The Corporation. I do not know how they do it, but they do, and their son is such a handsome, intelligent, loveable little guy.

Hearing Dillion's voice brings my attention back to his office, "I'll inform them when they are in the office next. I can see them, moving in there, straight away."

"Where are they, anyway?" I had noticed their desks were vacant when we walked by them.

"They are on assignment, an undercover stint for another few more days. Lexi and Jett should be back in the office by Monday."

"Let them know we said hi and we will catch up with them soon."

"I will. You make sure to take care of yourself. And you Branx, look after our girl here. You are one lucky man to be married to her. Also, congratulations on becoming parents."

Branx says with a big smile, "Thanks, Dillion. I am excited and cannot wait to become a father."

We soon stop speaking when we hear the message tone on Branx mobile phone. Branx gives me a shake of his head, knowing who just sent the message. Sadly so do I.

"We better go. Until the *Ceremonial* day, bye, Dillion."

With tight hugs goodbye, we make our way towards the door when another ding comes from Branx's phone. It soon becomes apparent from the tone, Brodlyne has sent Branx another message. Geez. What does she want now?

Stepping out of Dillion's office, we pause out in the hallway.

I can see the surprise and annoyance as Branx reads the new messages before he looks up at my face.

"Alex, I have to go and see my mother, she is worried sick, thinking something has happened to me." What the…? That bitch knew we were going away for three weeks. Talk about being manipulative.

"Branx, leave a message, we gave her our information, including a contact number. If she was that concerned she would have made contact with my grandparents, your mother has their mobile number, for emergencies. If anything happened to your mother, security would have notified my parents, and they would have been on our doorstep straight away."

"Alex, I still have to go and see her and hand in a copy of my resignation." With his mind full of anxiety, Branx is not sure what he really wants to do regarding his mother. "When you become the next Queen, I will be required to learn how to be your right-hand man, just as your father is to your mother. You are far too important to me. Mother will have to learn to understand, you and our child will come first."

"Aww, honey. You will be a fantastic father."

With a shake of his head, I can see the frustration racing through him. If he only had a father, he might have a different perspective on life and fatherhood. Somehow, Brodlyne also robbed him of a father.

"Really Alex? I never had a father, so how am I going to know if I am doing the right thing?"

"Branx, you know right from wrong. You know how to use your manners. You know to treat women with respect and protect them. Also, you know how to love. Because, if you can love me, you can very easily love our child."

"I don't know, Alex. What happens if I mess up?"

Wrapping my arms around Branx, I press my pregnant belly into to his front, feeling my little girl starting to move, indicating she is beginning to be squashed between her parents. Moving my belly-bulge a little to the side allowing our daughter more room to move.

Our daughter is growing bigger and making herself known, pressing her body against our hands when she can. Looking down, Branx presses his hand against the growing little bulge as I say, "Well, we will mess up together."

"At least you grew up with your family around you. I only ever had my mother."

"For all her faults, you still turned out to be my perfect man, Mr Rayden."

"I love you, my beautiful, talented wife," Branx says as I feel the warmth of his hand penetrate through to my belly.

"I love you too, my sexy husband." With another brush of our lips, we deepen our kiss and all thoughts of anyone else, ceased to exist.

By 6.00 p.m. Branx and I travelled from Darshia via the portal back to the human realm to the city. With me in the driver's seat, allowing Branx time to read some of his emails and think about everything, including everything I found out about our ongoing case and of course the death threats and paid hit on my head.

I was not happy to see a message from the accounts department, requesting my presence to sign some final paperwork, asking me just over an hour ago to drop by at 6.30 p.m. for the last minute meeting with them and with HR.

I had also found it strange and suspicious how Brodlyne had become persistent, pushing the issue for Branx to meet with her to have dinner. Not feeling comfortable at all regarding these unexpected meetings, I would prefer to stay with Branx, especially when he is to meet Brodlyne for dinner in twenty minutes.

Knowing I will be catching up with him at the restaurant later, relieves a little of my anxiety. "Don't forget to order your taxi, babe. Otherwise, it might be a long wait, and I do not want to be spending too much time alone with my mother." Branx looks over to my face and smiles before turning his head and continuing reading his emails.

I feel better knowing Branx will be driving my car to the restaurant, using their valet parking, allowing me to travel by taxi without all the added stress of trudging through traffic, only for me to be dropped off at the front door and walking straight into the restaurant.

Thankfully, with our health fully restored thanks to all the peaceful days relaxing by the water, and eating all the delicious foods rich in protein and iron aiding in the consumption of our blood. No one would know, Branx was on death's door two weeks ago with massive external and internal injuries. I am so relieved my blood was able to save and heal him.

The only thing I have noticed Branx seems to display more paranormal talents, these gifts seem to have increased and enhanced in some way or another. As long as Brodlyne does not notice the difference in Branx, we should be fine.

Branx has decided to fill in his mother on our pending birth of our first child over dinner. I'm still feeling apprehensive about going anywhere near Brodlyne since her outburst back at the hospital three weeks ago.

In one way or another, I fear not just for my safety, but that of our unborn daughter.

"Branx, did you mention to your mother about me arriving late to the restaurant?"

With a shake of his head, Branx says, "No. Mother was aware of the meeting you have with HR though, which I thought a bit strange." I glance over to Branx and notice the concern in his eyes. At least the two of us feel the same regarding these last minute meetings. "She made sure I will be meeting her at the restaurant at 6.30 p.m."

Hmm. Brodlyne seems more pushy than usual, and I wonder what is really going on? With her dinner reservation and my meeting at the same time, this is one way for Branx to be alone with her.

Turning his head towards the side window, I can see Branx is contemplating about something. It must be something essential to cause the pained look on his face. "Alex, I have changed my mind. I do not care if I am late. I have a feeling I need to stay with you."

The ache in my shoulders starts to lift away with Branx words. "I am grateful you decided to come with me. I do not know what is happening at the office. Surely, Dillion would have said something when we were both with him this morning."

Hmm. Something does not add up, and it has something to do with Brodlyne. I just know it.

Chapter Twenty-Seven

ALEX

PULLING INTO THE UNDERGROUND CAR PARK at the Corporation headquarters, I soon parked our modern, four-door car in my parking space. Just as I step out of the car, I start to glance around the car park, and it finally registers the rest of the parking area is empty, which I thought to be strange in itself. Where is everyone?

Relief filled me when Branx said he changed his mind about leaving me to meet his mother when I turned into the underground car parking area.

Branx mentioned he should be walking me to my appointments — protecting me, even though he knew it would make him late to the dinner reservation with his mother. I glance up and scan our surroundings; something is off.

Branx reaches the elevators first and hits the up button. It is not long until the elevator arrives and the doors open, Branx steps inside the elevator. With a prickling feeling crawling along my back, the pressure increases.

The presence of danger builds around me, with a wiggle of my fingers and a few well-placed words inside my head, my magic begins to flow through my body, protecting the child I am carrying.

I look back towards Branx and watch him hit the button for our floor. With a frown, Branx meets my eyes and shrugs his shoulders, and he smiles and mouths 'sorry, habit' as he starts to hit the button for the floor for the accounts department and also the level for HR. With several numbers lit up, it looks as if the elevator will be stopping at several levels this evening.

Just as I go to lift my foot, the sensation of *do not enter* increases — warning me not to step any further onto the elevator. I do not know what it is, but something is definitely wrong here, the sensation of doom increasing, and its close by. Looking back up to Branx's face, I notice concern written on his face, he knows through our link; I am sensing something.

"Alex, what is it. What do you sense?"

Just as I take another step towards Branx, I start to shake my head to the strange sensations bombarding me as my hand reaches for my head, a wave of dizziness hits me, making me miss a step and stumble right into Branx. With quick reflexes, he steps to the threshold of the elevator, capturing me in his strong arms, preventing me from falling. That is all I need, is to face plant here at work on the hard flooring and become the ex-employee laughing stock by the end of the week.

"Alex, don't even try to say there is nothing wrong. I knew not to leave you alone. That doctor of yours should never have said you are physically okay to leave Darshia."

Until I opened my eyes, my brain did not contend with the darkness of my closed eyelids. Oh, shit. Something is interfering with my body, the question is, what is it? Thinking I should turn around and sit back in the car, my eyes meet Branx's and I manage to say, "Branx, I need to sit down, can you take me back to the car and open the car door for me. Something is wrong here; I am not feeling safe in the car park. I think we should leave."

Immediately, he assists me back to our vehicle. With my butt firmly back in the car, only this time in the front passenger seat. Branx quickly runs around, sitting in my driver's seat, closing the door with a solid thunk. "Alex, tell me the truth. Is it me meeting my mother or is there something truly wrong nearby?"

With my feelings hurt, Branx has the nerve to say those words to me in the first place, turning my head to look him straight in the eye. "Thanks for those generous words, Branx." Trying to remain calm enough. If I become too worked up, my magic will start to leak through, and anyone nearby will see I am more than human. "Look, forget it, I'll come back tomorrow. I think it might be best to leave and head back to our apartment."

Seeing the guilt and hurt in Branx's eyes, he realises he hurt me when he unleashed his verbal assault.

"Look, Alex. I am sorry. My words came out wrong. I should have realised with all your magic; you would not pretend and make something up. It is just my …mother. She has me in knots. If you say there is something wrong here, I should take notice and listen," Branx quietly says and looks back down towards my lap, noticing the small sparks emitting from my fingertips. "I remember you had said something the day we had been captured; you had felt something wrong. Somehow you sensed something more was going on, than just a few BPE. As it turned out there had been over ten of them and looked how that turned out. I could have lost you."

Not in the mood for Branx and his guilt trips, I say, "Branx, either you can drive me back to our apartment or head for the restaurant. It is up to you. However, I am not sitting here waiting another minute; I am sensing we need to leave. If you do not want to drive, I will, whichever way you decide we need to leave this building immediately for our safety."

With a sigh, Branx places his seat belt on and turns the key in the ignition. Movement catches my eye in my field vision, I glance up and watch as the wide open elevator doors begin to move and slowly close.

Once the car is started and set in reverse, Branx disengaged the handbrake, and we begin the process of leaving our allocated car spot.

Knowing to keep quiet, I do not want to fight with Branx, especially knowing his mother will try anything to separate the two of us. Attempting to drive a wedge so deep between us, forcing both Branx and me to separate forever. If only the woman knew Branx and I are *soul mates*, and the separating forever type of thing does not happen.

With the feeling doom and the urgency of evacuating the building growing by the second, thoughts fill my mind, we need to move faster before it's too late. It will not be soon enough to get away from this superstructure of concrete, metal and glass. Relief quickly fills me, when the car drives onto the exit ramp. My hand protectively rests on my belly; all going well I will feel better in a few minutes.

JUST ABOUT LEAPING OFF MY SEAT AS MUCH AS one can while held in place by a car seat belt, I reach up, covering my ears with my hands; a loud explosion noise fills the car, scaring the shit out of me. Glancing around looking for the cause of the massive sound and feel a big hard mighty shove to the vehicle, the force of the explosion sends us airborne.

I scream when I feel the car leave the pavement as we go into the air. I hope and pray we do not flip or crash into another vehicle or part of the building. With my eyes squeezed shut, I feel the car land with a hard jolt, thrusting my body forward, hard against my seat belt, then thrown back painfully against the car seat.

Oomph.

Feeling as if something rammed the car, my head is thrust sideways towards the window, at the same time the interior of the car fills with powdered dust.

Aaargh. What in the world?

White fabric suddenly surrounds my head. Oh, my goddess. What the…? After a second or two, my brain resets.

Oh, geez, the airbags, they have deployed.

Closing my eyes to the airborne dust; my brain is painfully catching up to our circumstances, wondering why everything is deathly silent. My eyes fly open, and I do not hear my grunts or screams, I do not hear anything, all I know, the tightness of the seat belt alone will leave bruising, and I am going to be sore.

Reaching up and trying to pull at the exploded airbags, I try to see what is happening around us. Branx continues his hardest to keep the car under control his hands struggling with the steering wheel, while an avalanche of dust and debris rain down around us as the car finally exit out onto the road with bone-jarring movements.

Knowing full well, Branx cannot see anything in front of him, with the driver's side airbags deployed all around him and the white powdery dust in his eyes. Pulling and pushing at the deployed side airbags, I turn my head and stare open-eyed out my window through all the rubble dust, I watch the building we had just been in, crumble and disintegrate in a gigantic plume of dust, in front of my eyes.

Holy shit.

Chapter Twenty-Eight

I think I am in shock.

Nah, I have to be dreaming.

Surely, headquarters is still standing and not a pile of debris, rubble and dust.

Looking back out my window, all I can see is the air, thick with concrete dust, rubble, and debris everywhere, where headquarters was standing only ten minutes ago. Glancing around, trying to take in the carnage around us, the building we have been going to for the past four years is now a gigantic pile of twisted construction, debris and concrete. The whole building is now gone.

Slowly it dawned on me, Branx should have been talking, screaming, yelling about something by now. Instead, all I hear is quiet, an eerie quietness filling our car and my ears. Slowly I turn my head towards Branx and see him with his phone to his ear. His mouth is moving, but I am not able to hear a word he is saying.

Then it dawns on me; the blast has affected my hearing. I hope my ears start to function soon. I look back up to Branx and notice he is talking to someone, while he is looking at me.

Not sure how loud my voice will be, I better let Branx know, my hearing is shot. "Branx. Honey, can you hear me?" Looking at Branx, I notice the strange look come over his face.

"Honey." I start to shake my head and touch my ear, "I cannot hear anything. All the noise, everything, is quiet. I think the blast has affected my hearing. Can you still hear everything?" I asked, pleading with my eyes.

With a nod of his head, Branx touches his ear. Letting me know he can still hear. With a sigh, I nod my head. "That is great. Can you phone my parents, they are going to hear about the explosion. Oh, and request for Riley and a team to be sent out. This…" Waving my hand out the window towards the destruction, "was no accident, and someone tried to kill us, well maybe me again. But, why in the hell would anyone blow up a whole building?"

With a shrug of his shoulders, Branx goes back to his phone call. I wonder whom he is speaking to and if it is to the emergency services or his mother.

Chapter Twenty-Nine

ALEX

WITHIN MINUTES WE ARE SURROUNDED BY THE emergency services, it also does not help with our car damaged and blocked in from all sides with all the building rubble, debris, and other smashed vehicles, spreading out onto the road, I am not able to open my car door. It had taken me a few minutes to realise there had been other cars driving along the adjacent road with the building when it exploded. Cars, which are now crushed or damaged sitting were the debris of metal, concrete and other vehicles had struck them.

The firefighters and ambulance officers soon retrieve me out of the damaged car and two persistent ambulance medics escorting me to the back of a waiting ambulance. Not wanting to leave Branx and become separated; I soon find I have no choice in the matter when I find myself still unable to hear, and no one will listen to me. Feeling lost, angry and extremely frustrated, I start to watch the ambulance doors close.

At the last second, I see a hand appear, preventing the doors from shutting. Concerned for my safety, I start to send out my magical power to protect myself. The doors open widely, and relief engulfs me to see Riley and one of his men standing at the back of the ambulance in the open doorway. I glance back at Riley with a smile on my face when I notice he is speaking to me.

With a shake of my head and my hand up to my ear, I say, "I still cannot hear anything, Riley. Do you know where Branx is? I have lost him." Watching Riley say something to the guy next to him before turning back towards me and quickly jumping into the back of the ambulance with me.

What is going on?

With the look of annoyed facial features on the ambo medic while his hand gestures flow about in the air, I have the feeling he is arguing with Riley? I continue to watch them, and the conversation looks heated between them until Riley turns and smiles at me — I think he won the heated discussion.

'Princess Alex, can you hear me this way?'

Nodding my head quickly, with a big smile, *'Yes, Riley.'* Relief fills me — I can still communicate with my mind. Yay me. *'Riley can you reach Branx, because, I have tried and there is no answer. We had been together in the car, but as soon as the emergency services showed, Branx and I were separated.'*

With a nod of his head, Riley went on to say, *'Yes, Princess, Branx is safe, and I am leaving some of my men with him. I do not feel he should be left alone. Branx mentioned he was meant to be meeting his mother at a restaurant. After several failed phone calls, Branx thinks his mother might be in the destroyed building, instead. With the ongoing investigation, we have been following Brodlyne, and she is not here or at the restaurant. As far as I am aware, Brodlyne is across town.'*

'*What do you mean she is not at the restaurant? Of course, she is there. Branx had a dinner meeting; well we both had a dinner meeting with her at 6.30 p.m. We arrived a little early for my appointment with HR and the Accounts Department, when I started having a strange feeling... In the end, Branx and I got back in the car and started to leave. I had thought it strange to find the car-parking area vacant.*'

With a pause, Riley says, '*I do not know what to tell you, Princess. Brodlyne is across town as we speak.*'

'*What?*'

'*Princess, you need to calm down, the paramedics are looking at us strangely.*'

'*Oh, shit. The humans do not understand the mind talking of a Dark One.*'

Looking at the ambo medic sitting in the back with Riley and myself, I smile at him and shrug my shoulders. Touching my ear and shaking my head to let him know, I still am not able to hear anything.

The ambo nods his head and as I watch him write something down on his clipboard. After another minute, he lifts up the clipboard with his capitalised handwritten questions.

DO YOU HAVE ANY PAIN? CAN YOU HEAR ANY NOISE AT ALL?

I shake my head. "No pain that I know of and there is nothing but silence."

The ambo paramedic nods his head, and then he lifts his medical equipment and shows me he wants to take my blood pressure and listen to my heart. Nodding my head, I move my arm towards him so that he can secure the blood pressure cuff to my arm.

Thinking I had better inform him, I am pregnant before he tries to administer any types of drugs to my system.

"Excuse me; I think you should also know I am pregnant. I do not know if my husband informed you or not before we left the explosion site."

Watching for the ambo paramedics reaction, I was not expecting his reply, as he wrote it down.

WE WERE NEVER TOLD OF THE PREGNANCY.

Looking over at Riley, I start to have a strange feeling, once again.

'Riley, please tell me, one of the royal guards are following us in one of the cars.'

'Yes, Princess. When it comes to you, we do not take risks. I have been keeping in constant contact with Gilson. He has sent for another two cars.'

'Why?'

'Why is a good question, but he just informed me we are not heading towards the nearest hospital?'

'Oh, shit.'

'Yes. Oh, shit. Indeed.'

'Riley, I think we are in trouble. Have you been able to hear the driver communicate with anyone?'

'Yes. Well, I am in the process of listening and reading the drivers mind. He is speaking with someone right now. He is arguing with whomever

he is talking with. The driver is angry about finding out you are pregnant. That was not part of the plan.'

'Plan. Crap. I think they had this ambulance as a backup, just in case I escaped the exploding building.'

'Yes. Indeed.'

'Riley have you notified your other guards who are staying with my husband.'

'Yes, Princess. Branx has received the information, and you are in the process of being transported to the hospital. Including the informed, your mother-in-law is on the other side of town, only now arriving at the restaurant with several men.'

'Oh, shit. Now that is going to go down well.'

'You could say that. Finding out his mother is safe and not in the exploded building, set his mind at ease, as for the men accompanying her we still do not know who they are. Regarding you being removed from his presence, let me just say, he was a bit angry.'

Ooh, crap. This information is going to have Branx's blood pressure rising sky high. This is one time, I am nearly glad not to be anywhere near Branx. He will be just about spitting nails right about now.

Riley nods his head, and he had been listening to my thoughts and replies, '*Your husband has just been informed, regarding this ambulance not heading towards the closest hospital; he is demanding to follow us immediately.*'

'*Riley, I still cannot reach him with my mind. It is like someone has placed a short range blockage on me. I need you to inform my mother please even if you have to send a text.*'

'*Right away, Princess.*'

'*Oh, and Riley. Keep someone on Brodlyne's tail. I want to know what is happening. I need to know if she is there of her own free will or someone has coerced her. Who knows who these men are?*'

'*I'm already on it, Princess.*'

Knowing, Riley and myself will have to

play dumb and wait out this little ambulance ride. Hopefully, we will soon find out who is behind the explosion and my attempted kidnapping.

What a way to spend the evening, I wish I can hear and also communicate with Branx.

Chapter Thirty

ALEX

ACCORDING TO THE AMBO PARAMEDIC, MY blood pressure is in a healthy range, and we should be arriving at the hospital any minute now.

Riley and I casually look at one another, wondering what these people are up to and where they are taking us.

'Riley, can you see anything? What does Gilson have to say about this little detour? Where are we?'

'Believe it or not, we are nearly at the same destination as Brodlyne.'

'What…?'

'*Princess, please calm yourself.*'

'*Riley…*'

'*Princess, be ready to move. We have just turned into the same street. Just wait for my signal.*'

Oh, shit. Okay, now it might be wise to remove the blood pressure cuff from my arm slowly.

Sitting up, I attempt to undo and remove the cuff. Feeling a firm, handgrip on my shoulder, digging into my flesh. Ouch. Looking towards the hand, damn, now that is a large rough looking hand.

Uh-huh. I think I might be in trouble. Slowly lifting my eyes, I look up and straight into a pair of intense amber eyes of the paramedic. *Oh, crap.* I think this guy might be a shifter or some form of Paranormal Entity.

'*Ah, Riley. A little assistance here would be useful.*'

With his back to me, Riley is busy looking out the window.

'What have you done now, Princess?'

'What, Me? What have I done?'

'Princess, you just had to sit there and wait until I gave the signal. Now, this guy is starting to show his true form, and I think we are in a little trouble in this small confined space.'

'Gee. You think? I would never have guessed.'

'Don't be smart with me, young Alex. Your mother has never removed my ability to punish you or your siblings. Remember that.'

'You wouldn't dare.'

'Wouldn't I?'

'Well. Well, my husband might have something to say about it.'

'Alex. Alex. Tsk, tsk. Since when do you hide behind someone else?'

'Riley, get back on track here, will you? Remember — inside the ambulance — small space. Oh, and don't forget trapped inside with a Paranormal

Entity, who looks like they might shift any second.'

'Oh, Princess. My man Gilson is still tailing us, with five other of the royal guards, oh and your husband is not far away.'

'Please don't allow, Branx to get hurt.'

'Princess, you and your unborn child, are my main priority.'

'Riley make sure Branx will be okay.'

'No, promises, Princess. However, just for you, I will try my best.'

'That is what I am afraid of.'

'Are you two finished with your conversation, or can anyone just join in?' Hearing the ambo paramedic's voice, through the mind-link I have with Riley.'

Looking back at the ambo paramedic, I give him a slight smile and shrug my shoulders. "Sorry. I am still trying to see if there is anything I can hear. I just needed to move. Maybe if I sit up the different angle…"

With the look of disbelief from the ambo paramedic, I might as well stop speaking. He is not going to believe me, as I pull the blood pressure cuff away my arm, passing it back to the angry looking ambo paramedic, his eyes no longer resemble anything human.

"Here you go, you can put it away now. What hospital are we at, I need to inform my family," I say.

Judging by the look on both the medic and Riley's face my voice might have been a touch too loud for such a small space.

With a shake of his head, the medic snatches the blood pressure cuff from my hands and says something to Riley. Bugger I missed it, Riley has blocked me off from the mind link.

Just then, the ambulance comes to a sudden stop, making me jostle forward. I keep looking from Riley to the ambo paramedic, waiting for something to happen. I would appreciate my hearing right about now, and I need all my senses to communicate or protect myself.

Now is someone going to jump out at us with guns? Will there be shooting? When can

I start to use my magic? Oh, and the big question on the tip of my tongue. Where in the hell are we, because I feel like we are in hell and I require my very own angel to come and save me.

No sound, still deaf to the outside world, I wonder what is happening. I look back to Riley and try to speak with him.

'Riley. What is going on? Where are Gilson and the others?' I nervously ask as I look around, wondering what is happening.

'Princess, get ready. Gilson and the others are here. However, so is a large group of Paranormal Entities. The others have just notified me, these beings surrounding us are of the bad variety.'

Oh, bugger.

'Riley, maybe, they need to assess the area before engaging with the enemy. Are these men our enemies, or the enemy of their enemy? Were others involved? What has Gilson found out so far?'

'Ms Alex, Princes of Darshia, your life is a little more important don't you think?'

Next thing I know, the double doors of the ambulance are ripped quickly opened, and an angry looking Brodlyne is standing there looking at me with a gun trained on Riley.

Shit.

So much for *Dark One* reflexes.

'Hey Riley, let me link with your mind, I want to know what the Bitch is saying.'

Riley stares at Brodlyne and starts talking, and I am missing the conversation. That is it, they have kidnapped me, and no one is informing me, what is happening.

"Hello. Can anyone hear me, because I cannot hear anything? Why are we not at the hospital? A doctor would be good right about now, to find out why I have no hearing," I say to anyone who will listen. I do not care how loud I am, because I know from the reactions of everyone around me I am very loud.

With a tilt of her head and her trademark feral grin, Brodlyne points her handgun towards me.

Bugger. Maybe I should have waited to speak...

Just then, from the surrounding darkness,

someone else joins our little party at the back of the ambulance. A stranger, a man, dressed from head to toe in black comes up and starts speaking with Brodlyne.

The silly thing is as soon as I saw his face my breath hitches. *Oh my*, this man looks similar to Branx. He can pass as an older version of him, who is he?

Brodlyne starts to shake her head at the stranger and begins to wave the handgun about, even though the stupid woman still has it facing me. With super quick reflexes, the newcomer disarms Brodlyne and passes the handgun to one of his men. Wow. These people are multiplying, with another five men dressed in black appear, I wonder who in the hell they are. Also, are these men the good guys or bad?

Chapter Thirty-One

ALEX

Just as Riley assists me down from the back of the ambulance, my senses go on full alert. A familiar presence appears out of the darkness; my head turns just as Branx comes racing up to me. Nearly sending me to the ground, with the impact of his muscular body against mine. Branx manages to keep us upright, with his arms wrapped tightly around me and instantly feel him at my mind shields.

Relief soon fills me, as I am finally able to sense him within my mind. Okay, let's hope I can hear him in my head through our connection, '*Oh, thank God baby, I had been so worried, what have I missed?*'

Giving my head a slight shake, I reply, *'I have no idea. My hearing is still gone, I cannot hear a thing. Your mother just had a gun trained on me, until that man over there, dressed in black, who- by the way, looks like an older version of you. Anyway, this new guy walked up and disarmed Brodlyne, and they have been arguing ever since.'*

Branx turns his head looking the stranger up and down.

'I have never seen him before.' Branx mumbles before turning his head back towards me and says, *'Hang on …what do you mean, your hearing has not returned. You should be able to hear by now. Why are you not at the hospital?'*

'Well, I have been asking that question myself, but no one will give me an answer. Oh, and the people who kidnapped me in the first place, let it slip they did not know I am pregnant. So, me being pregnant was not part of the plan. Whatever that plan might be?'

'What plan? Who are these people?' Branx queries, his voice full of concern. *'Alex, are you feeling okay, should you be standing.'* Branx

continues, while his hand gently rubs my belly, assuring himself the baby is okay. *'Maybe I should escort you to the car and have Riley take you back to Darshia. I still have to speak to my mother. I need to know, why she pushed the issue about you attending that appointment, the appointment where the building blew up.'*

'Branx, your mother is not stable.'

'Alex, please. I still need to speak with her.'

'Branx are you serious? The woman just had a loaded gun trained on me. On me, Branx. Remember me your pregnant wife?'

'Alex, please understand.'

'No, Branx…'

Just then, the stranger who resembles my husband approaches us, interrupting our little chat. Lucky for me I can listen through the mind link with Branx as this stranger begins to speak.

'Hello, young Branx. I am sorry to disturb you,

but we need to talk. You can leave the young lady here, or my men will escort her to your home.'

What the... *'Young lady. Escort me home.'* Yeah, I do not think so.

I shake my head in annoyance towards this stranger and reply, "Hey buddy, how about you start with introducing yourself to my husband and me first. Oh, and I am not leaving my husband anytime soon. Also, see these other men behind me, they are with me. So if Branx and I stay, so do they."

The stranger with the same eyes as Branx, turns and looks at me and studies my face, before looking over at Riley and then the other men. After a few seconds, the man's eyes widened, and then he looks back at me, looking straight into my eyes.

Hearing his voice through my mind link with Branx, he asks, *'What is your name child?'*

"Hey, I am not a child."

'Okay, I will rephrase the question. What is your name and where are you from?'

"How about, you inform us of your name first, and where you are from? Also, how do you know Branx's mother Brodlyne, over there?" My head nods in her direction.

My eyes catch the worried look on her face.

'What? Brodlyne is not Branx's mother. Who gave you such lies?'

Is this guy for real? Of course, Brodlyne is Branx's mother. "Well, Brodlyne of course," I reply with my eyebrow raised in question. "Since the day I met Brodlyne, when I was seventeen, she has always informed me or anyone else, that she is Branx's mother and Branx's father has never been in his li-".

'Look, young lady. Brodlyne is definitely not Branx's mother, she might be his aunt, which we really cannot help, but she is not Branx's mother.'

What? Aunty?
"Hang on a bloody cotton picking minute. You are informing us, that woman over there. The woman, who has always hated me from the start, is not my *soul mate's* mother."

'*Soul mate.*' The stranger, looking from me to Branx and back again. '*You and Branx are soul mates?*'

"Yes, genius. Branx and I are *soul mates.*" With my hand gently rubbing my belly, the stranger's eyes follow my hand in its movements.

'*One of my men has mentioned you are pregnant. Is this true?*'

Finally, Branx starts to speak, in a pissed off stern voice. '*Look, I do not know who you are. We noticed you have avoided answering the question of who you are and where you are from? Now, are you going to answer the questions, because I need to take my pregnant wife back to her family home and I need to speak with my so-called mother? Now, who are you?*'

The stranger, taking far too long to answer, turned towards Riley and started speaking to him. What the...?

'*Riley, what in the world are you doing here? Whatever happened to the bitch Alexettia?*'

Wow, this guy knows Riley and my Grandma Ma?

Riley quickly moved beside me, with a slight smile, as he raised his hand to shake the strangers.

Okay, back up a bit. What are these two doing shaking one another's hands as if they are old friends?

'What in the hell are you doing here, Bravaile. I see you still have your little shadows. Do you mind filling me in, why your men kidnapped the Princess here?'

With shock registering on his face, this stranger whose name turns out to be Bravaile which still means nothing to me, turns and looks at me.

'Please tell me; you are not related to Alexettia.'

With a laugh and a shake of my head, I reply, "Dude. My mother is going to kick your arse when she arrives. Yes, my mother is the Queen and my Grandma Ma — Alexettia, passed before I was born. Just because my grandmother is no longer here, you still do not get to call her names."

'Alexettia dead! Hmm. Come to think of it, I vaguely remember hearing something about that, and her long-lost great-granddaughter arrived to take over the role as Queen.'

"My mother arrived before Grandma Ma had passed; my mother had saved Alexettia's life more than once back then."

'Your mother is — The Alexia?'

"Yes."

'Well, I'll be damn. I like your mother. I met her years ago.'

Sensing my mother approach from the shadows is reassuring, closely followed by my father. Feeling Mum extending her Queen powers, causing the hair along my arms to rise, a bit scary.

'Well, that is good to know, Bravaile. In the brief time, we met all those years ago; you gave me the impression you prefer to get a job done yourself. Now, do you mind informing both Drake and me, why you have my daughter, come now, time is ticking.'

With a quick flick of his head and body, Bravaile meets my parents head-on. *'Well, well, well. Hello to you too, Alexia and of course your husband, Drake. How are you both?'*

'Bravaile answer the question. Why do you have my daughter?'

Bravaile turns his head, looking back over his shoulder, staring me right in the eye first, before his eyes meet Branx. *'Glad to see you are still direct and to the point.'* Bravaile turns and faces my parents before answering. *'Well, Alexia. It turns out your daughter is married to my son.'*

What... Wow. This is new. Son? Oh, my... what? Confusion hits me. This stranger is the father, Branx was told he never had?

'Bravaile, really? You are claiming Branx as your son, in front of all these witnesses,' My mother says as she waves her hand in the air, indicating all the people about us. *'Why have you kept out of Branx's life all these years? The poor boy thinks he has been abandoned, left with this poor excuse who claims to be his mother. Why would you leave such a child in the hands of*

Brodlyne? Where is Branx's, birth mother? Also, do not think I have noticed you still have not answered why you have my daughter.'

'Alexia, for one, I had no choice, but to leave my son to live with his aunt after his mother died giving birth to him. Everyone thinks my newborn son died, along with his mother. My beautiful wife and mate died because we were attacked. Attacked by assassins.'

With a nod of her head, my mother says, *'Yes, I know all about assassins. They become extremely annoying little buggers. Tend not to give you any peace, when they have their focus on killing you.'*

With a nod of his head, Bravaile agrees before saying, *'well yes, that is indeed the case. As for Brodlyne, she had just completed a long-term undercover case and had just started her month's downtime break when she arrived. Xaiverly managed to convince Brodlyne to look after and raise Branx as if he was her own child before Xaiverly slipped into a coma and died. Brodlyne agreed to protect Branx from the ones who caused Xaiverly's death and to seek vengeance.'*

'Wow, that is a big story. Sorry to hear you lost your mate in such tragic circumstances. However, you still have not explained to me, why you have my daughter?'

With a lift of his chin, Bravaile finally answers, *'Brodlyne.'*

Just the one word — One name, and we all turn to look at the woman, in question.

'What has Brodlyne got to do with my daughter being taken?' My mother demands.

With a shake of his head, Bravaile replies, *'Brodlyne does not like Alex and wants her away from my son, she said, Alex, is a menace to my son's life and needs to be exterminated.'*

'Oh, really. Did Brodlyne also inform you, my daughter and your son are soul mates? Also, they have been mated and married since Alex turned eighteen? Oh, and Alex and Branx are expecting their first child?'

With a shake of his head, Bravaile replied, *'No. She did not.'* Turning and facing Branx and myself, he went on to say, *'If I had known, my son had found his soul mate; I would have made myself known to him years earlier. If I had known, that little girl you had nursed that day, was, in reality, my own son's soul mate, I would have involved myself in my son's life. Explaining what he is and what he will become.'*

What? What is this man going on about? What is this man? My eyes grow wide, wondering what we have become involved in as I see the shock on my husband's face.

Hearing my mother's voice brings my attention back to the present.

'Bravaile, if your son had met my daughter sooner, all your secrets would have been exposed, and your son's life would have been in more danger than it already is. Why try to kill my daughter, though? You do realise, that in itself is an act of war against Darshia.'

Oh, shit. This conversation is significant, especially if my mother is bringing in war and Darshia.

'Alexia, I apologise. I did not know your daughter to be a Dark One or a Princess of Darshia.'

'What, you think ignorance, will prevent a war. You tried to kill my daughter.'

Lifting both his hands in a surrender gesture, he replies, *'Hey, now, I have not tried to kill your daughter.'*

'What do you call what happened to both Alex and Branx over three weeks ago and today?'

'What are you talking about?'

'Are you denying, their capture? Branx would have died if it had not been for Alex.'

'What.' Bravaile turns and faces Branx, with his eyes nearly bulging out of his head. *'My son...'* Shaking his head, he then turns and faces Brodlyne and yells, *'Brodlyne, get your pathetic arse over here and explain yourself. Remember the oath you had taken, to protect my son at all costs or forfeit your own life.'*

Cowering Brodlyne scampers over to us with her head bent forward and eyes downcast. *'Yes, Bravaile. How may I serve thee?'*

Oh wow. *How may I serve thee…* This is interesting, very interesting.

'Brodlyne, do you know who Alexia is?'

Brodlyne turns her head up and looks over to my mother, with a nod of her head Brodlyne replies, *'This is Alex's cousin.'* With a sneer, Brodlyne asks, *'Why do you ask, she is nothing to us.'*

Struggling to remain quiet, I know if my mother or father does not say anything, Branx will.

Instead, Bravaile speaks first, *'Brodlyne, you know of Dark Ones, do you not?'*

With a nod of her head, she answers, *'Yes.'*

'Then Brodlyne, why are you treating Alexia here with so much disrespect, for she is the Queen of Darshia. Oh, and by the way, Alex here is Alexia and Drake's, their youngest daughter. A Dark One and the Princess of Darshia.'

Shaking her head from side to side, in denial, *'You must be mistaken, Bravaile. Alex is only a human. She is not a Dark One. She…she…'*

With that I open my mouth slightly, allowing my incisors to drop, exposing them as well as releasing a little of my magic to seep through and spark out of my fingertips. Anyone standing by will now know, I am indeed a magical *Dark One.*

With shock nearly a permanent feature on Brodlyne's face, she continues to shake her head in denial, taking a small step back. *'No. No, no, no. Oh, my God. How did I not know about this?'*

With disgust at the forefront of my feelings and emotions, I finally say to her, "Now you know, why and how Branx survived the capture and attack against the both of us. This…" I start to wave my sparking fingers in the air, "is why Branx lives today."

Branx moved his body behind mine and wrapped his arms around my middle, placing his lips against my neck and one hand protectively over my belly.

Through our link, I can feel his emotions and his love for the baby and me. *'I love you.'*

Branx, whispers in my ear, feeling his breath touch my ear with each word he says, making sure anyone nearby would hear him. The catch is, I still do not have my hearing. I can only verbally understand everyone through the mind link with Branx and my mother.

Chapter Thirty-Two

ALEX

"**H**ERE ALEX, I GOT YOU A CUP OF TEA AND A slice of fruitcake," My father quietly says placing the items on the step beside me.

I do not know where he got them, but I am thankful. Smiling up at my dad and thanking him with a kiss on his cheek. My dad still remembers my love of fruitcake and chocolate, something I have loved to eat since I was a little girl.

"Are you having enough blood, baby?" My father asks, "You make sure Branx is there for you, if you are anything like your mother, you will crave blood more than usual."

Nodding my head at my father's words

and loving his protective and caring nature. "Yes, Daddy that is why Branx walked me over to here. So we can have some privacy and for blood."

Branx noticed this quiet spot earlier and walked me over to this secluded place away from prying eyes so that I can consume his blood in private. One, to see if that might help with my hearing and Two, the baby would benefit from the feeding of Branx's delicious blood.

Plus, I needed to sit down and rest. Not forgetting the new elephant in the room — we still have to discuss the news about his crazy — aunt and not as we have known her, his mother. Oh, and his mysterious father, Bravaile.

Finally, after all this time, since the explosion, my hearing is back.

Yay, me.

Maybe I should not have been so eager now I can hear Brodlyne, my mother and Bravaile arguing. Even though I am not near them, I can still feel the tension from where I am sitting. Things are getting pretty heated. I bet my mother ends up zapping someone soon.

And yep, there is it is now.

With a bright light, flashing over the parked cars, I hear a scream. With a tingle ghosting over my skin, I feel a rush of magic in the air. Knowing full well, my mother has just zapped Brodlyne, with her magic.

Well if my mother didn't, I would have. Brodlyne is a real bitch.

Brodlyne had the nerve to say, I am not Branx's *soul mate*, and we are not legally married and a few other nasty little words. My mother, oh how I love this woman, refuted Brodlyne and said, our family was there to witness the wedding, and she had also seen the proof of the *Joining Ceremony*. Oh my Gods, now that is TMI.

My mother has never mentioned anything regarding the condeam. Gross, as if we need to hear, what a condeam is and how it is used in the *Joining Ceremony*, to prove the couple are mated for life. I do not see how looking at what resembles a broken condom covered in our combined sexually fluids proves and makes a couple mated.

Well, I suppose, it notifies the officials that the said couple has had sex and if I remember vaguely, you have to say some type of sacred vows to one another at the height of passion — words I was never told anything about.

After the words, you feel as if your body become one with that of your Mate and just as you are orgasming, you bite one another and consume the other's blood to seal the act of a *Mating Ceremony*. Did I happen to mention the bright lights surrounding you…yeah well there is. It just about scared the crap out of me when I saw them and I swear we lifted off the bed also.

As in my mother's case, even though my parents already had my twin siblings Alley and Damien before the Ceremonies had taken place. My mother had been expected to conceive again to activate her full Queen powers, and by conceiving with me, this enabled her abilities to take full effect.

I will have to speak with her, to see what will happen regarding me, seems I am now next in line to become Queen and with it the uneasy feeling of replacing my mother. Maybe I might be able to persuade her to stay on as Queen a bit longer, more than thirteen months remaining. I do not know, if I will be competent in becoming the next Queen, seems my older sister will be marrying her *soul mate* and the father of her child and moving away as Alley will be the Queen of her husband's vast kingdom.

And so, Alley thought she would never meet her *soul mate,* and somehow she did unknowingly several years ago. Fighting for her life in a massive assassin attack while at a Paranormal Entity event. The event is similar to a mini Olympics, where *Dark Ones* from all kingdoms compete against all types of Entities in combat, including different forms of martial arts. As Alley is older than me, she just qualified with her age to enter; our parents allowed her to attend and compete — under a fake name of course.

Alley had met her *soul mate* at this competition, and the pair of them became trapped for several days. Thinking they are not going to escape or survive, Alley and her *soul mate* Philip without realising it performed their own *Mating Ceremony.*

Let me put it this way; Alley ended up pregnant after that trauma filled event, where over several hundred *Dark Ones and Entity's* had been assassinated and over 200 *Entity's* injured. Several months later, Alley found out she was pregnant she tried to track down the guy, she had hidden away with, only for Alley not able to find him.

Under the impression, he was one of the *Dark Ones* killed in one of the later attacks where several *Dark Ones and Entities* perished; Alley became heartbroken.

By some miracle, Alley was not dependant on her *soul mates* blood and instead, was able to survive her pregnancy drinking our mothers, unique Queen blend, just as we had as children.

In the end, it turns out both Alley and her Philip used fake names, which helped save their lives.

To make another miracle come true, my sister's betrothed — a betrothal which had previously been arranged to unite our two Dark One kingdoms, before Alley turned eighteen — Alley's fiancé Philip arrived early to Darshia for their official engagement party, earlier this year.

Well, to cut a long story short, after officially meeting for the first time, both Alley and Philip were both in shock to realise they are seeing the lover they had all those years ago. In which they both had survived that event in which they both thought the other had perished when they had fallen in love and conceived their daughter.

So, this now leaves me in the position to take over from my mother and lead Darshia as the new Queen. A position I would rather not have, but a prestigious job I have been taught, right along with my sister Alley.

Chapter Thirty-Three

ALEX

"ALEX, WHAT ARE YOU THINKING ABOUT?" My mother asks when she sits down beside me.

"Just different things, Mumma. Branx, his mother who is now his aunt and ...this stranger who is Branx's long-lost father. Oh, then there is me, taking over your position and becoming Queen of Darshia. You know nothing major."

Nothing like feeling sarcastic when everything is starting to weigh you down.

"Alex, ask me, anything you want. Tell me anything. I will always be here for you. Just remember, never, never give up. You are my baby girl and remember. I will always love you," Mum says as she wraps her loving arms around me.

With a sigh, I rest my head on Mum's shoulder. "Thank you, Mumma. Can you remain Queen a bit longer? I think there is a lot of stuff to work out with my husband before I can take on the role of Queen."

"Oh, my baby girl. There is so much for you to learn, as part of your Queen duties. So much for you to know about Branx's father and what Paranormal Entity he is. Now I know about Bravaile, I soon realised what I had been sensing about Branx, all these years. Remember we knew he had a Paranormal Entity in him, but we could never determine what type. Well, now I know the truth."

Turning my head, I look my mother straight in the eye and ask, "What is he?"

"Alex, you should be speaking to Branx first."

"Mother, just tell me. What kind of Entity is Bravaile and what about Branx's mother, what was she?"

"What do you feel, what do you sense with your magic, when Bravaile is near?"

Hmm. Giving my mother's question some thought, I do not really know. When I had first came in contact with Bravaile, I had no hearing. Thinking back, I do seem to recall there had been something... whatever it was, it seemed to affect my other senses; it had been as if something was blocking my power, my abilities.

With my mother's guidance once more, I reach out with my mind, I concentrate on Bravaile. Ever so gently I release just enough power to leak through to brush silently over him, to invade his mind, his body. Just the way my mother had taught me earlier this year, when she had explained to me, how she could breach and read anyone's mind, without that person detecting.

Ever so carefully I find a way through and breach Bravaile's mind shields and into his memories.

Feeling my mother beside me in Bravaile's mind, I listen to Mum, explain each process, each step while I work my way through each layer.

Layer, upon layer, seeing, hearing and witnessing what this man had done, completed, accomplished and killed throughout the years. Some of it was terrifying, while other parts heartbreaking and challenging. The further I submerged myself, the more I learnt until I found the other piece of the puzzle I had been searching for, when he and his pregnant wife had been set upon and attacked.

Seeing the people who had tried to kill them and listening to the little bits of information from one of the assassins. The ones who had ordered the hit on their lives and why. Witness Bravaile in action, fighting and managing to kill all the killers, only to fail his beloved wife — Xaiverly.

Within hours, Xaiverly had gone into labour and given birth to her son, only for her to lose too much blood from the injuries she sustained and died in Bravaile's arms, while her sister looked on, holding a sleeping, baby Branx.

Able to see and witness the conversation Bravaile also had with Brodlyne and the life pack agreement to protect Branx young life or forfeit her own.

Whoa. Branx's mother was a shifter, a wolf shifter just like her sister, Brodlyne. Oh, my God. Brodlyne is a shifter. Wow, she has kept that hidden rather well throughout the years. I never detected a thing. As for Xaiverly, her clan had been against her joining with Bravaile and mating with him. As for Bravaile, he is one of the turned vampires.

The jury is still out, whether he is good or bad.

Oh, my... Vampire. Not *Dark One*. He was never a *Dark One*, only a turned vampire, and it happened before he met Xaiverly. Vampire slayers had killed his creator over a hundred and eighty years ago. As for Bravaile, his older sister had been Riley's mate, the woman who had been killed, thanks to Grandma Ma and her possessive nature. Trasay, Riley's mate had left behind a son, Travis would play with Alley, Damien and me throughout the years until he left Darshia and found his *soul mate* on the other side of the country while travelling around the world.

Ha. So that is how Bravaile and Riley know one another, they were brother-in-laws.

Chapter Thirty-Four

ALEX

"**W**ELL. HOW DID YOU GO, ALEX? DID YOU dig deep enough, or only the surface layers?" my mother's voice drags my attention back to the step, we are sitting on, and feeling the hard cold, rough surface against my fabric covered butt.

"Hmm. Let me see. I had seen what Bravaile went through over the years. I had seen and felt the attack, the birth of Branx and then the death of Xaiverly. Witnessed the pact when Brodlyne accepted the oath to protect him."

"Yes. What else?" My mother nods her head, encouraging me to continue.

"Ah. Um." Biting my bottom lip, moving

swiftly through my thoughts until I find something else, "Both Xaiverly and Brodlyne are shifters, wolf shifters."

"Yes. Keep going." A smile forms on Mum's face.

"Bravaile is a turned vampire."

"Oh that is good, but you are missing a couple of key points." Huh. What key points? I thought to be a turned vampire, and the sisters come from a clan of wolf shifters had to be the main points?

"Alex, you are missing, the real reason why you're here and why Brodlyne not only despises and hates you, she also wants you dead."

Whoa, what?

With the other Entities and *Dark Ones* heavy in discussions, I finally finish a few more mentally draining lessons, with my powerful mother. I am starting to master the ability of manipulation and breach into another being's mind. I never thought I would be able to perform these acts before becoming Queen. Mum, once again reminded me, *I am her daughter, and anything is possible.* I already have the royal power and the ability; all I have to do is learn and practice my abilities.

After thirty more minutes of practice, the ability to mind talk or unbeknown to the subject I had been practising on, I soon discovered my abilities, improving and remarkably similar talents to my mother. The ability to slip into someone's mind, so quick and easy, was just like a hot knife slicing through butter, and I soon found out the real reason why I am here.

After leaving the *Bitch from Helz*, um I mean Brodlyne's, mind with uncertainty I do not know what to think. With my head shaking internally with everything, I have seen. I now understand why she hates me and what her sick plans had been for my *soul mate* and husband.

Feeling the contents of my stomach making its way slowly back up towards my mouth, I try to swallow and push everything back down. This woman is one sick mother fu... Yeah, I am not going to finish that thought.

Trying to reign in my temper, I make the decision it is time to have a little chat with my newly found father-in-law.

Especially on the topic of a couple of the

conversations, he had been involved in before Branx was born, these details in the planning of the takeover of several Kingdoms. Darshia had been on the list of potential countries to be dominated. Only for the contents of such plans and other secrets to be removed from his mind, well not all the contents details. With my gifted talents, I can find all the tampered pieces and assembled them back together again.

The most bizarre information is what I managed to come across, so deeply hidden within Brodlyne's mind — bone-chilling information. Also stumbling across how Bravaile overheard the details from a conversation between Brodlyne and another — they had been discussing the assassin attempt on Bravaile's life, which of course resulted in the death of his beloved *soul mate* and wife — Xaiverly. Only for this information to be removed from Bravaile's mind and with it, the attack and threats of war between the Vampires and *Dark One*'s Empires.

If Brodlyne wanted her brother-in-law dead...then why did she want to see her sister killed? The point of all this is and still do not understand, why keep Bravaile alive when these people wanted him dead? I am still missing something here...

But, what?

WITH EACH STEP, I KEEP MY EYES PEELED AND my senses open.

With Branx speaking with his aunt, under one of the streetlights, I can guarantee things will be heating up over there, especially when you can see Branx waving his arms about in the air.

Sensing Riley not far from me, for once I am glad he is keeping a short distance. With all the bloodthirsty enemies around us, it is a relief to know, more of my mother's guards are hiding amongst the shadows. While Darshia is on high alert, my older brother Damien is back at the castle overseeing to the safety of our people and keeping an eye on our younger brother — Dane.

Our parents made sure, all four of us kids were taught, to handle the security and safety of Darshia and its people; it has been drummed into us from an early age. As Damien is older than Dane, the poor kid will have to sit on the sidelines, as per our parent's instructions.

Even though Damien will keep Dane right by his side, involving him in everything, which will make me happy, because that is what the four of us kids have always done. We learnt to share the responsibility and listen before stepping forward and proceeding.

I still call my cocky little brother, Dane, the Kid, just to annoy him. He is old enough to know how to handle such a situation, after all, I know for a fact, Dane secretly, joined the Dark One Secret Forces. A particular unit designed to infiltrate bad situations, to retrieve and ascertain the 'said item' and return to base.

After all the years Dane spent hanging around Riley and the royal security, he has grown into a force to be reckoned with. The kid has been away on several missions, worry the heck out of me.

Only by chance did I find out about Dane's secret life when Dillion had informed me regarding a secret mission, I had been working on. I soon found myself surrounded by a special group known as the Dark One Secret Forces, and who was in charge of the mission — Dane, in all his six foot plus muscle glory.

Knowing Dane, he will be having a few words with our loving parents, how they keep leaving him out of all the crucial decisions regarding the safety of Darshia. It is only a matter of time before our parents will find out about Dane's extra activities, I do not want to be anywhere near Darshia when the shit hits the fan between them.

As for the feeling in the air, something is about to happen, whatever that bad feeling is, it is not going to be good.

Now to find my father-in-law and have that little chat.

Chapter Thirty-Five

ALEX

"ALEX. THANK YOU, FOR EVERYTHING YOU have done for my son. I know he is only alive because of what you managed to do." With an annoyed look on his face, I watch Bravaile glance over towards Brodlyne. Then to his son, and back to me with a smile. "Please forgive my lack of manners. Dealing with Brodlyne is much to be desired right now."

Hmm. Do I have enough time to search Bravaile's mind, before I have to start speaking in turn? I return Bravaile's smile and nod, as my eyes travel over to Branx.

"Bravaile, you're probably expecting me to ask you several questions," pausing, my eyes return and focus back on Bravaile, as I slowly fill my lungs with air. "Which in fact I do. However. I require speaking with you in private for a few minutes."

With a slight frown, Bravaile replies, "Surely, whatever you have to say, you can speak freely here. All my men know my business."

With a slight shake of my head, I nod my head, lifting my hand to indicate for the both of us to walk over to the park seat to sit down.

"Oh, I am sorry. It would be better if you were sitting down. Yes, let me lead the way and escort you to the seat."

Sometimes I find being pregnant does have its advantages.

With another smile and nod, we both make our way over to the other side of the street and sit down on one of the vacant park bench seats. Just as we start to sit down, I allow my senses to flow out and around us. Checking what kind of privacy we have. It soon becomes apparent; we are surrounded by a variety of different Entities, allowing us no privacy. Great, looks like I'll attempt to use a couple of my talents to complete this conversation. Hmm, with my witch and *Dark One*, abilities, let's see if they work with a turned vampire.

Looking first at Bravaile, it only takes a matter of seconds to place a magical shield around us, I smile at Bravaile while my mind branches out, looking and seeking a break in his mind shields. First, it seems impossible; I start to give up until I remembered what my mother just taught me, less than twenty minutes ago. Wow, I had begun to believe, my mother had been the one to allow me to breach Bravaile's mind. Glad to know, it was me after all, I had been successful in breaching his mind, now for the next step.

Using my new hidden talents, I try again and soon breach Bravaile's mind shields at the same time placing my shields around our minds to prevent anyone from hearing our thoughts.

'Please, do not be alarmed, Bravaile,' I say, even though Bravaile nearly jumps out of his seat and quickly looks around, until his startled eyes land on me. *'No one can hear us like this. As I said, we need to talk in private.'*

'But how?' With concern written in his eyes, Bravaile started to emit nerviness, instantly I begin to feel his fight or flee instinct kicking in as his eyes dart around

us. *'How can you do this? No one should be able to breach my mind. No one.'*

'Well, Bravaile, your mind is not as protected as you think.'

Geez. Why do people who presume to think they are all powerful are sure their minds are safe?

'What kind of witchcraft are you using on me?'

With a shake of my head, I reply, *'I can assure you. I am not using any witchcraft on your mind. I am only using my Dark One abilities. Don't forget, as you said earlier to Brodlyne, I am the Princess of Darshia, and I will be the next Queen. When I finally agree to replace my mother, that is. Which by the way, will not be happening anytime soon.'*

'So you are telling me, as you're a Dark One princess, you are capable of such, and yet the average Dark One cannot?'

'Something like that, yes.'

'Can you hear my thoughts?'

'I can if I want to. But don't worry, I have far too many other problems to deal with, than adding more from your mind. But then, what we have to speak about, does concern you and your lost memories.'

With a look of disbelief, Bravaile says, *'Lost memories. What lost memories?'*

'If you allow me to speak, I will fill you in on what I discovered. Just hold my hand, and I will show you.'

'This better not be a trick, Alex.'

'No. No trick. Just the truth. Oh, and I want the truth from you as well in return.'

For the next few minutes, I replay, what I have come across in Brodlyne's mind. Demonstrating the fact, Bravaile has had his memory tampered, and Brodlyne with another unknown male is the cause. Especially the missing information and the impending attack on Darshia. Which Bravaile denies any involvement — arranging the attacks on *Dark One* kingdoms.

The biggest shock to Bravaile is the

involvement of Brodlyne in the assassination attack, which leads to his wife's death. He is shocked to find out, the one person he thought he would be able to trust with his son's life is the one to kill her own sister. Bravaile, always wondered how Brodlyne arrived so soon after the attack.

Feeling his anger increase, especially when he learns of Brodlyne's deception of her true nature, and why she agreed to raise Branx. She had been planning to conceive a child with Branx when he became old enough. A child to use as her pawn to gain control of the Vampire Nation.

In the time frame, Bravaile and I been mind talking, there was at least ten individual attacks on our minds. Whoever they are, they are determined to know what we are discussing. Maybe they should learn, not mess with a *Dark One*.

"Alex, thank you for allowing me to see and speak to you regarding these matters—"

Cutting Bravaile off, thinking it will be wise to explain I am not the only one who knows this thought and memories. Just in case he decides, I am better off dead, instead of alive seems I have access to all the confidential information.

"Bravaile, I will inform you, I am not the only one who knows of this information which we have uncovered today. Just on the off chance, you thought I might have been the only person other than yourself with such knowledge."

With a sly glance towards me, Bravaile replies, "I would never contemplate such a thing, young Alex. After all, you are my son's *soul mate* and the mother of my grandchild."

Hmm. With a lift of my eyebrow, my thoughts automatically think, bravo Bravaile. I noticed how you carefully worded your answer. What are you hiding? What is Bravaile up to, now?

With a slight nod of my head, I say, "Bravaile, you still have not mentioned what your plans are regarding Brodlyne? She has betrayed us all."

With a straight face, Bravaile says, "Alex, when I decide on a plan of action I will notify you, how does that sound?"

Shaking my head to his comments, no it is not good enough, what is Bravaile hiding and why does it seem he is protecting Brodlyne in some way?

"Bravaile, if I did not know any better, I would say, you are avoiding the truth."

Standing back up, I turn and face my new father-in-law. "By the way Bravaile, if you think you can lie to me and cover it up, you will find yourself dead. If you know anything about my mother, then you know she killed her father-in-law, for his attempt on her life. And I will not hold back if I am forced to do the same."

Feeling the weight of his stare, I turn my head, and notice Branx has been watching me, I nod in his direction and link my mind with his. *'Hey honey. Did you finish your little conversation with Brodlyne?'*

'Yes. Why?'

'Why, is an excellent question.'

'Alex, what do you know that I don't?'

'A lot by the looks of it. I have also just had a little chat with your father on the hidden subject matter. Meet with me by the castle car, one of the guards has just delivered tea, coffee, sandwiches and cakes again, and I will fill you in.'

'What hidden subject matter?'

Now, this is one conversation, I would prefer to have something in my belly before discussing with Branx. He is not going to like it. Not one bit. On the other hand, is he going to believe me?

Chapter Thirty-Six

ALEX

YUM. I LOVE CHOCOLATE CAKE, AND THESE
sandwiches are yummy as well, eating for two
has its benefits. Oh, how I needed this cup of
tea. I did not realise, how cold my body is
until I was a third of the way through my hot
brew. Sitting on a seat near one of the castle
cars, it is not long before I finish eating
another slice of scrumptious cake and
sandwiches, with a fresh cup of tea in my
hand.

I turn and face Branx when I feel him at
my mind shields, *'Baby, are you going to avoid
talking to me or are you ready now?'*

'*Honey. Remember I love you.*'

'*Yes, I know that, Alex. Now stop stalling.*'

'*Branx, I would like for you to hold my hand, and from there I will allow you into my head, into my memories and thoughts and we will also travel into Brodlyne's and your father's. There is going to be some information you will not want to believe. There will be information and visions, which will make you extremely angry.*'

'*What is going on, Alex? What are you going to show me, to make me extremely angry.*'

'*I am sorry, Branx.*' A big part of me does not want to travel this path; this information is going to destroy my beloved. '*You have to promise me Branx, not to act before you have all the information because I do have my mother and Riley ready to prevent you from leaving me from this area and attempting to do something stupid and dangerous.*'

'*Okay, baby. I do not know to be worried or nervous. What has you so concerned for my safety?*'

I am nervous and worried, Branx will try to do something stupid and get himself killed or worse if Brodlyne manages to get her hands on Branx. Just wait until he finds out what that She-Devil has planned for my *soul mate*. No, wonder why she had been so adamant regarding Branx and that other woman, Angela. Brodlyne would have used poor Angela as her pawn in this sick game and taken advantage of the situation until Brodlyne succeeded in her diabolical plan.

'Branx, what you are about to see, is going to hurt you. Not physically, but it will hurt emotionally. However, you need to know, as much as possible, because we need a solution to work our way through this if we want to survive tonight without getting hurt or worse killed.'

'What?'

'Branx, please remain calm.'

'How can I remain calm?'

'Honey, please try. Try for our baby and me.'

'Okay, Alex, I will try.'

'I am going to kill her. What in the hell did she think she had been thinking to do that to the person she called a sister. A person whom she had once called her family.'

'Branx, I need you to sit back down beside me, please. You are starting to attract attention. Come on, Honey.'

'Alex, I know I know. That evil bitch is not my aunt at all. She is just a power hungry, using bitch who wanted my father. Now I am a grown man, that bitch thinks she can have me as her mate.'

Watching Branx, struggle with the overload of information. How does anyone move to pass this situation, finding out, the person whom you loved with all your heart, which you also thought to be your flesh and blood — your mother, used to drug you.

The She-Bitch had been raping Branx and milking his seed for experiments. Oh, that bitch Brodlyne is going to pay. First, I need to find out a little bit more information to see where she had taken the seminal fluid belonging to Branx and who the doctors had been and if they had impregnated any other female, all those years ago when we were teenagers.

'I had seen the images, Alex. What she has done and what she planned. Those foul, vile, disgusting things she did to me, while I had been drugged. Those images of me, from when I was in high school, they are sick. She is sick. I should just shoot her, right now.'

'Branx. Branx, honey look at me.'

'Alex, I feel sick.'

With my mind, linked with Branx, I can see, when the reality of what happened to him before we were together is starting to sink in. The shock of the assaults, the *Bitch from Helz* has caused. Because I can travel deeper, I also came across another assault to Branx, only four months ago. Making my stomach revolt, Branx is not the only one feeling sick.

It happened when I went back to Darshia for Alley's engagement party to Philip. Branx had been deep into a case we had been working on and was not able to travel with me that weekend. Instead, Brodlyne had arranged for Branx to stay at the apartments at Headquarters, the high-quality suites available to the staff and clients to use.

Brodlyne had once again managed to drug Branx, using my husband for her own, perverted, sick pleasure. I had seen what she had done to him, including the physical rape with her body, not just her hands but the devices she had used for the collection of semen.

She had planned to conceive, as far as I can work out, something happened, and Brodlyne did not conceive that weekend. It turns out; the *Bitch from Helz* was fertile when we had been attacked over three weeks ago. She had been planning on milking Branx, once again, maybe she should have consulted the BPE and they might have handed him over instead of nearly killing him. Brodlyne had been that desperate to have me out of Branx life; she wanted me dead.

Focus Alex. How am I going to get through to him? My heart is breaking for my husband, and I feel I might be losing him, minute by minute with the hideous torment swirling around in his mind.

'Honey, keep looking at me, keep your focus on me,

baby. We are going to think of just the two of us. You are going to feel my love wash over you. That woman will never touch you again. Do you understand? After tonight, we will be travelling back to Darshia with my parents and tomorrow we can go back to the private beach once more. How does that sound, Honey?'

Feeling anger and hatred build within, my beloved, lover, friend and husband. A force building and gathering so fast, I am afraid of what is happening to Branx. At least my parents and Riley are ready, and I hope with all my heart we are enough to prevent Branx from losing himself.

'Alex, I want that woman dead, do you understand me, because I will kill her myself.'

'Okay, Honey.'

'Baby, does my father know what Brodlyne has done to me?'

'Not everything, no.'

Through clenched teeth, Branx, asks, *'What does he know?'*

'He knows, Brodlyne is not your aunt. Also, Brodlyne wants to use you so she can conceive. However, he does not know what she has done to achieve that.'

'Alex, I do not want anybody else to know.'

'Um. Branx.'

'Alex. Who else knows?'

'Ah. My mother…'

'What? That is just fucking unbelievable.'

'Branx, my mother knew before I did. When my mother was assisting me earlier, we had gone over a couple of lessons of breaching others minds. It was Mum, who pushed for me to look deeper into Brodlyne's mind. I thought I had dug deep enough. As I found out, no I had not. Mother has since said she is not going to share this information with my father. It is a private matter for you and me to sort out first.'

'Alex, I do not want anyone else to know at this stage. I feel disgusted, used, and dirty and most of all betrayed.'

'Honey, you have every right to feel that way. I am here for you. I love you.'

Wrapping my arms around my husband, with my magic I place a calming spell allowing it to cover him slowly, as I say, *'Branx, please do not let this woman get under your skin. You are not dirty. You are my loving, sexy husband, whom I love with all my heart. Do you understand me?'*

'Oh, baby. I love you.'

'I love you too, Branx.'

AFTER SEVERAL MINUTES, I FINALLY HAVE Branx calm enough to eat something and finish drinking his coffee. Knowing he has consumed something eases my conscious, especially when I start to sense and feel something is about to happen, something terrible and the feeling is increasing by the minute. Why do I have the feeling Brodlyne is behind this uneasiness...

Sending out a message to my mother, when I am not able to see her close by.

'Mum. Where are you?'

'Alex, I am with your father and Riley. We are busy discussing…'

I interrupt Mum, *'I need to speak with you. Branx knows. He has seen most of what Brodlyne has performed on his younger self. Well not all, I do not want him to know everything today. His heart is breaking enough. If he found out everything, I think he will snap.'*

'Alex, I think you are right. Now, I would like you to take Branx, to one of the palace cars and wait there until I arrive. Do you understand?'

'Yes. What is happening? I can sense something bad is about to happen.'

'Good to know you can also sense it; I would advise you to get your arse moving, now.'

Oh shit. When my mother says move, you move. My senses had been correct, something big is about to happen.

'Yes. Mother.'

'Alex, remember, I love you, baby girl.'

Uh-oh. For my mother to say, *'I love you'* she is worried and concerned, which is not like Mum at all.

'I love you and Daddy too.'

Ah, bugger it. I think I am officially starting to stress out. Feeling my heart rate increase, as sweat forms and slowly drips down my forehead. Time to get Branx moving and to somewhere safe.

In the next few minutes, I manage to convince a confused Branx to get up as Mum instructed. We walk to one of the palace cars and sit inside waiting for my mother to arrive.

With my senses screaming, whatever is going to happen is about to start.

With a tap against the car door window, I just about jump off my seat. Turning my head, I find Bravaile standing there indicating to open the window.

With my mind, I ask him, *'What is it Bravaile?'*

'Alex, I need to speak to my son.'

'I am sorry, Bravaile. Branx just received some devastating news. He is in no shape to have a civil conversation with anyone, right now.'

'What devastating news?'

'All I can say, it is to do with Brodlyne and what she has done to Branx. Without his permission, I am not going to divulge the traumatic information. Information we came across buried deep down in her memories.'

'Alex, what had Brodlyne done?'

'I am not going to break my husband's trust. I would suggest you ask the She-Bitch, I mean Brodlyne, yourself. However, then, she will most likely lie to you anyway.'

'Alex, tell me, what has she done to my son?'

'Bravaile, when Branx is ready, he will inform you. All I will say for now, if Brodlyne happens to die tonight, Branx would be happy about it and so would I. She does not deserve to live after what she has done.'

'I will discuss this with my son; at a later date. I

am here to say; I am leaving. I have another business problem, which requires my presence. I will be taking Brodlyne with me.'

With the window slowly opening, the tension in the air is ripe, whatever is about to happen is here.

'Bravaile, I can sense something is about to happen. Something bad. I would suggest being extra careful.'

'Thank you for the warning, Alex.' Lifting his hand, I notice something clutched in his fingers. *'Here are my private contact details.'*

Bravaile passed me his business card through the open car window, turning the heavy embossed card over, as I scan the handwritten message on the back.

'I would like to be able to be in contact with Branx when the hostilities are not so thick in the air.'

'I think he might like that. Good-bye, Bravaile.'

'See you another time young Alex. And continue to

look after my son, for me. I place my heart in your hands. Care for it well.'

With that, Bravaile turns and heads to the other side of the street. With my finger pushing down on the window button, I continue to watch my father-in-law as the car window slowly slides up to close.

Hmm. I know Branx is sitting beside me. First I had thought Branx is just deep in thought, but with what I am sensing, it is as if his inner self-has left the vehicle. All the overload of information he has learnt tonight, Branx is demonstrating he is not mentally able to handle what he discovered. I am amazed he did not go after Brodlyne and seek justice for the atrocities she has performed.

Turning my head enough, I notice the blank look on his face. Oh no, this is bad, extremely bad. I try to reach out to him, with my mind. The only thing I find is silence. No, my mind screams. Branx has gone into shock.
Shit.

Just as I start to turn my head to look for Mum, various loud noises erupt outside the car cause my body to jump in my seat.

Turning my head, I glance out the windows'. My mouth opens wide at the vision in front of me. Oh, my Gods. This is bad, so very bad. Right outside from the protection of the palace car, a war is raging. Guns, claws, stakes, swords and blades of all sorts flying, high and low.

Hand to hand combat as a full frontal attack launches around us. Entities are either falling to the ground or turning into dust and floating away in the breeze. Quickly glancing around the chaos, searching for my parents and Bravaile.

Relief hits me when I see, both my parents are climbing into another car, and of course, I catch a glimpse of my mother pointing her handgun and shoot several shifters and vampires, while Riley scrambles in after my parents. Feeling the car I am in start to move, I soon realise, we are leaving.

Just as I am turning my head away from the messy, violent, bloody massacre, is when I notice, Bravaile, at the corner of my eye, stumble, followed by his body hitting the ground. Oh, no. With a hitch to my breath, I watch in slow motion, and scan his body, waiting for something to happen within those milliseconds. All I witness is Bravaile lying in a solid heap on the ground, and he did not turn to dust.

Yelling out to my driver, I have him manoeuvre the car, as close as possible to Bravaile. Retrieving one of the several handguns from the side compartment in the car and quickly making sure it is loaded and ready to go with several full clips of ammunition beside my leg. Switching the gun's safety off, I decided to open the car door carefully, and taking a deep breath in and wondering what in the hell I am doing.

I lift my left hand up, within seconds, my fingers start to tingle and glow. As I scan my surrounding area, distinguish the difference between the good guys and the bad and begin to release my powers. Sending several shifters and vamps flying at the same time shooting the handgun with the other hand, sending silver bullets straight into either a direct headshot or dead centre of their heart.

With my powers building; sending several vamps up in balls of flame before bursting into a dust cloud. The body count starts to grow until I can climb out of the car.

With Bravaile's shoed foot nearby, I reach down and pull him towards me, dragging his heavy body along the ground, at the same time I continue to shoot hitting four more shifters. Only to feel several bullets fly far too close to my head, hitting the side of the car.

With a burst of power, I send it out and around me, sending anything and anyone near me, flying off their feet, hopefully giving myself enough cover for what I am about to do.

Placing the gun down allowing me to use both my hands I pull Bravaile's body as hard and quickly as I can, dragging him across the last foot of pavement and heaving his body half into the car.

Even though this had felt like a considerable amount of time from when we pulled up near Bravaile, in reality, it was most likely no more than forty seconds.

With another hard heave, I manage to lift and pull an unconscious Bravaile across the seat of the car allowing me to slam the door closed as I yell out to the driver to — *"go and head for Darshia and straight to the hospital."*

Chapter Thirty-Seven

ALEX

SITTING BESIDE BRANX, WHILE HE SLEEPS IN the hospital bed, I had failed to notice a stray bullet had hit Branx until after sitting back in the car and smelt his fresh blood.

I'm cursing myself, for not protecting him. With thoughts only of saving him, I soon had my wrist open, dripping with blood and forcing it into his mouth for him to feed. After several tries, Branx started to respond and drink. Thank goodness. Once we arrived at the hospital, the medical staff had taken over, removing the bullet and patching him up, until my blood started to heal the wound.

Sensing my mother, approach the closed

hospital room door, I send her a message via our mind link, '*Hi Mum. Branx is still asleep. Did you bring me any food and a change of clothes?*'

Just as the door started to open, my mother replies, '*Yes, Alex. I have everything here for you. Now eat and drink, then I want you in that bathroom over there and go and shower. You are still covered in blood.*'

'*Okay, Mum.*'

With the food and drinks placed on the little hospital table, I am soon eating the plate of roast beef with vegetables and drinking the bottle of juice. Once I finished the juice, I start on the bottle of water. Finding I am more hungry and thirsty than I first thought. Must be the pregnancy and my hormones.

With the soft loving touch of my mother's hand on my shoulder, her voice interrupts my racing thoughts, '*Alex what you did tonight was extremely brave. Bravaile is thankful to you, for saving his life. Even though he is angry, you allowed Branx to be shot because you stopped and opened the car door.*'

Typical male! Bravaile is giving a backhanded thank you, for saving his miserable life.

'*Mum, what else was I to do? Leave him there to die, because he would have if I had done nothing and left.*'

'*Alex, we both know you saved Bravaile's life. For you — someone who does not know him, risked your life to save his. Bravaile is only angry to find so many of the Entities had betrayed him, as he feels he had failed in protecting his son. Then there is the fact, far too many lives slaughtered tonight.*'

'*Mum, what about Brodlyne, did anyone find her body or see her escape?*'

With a shake of her head in disappointment, Mum replies, '*Two of our guards had witnessed her escaping with two others. The guards had opened fire at them, killing one male and hitting and injuring Brodlyne. They had been about to go after them when several shifter and vamps surrounded them.*'

Oh, no. '*Did these two guards, survive?*'

With another small shake of her head, my mother replied, '*Sadly one had been killed, the other only barely escaping.*'

'*Have you read this guards mind, to make sure he is telling the truth?*'

'*Yes, Alex,*' Mum says dryly, with an eye roll. '*I made sure of the facts before arriving here.*'

'*Mum, how many of our people died tonight?*' That thought has plagued my mind, far too much, while I have been sitting here.

'*Sadly three of ours. From what we have been able to gather so far, at least sixty-five other Entities died, with the exact numbers we will never know, because it is hard to work out who was on which side. A few of our people had witnessed what you are capable of; they had seen your Dark One and Witch abilities. Do not be surprised if you find a few of our residents wary of you, some enabled and others in awe.*'

Just great. This is all I need for the residents of Darshia becoming scared of me.

'Alex, our people needed to know, their next Queen will be able to protect her people. Also, you have demonstrated you have the abilities to do just that. Now go and shower. I will remain here until you come out.'

'Thank you, Mumma.'

Giving one another a hug, I feel my mother's love for me through our connection.

'I love you, Mum.'

'I will always love you, my baby girl. And don't you forget it.'

Releasing my arms around my mother, I moved to the bags my mother carried in, picked them up and started for a well-earned shower and change of clothes.

It does not take me long to be showered and dressed, feeling human and clean once again and sitting next to Branx.

'Mum, what are we going to do about Brodlyne; I need to find out more information about her experiments. Did you find anything out and if any

other female might have been impregnated with Branx's seminal fluid?'

With a shake of her head, Mum says, *'Even though I travelled deep within Brodlyne's mind, I do not think any other female has successfully been impregnated. Most likely due to the fact Branx has been mated to you for all these years, making Branx infertile to any other female.'*

I release a sigh, and my shoulder sags in relief to the news.

A noise behind me has my head turning towards, Branx. Pushing the chair back over to beside the bed, I place my hand back over his limp one. At least this time, his hand has more warmth to the touch.

With my mind, I reach out to his, and finally, I can sense he is there, *'Hey honey. You're in the hospital again. How are you feeling?'*

Sensing confusion and pain emitted from a drowsy, Branx. He asks, *'Alex. What's going on? Why am I in the hospital and which one am I in this time?'*

Oh, no. Poor Branx. He must be baffled

as he only just got out of one hospital and now he is in another. Now to rip that band-aid off and break the news to him — he's been shot.

'Branx, you had been shot. A bullet which was meant for me missed and hit you instead.'

With a frown, Branx asks, *'Alex, why was someone shooting at you?'*

'Branx what do you remember last?'

I can see, Branx is confused. *'I am not sure, Alex, my mind is a little fuzzy.'*

'Okay, honey. I'll let the doctor know you are waking. Are you in any pain?'

'A little, my shoulder hurts.'

'You had been shot in the shoulder with a silver bullet that is why it is sore. My mother will stay with you, while I speak with the doctor.'

I slowly get up, lean down and press my lips against Branx forehead.
"Mum, I am going to let the doctor know,

he is starting to wake and in some pain. I will be back in a moment."

"Okay, Alex. I'll stay and keep Branx company for a few minutes."

"Thanks, Mum. I should not be long."

Just as I close the door behind me, I scan the area for one of the staff. Okay, this is strange, I wonder where the doctor and all the nurses have disappeared to? This place is empty, and I wonder what is going on?

Chapter Thirty-Eight

GEEZ, THERE GOES OUR QUIET ROMANTIC candlelit dinner and a heart pumping, sweaty night of sex. Being injured in the hospital is not what I had imagined for tonight. Being shot, totally blows, and my shoulder is killing me. I wonder if my mother is going to show up. Alex did not mention which hospital I am in, but then if her mother is here, I am most likely in Darshia.

My body feels like lead and whatever is packed in those silver bullets is deadly. Why does my brain feel so fuzzy? Whatever the drugs they have given me, have sent me on my arse.

Slowly opening my eyes, I am glad the

room's overhead lights are turned off; a small light must be turned on somewhere behind me providing just enough light for the room which I am thankful for. After blinking my eyes a few times, everything starts to come into focus.

"Hello, Branx. Glad to see you are back with us." Ah, shit. Nearly jumping off the bed from the unexpected voice, I forgot Alexia is still in the room. "Are you able to speak?" Alexia asks, from somewhere nearby.

With my heart racing, my eyes slowly glance in the direction of the female voice. And there she is, a very similar version of my beautiful wife. Alexia might be a Queen in Darshia, but she will always treat you with respect and kindness. That is more than a lot of people I know.

I try to smile, but it takes too much effort. I soon realise my mouth does not want to function when I tried to speak. *Shit.*

These drugs are playing havoc with my system.

Alexia must have noticed me trying to speak. Instead, she breaches my mind. *'Is this better Branx? I see you are having a little difficulty.'*

'Thanks, Alexia. My body is feeling heavy and does not want to respond.'

'That is understandable. Try to relax. Alex should be back shortly.'

'Alexia, what happened? Also, where am I?'

'Ah. Well, you are in Darshia for a start. To what happened, well, you know you were shot. What is the last thing you remember?'

'Hmm. Not much. My mind is fuzzy. What were we doing when I was shot?'

'Branx I think you better wait for the doctor to arrive. The doctor had to perform some extra tests.'

'What extra tests? What is wrong with me?'

'Before you were shot, you recently found out some devastating news. You were extremely upset and in shock.'

What type of news would possibly upset me to the point I go into shock?

'Branx, you should wait for Alex to come back, and speak with her.'

'Alexia, is Alex okay? Is Alex sick? Tell me.'

With a slight shake of her head, Alexia remains quiet.

Feeling my heart rate increase, it is a wonder the nurses have not come racing in with the loudness of it thumping against my ribs. With my mind racing, I wonder what is going on, if it is not Alex... My eyes meet Alexia's. Okay, it must be me.

'Alexia, what has happened? Tell me.'

With a roll of her eyes, Alexia says, *'Look, I can see you are not going to give up, and your heart is racing. Branx, I will give you the quick version. Tonight, you found out your birth mother had died after giving birth to you. Brodlyne — we were first told was your Aunt, but minutes before you had been shot, it became known, Brodlyne is not related by blood to you at all.'*

'What? Is this some type of joke?'

'Nope. Sorry. No joke. Brodlyne is not your

mother; she had sworn an oath to protect you after you had been born.'

This is nonsense, Brodlyne is not my birth mother, and she swore a what? *An oath. Okay. What about my birth father, is he even alive?'*

Looking straight into the face of my mother-in-law and trying to read her face and body language. This has to be some kind of joke? How can Brodlyne not be my mother? Also, *my father is alive!* Where has he been all this time? Hearing Alexia voice once again, I try to focus on what she has to say.

I need answers.

I continue to watch Alexia, and she hesitates. I can see she is carefully choosing her words before answering, *'Your father. Well, yes he is alive in his own way. If it had not been for Alex, your birth father would have died tonight.'*

'What in the hell, does Alex have to do with my birth father?'

'Look Branx. Do you remember being captured and tortured?'

Captured... Tortured... My mind starts to race.

Oh, no. Now that seems to be something I am starting to remember. Alex and I had been working on our case when we received a call from Brodlyne confirming the BPE had been sighted again.

Alex and I went to investigate. Only to find there had been far too many BPE and we had been captured and hurt.

Remembering bits and pieces from that horrendous time, until I woke up in the hospital, hearing Brodlyne and Alex speaking.

Oh, my God, *Alex is pregnant; I'm going to be a father.* We are going to be parents. Feeling ecstatic with pride and I try to smile, with the thought, I already love our baby — and my beautiful Alex... How do you start to love someone more when they are already your world, my everything.

Determined to remember more, Darshia appears in my mind, but why? What else happened...come on Branx think.

...Darshia, something to do with Darshia and handing something in... That's right we travelled back to Darshia to recover from my injuries, before visiting Dillion and handing in our resignations.

Oh, shit. The precinct blew up around us, and we barely survived the explosion. Also, Alex had been taken — kidnapped.

Holy shit. That is when we found out Brodlyne is not my mother and my birth father had been there. I met my father!

After that everything is still a little fuzzy. Why, what would affect my mind, severe enough to cause my memories to disappear.

Chapter Thirty-Nine

ALEX

DECIDING TO OPEN MY MIND, I GO ON THE hunt for the hospital staff. Eventually finding the doctor and some of the nurses in one of the staff medical break rooms.

I stay to the shadows and keep my presence unknown, I listen to the expert medical personnel. Listening to what they thought was bragging rights. Bragging about the mistreatment of Branx. Pity they did not realise I was already in the room with them before they had shown their true colours.

These staff members have since learned Branx's birth father is a turned vampire, which is something far too many *Dark Ones* detest and dislike. Overhearing their little snide remarks, they do not realise their future Queen had been listening to every word of their sordid gossip.

The most significant piece of offensive statements is the fact one of the nurses ended up administrating one of the medications at the wrong dose. Instantly feeling my magic surge through my body causing my fingers to light up and spark. The tips of my fingers hum and tingle, my magic waiting to explode and rush out and zap anything in its path.

Unfuckingbelievable is all I can think before my shock and annoyance turn into anger. Anger building, radiating from within and spreading like wildfire throughout my body, rage and the temptation of hurting these so-called people. How dare these so-called medical professionals, treat any patient in this way?

Reminding myself to calm down, slowly taking in a deep breath before letting it all back out again. I reach out with my mind to Riley and request his presence here at the hospital ASAP and quickly filling him in regarding the nursing staff. Sensing his annoyed and disappointed attitude towards the medical staff, he reassured me he would be arriving shortly. He also mentioned he would contact Doctor Brean, and have him come and examine Branx.

It soon dawns on me, my body is in full view of the staff break room, and these stupid idiots have not noticed a stranger with sparking hands is in the entryway. Unfuckingbelievable.

Morons.

What type of morons, are these people?

After listening to enough of their smut, I walk further into the room, the staff soon fall silent, realising someone different has entered the room, but then it might be the tone of my voice.

"Do you enjoy working here in Darshia?" I say, in a deadly calm voice. Watching the medical staff, yelp in fright and jump to their feet to face me. A couple of them start to bow their heads to my presence. It is funny how a room can grow silent when one enters.

"Maybe you are planning on moving to another hospital to work in? Hmm. I wonder what the Queen would say if she knew her subjects have been mistreating her son-in-law." Looking at each, and every, one of them straight in the eye. The worried looks they started to give one another, knowing they are in deep shit. Oh, yes. Deep shit is an understatement.

Hearing and listening, to their thoughts, these idiots do not realise how much of a serious situation they are really in. "Oh, I think you should sit back down. The Head of Security shall be here any minute to have a little chat with each, and every, one of you."

Hearing a couple of them gulp, they are starting to realise; they might be facing jail time for the mistreatment of a patient and the attempt of severe bodily harm to a Royal Subject.

I lift my hand and notice it is still emitting sparks. Oops. The look on their face is nearly comical if it was not for the seriousness of the situation — each one of them, keeping their eyes on my hand. The cat is out of the bag regarding my magic — oops.

"So you do realise, the patient you have been treating is my husband, and I will be the next new Queen of Darshia. What you have achieved today is close to a death sentence."

With my words hanging in the air, one of the nurses, the one who had bragged about the administration of Branx's medication, turns deathly pale, her eyes roll back in her head, and she collapses, hitting her head hard against the table before falling on the floor with a thud. The other staff look down at her, then back to me, then back down to their fellow staff member. None of them moves from their standing position.

Pathetic.

Shaking my head in disgust, I turn and walk back towards Branx's room. And just think, these people will be my royal subjects. Oh, help me now.

Chapter Forty

BRANX

TRYING TO MOVE MY MOUTH ONCE MORE, IT finally starts to function, even though the rest of my body feels like a massive weight. Sensing a disturbance in the air, the hairs on my arms begin to rise. Oh wow, the disturbance is Alex. Oh, shit. My baby is pissed off. I can feel her magic and anger from here. Someone is in deep shit, and I am glad it is not me.

Turning towards my mother-in-law to gauge her reaction and ask, "Alexia, would it be possible for you to go and speak with Alex? I think she might be a little annoyed."

With a laugh, Alexia says to me, "Oh,

Branx. From what my little girl is emitting, my daughter is one pissed off woman."

With a shake of her head, I can see, Alexia communicating with someone before her eyes turn back to me. "Branx, I better go and see to Alex, before Riley arrives. It is time to perform some Queen duties."

Oookaayyy. Something big must have happened out there.

All I know, Alex is blocking me from her mind.

"Alexia, before you go, is Alex okay?"

With a look back over her shoulder, Alexia replies, "Yes, Branx. Alex is a little upset. I better go and see to her before she lets her magic fly."

"Look after her," I plead.

With a wave of her hand, indicating she had heard me, as I watch the back of Alexia exit my hospital room and closing the door behind her with a soft click.

Hearing a female voice in my head, Alexia replies, *I always try Branx. Always try.*

With my head firmly back against my pillow, I close my eyes. Feeling fatigue setting in,

I wonder what is going on, out in the hallway for my beautiful wife to be so pissed off. I hope Alex remembers she is carrying our child.

ALEX

WITH FRUSTRATION I SHAKE MY HEAD, AND ask, "Mother, how do you do it?"

I can already sense her questions she has installed for me. "Alex, what happened, baby girl? Who has made my daughter angry?"

"Oh, Mum. I had gone out to find the doctor and nursing staff, as I had said. Only to overhear them gossiping about Branx. It is terrible, Mum, and cruel. To make matters worse, one of the nurses had wrongly administrated Branx medication. She could have killed him, and she had taken it in her stride to pass it off as a joke. A pathetic joke and I...I wanted to zap her with my magic. Make her pay for what she had done."

Stepping towards me and wrapping her arms tightly around my shoulder, my mother's words brush my mind. *'Oh, my baby girl. I am proud of you. You did not use your magic to hurt anyone; you could have easily wielded your magic to serve as punishment. You have shown great strength. See, you are learning, you will make a fantastic Queen.'*

'But... Mum. I want those staff to pay for what they have said and done to Branx. To me, they have shown they are not loyal to Darshia. A loyal subject and a health professional does not treat their patients in this manner. I have sent for our old family doctor to check on Branx and perform a full set of tests. I hope there is no damage caused by that stupid nurse, Mum; I feel so angry right now. Grrrr.'

Oops. Looking at my sparking hands goes to show how angry I am right now. Trying to take in a calming breath to settle my agitated hands. Feeling my mother's loving and calming embrace helps a little to calm me.

'Shhh. Yes, I know, baby girl. Let it out, and we will sort everything out, including the unprofessionalism of the medical staff. There will be punishments. That is a given. Come. Let me

take you back to Branx. Go and lay down beside him on the bed and rest.'

Pulling back enough so I can look my mother in the face, I say, *'I can't do that.'*

'Why not?' My mother asks with a cheeky smile and a wicked glint in her eyes.

Feeling my face heat of embarrassment. *'B…be…because you do not.'*

Hearing my mother laugh across my mind, do I want to know what my mother means by that laugh as she laughingly replies? *'Alex, as the future Queen, you can do that and much more. Believe me, I have and much, much more.'* Mum produces a sly smile, a smile I do not think I want to know what it entails.

'Mum. Why do I have the feeling, I do not want to know what you are talking about?'

'Because, you do not, that is why. All you have to remember is you can do anything.'

'Hmm. Okay. I do feel exhausted. Sleep does sound good.'

'That's the way, now go and join your husband in bed and rest. Riley and I will sort everything out. After all, I am the Queen and your mother. If I cannot sort it out, who can?'

Chapter Forty-One

FEELING A SLIGHT PRESSURE ON MY SHOULDER has me sitting up. My eyes instantly open and alert for danger. Instead, all I find is my old family doctor. Doctor Brean who has not physically aged in all the years I have known him. He smiles down at me, indicating everything is okay.

"Alex, relax. It is only I, Doctor Brean. The results have arrived for the tests I performed on Branx earlier; there are a few things we need to discuss."

I furrow my brow in thought, staring Doctor Brean in the eyes, and ask, "What tests did you perform?"

My brain busy trying to work out, had I been asleep when these tests had been taken? I don't remember him performing any tests.

"Doctor Brean, please just say what you need to. I have had a long day. I am not in the mood, to play games."

With a worried look on his face, Doctor Brean glances from my face to Branx, then back to me. Making sure to stay out of his head and thoughts.

Doctor Brean nods his head in understanding and says, "Princess Alex, the tests I had requested earlier has come back. Only one other has seen the results, and they have been sworn to secrecy or have their life cut short."

Oh, shit. For Doctor Brean to mention the sworn to secrecy stuff, this is going to be serious. I wonder if I should have my mum here for support.

With my mind I reach out to my mother, only to discover she is up in the baby nursery holding the newborns and gently rocking them back to sleep.

Oh, wow. I think my mother might be starting to get clucky.

Watch out, Dad.

'Excuse me, Mum.'

Thank goodness, my mother felt me at her shields. That is one thing we do not need, is for Mum to drop a newborn accidentally.

'Yes, my baby girl, what is it?'

'Can you come back to the room? The doctor is here, and he is about to explain the latest test results? It sounds serious, Mum.'

Watching Mum hand the baby back to the nurse and thank her. Mum turns and walks out of the nursery.

'I'm on my way, baby girl.'

With relief, I reply, '*Thank you, Mum.*'

Closing my mind to Mum, I focus back on Doctor Brean once more.

"Alex, I should warn you, the results are not good. Given the fact, Branx's father is a turned vampire, and Branx has been consuming your blood for a few years now."

"Doctor Brean, just say what you have to say," I demand.

"Alex, Branx is turning into a vampire with *Dark One* abilities, according to his blood work."

Okay, this is serious. How concerned should I be for my own safety and my unborn child? "Alright, so Branx is turning into a vampire. What does that mean long term?"

With concern in his eyes, Doctor Brean responds, "Princess Alex, to tell you the truth, I do not know. I've never dealt with turned vampires before, or a *Dark One* with vampire traits, this is something new for me."

Oh crap. That is just fantastic, thinking quickly I inquire, "Doctor Brean, out of the Old Ones, here in Darshia, who has dealt with turned vampires. The vampires which are not trying to kill everything that is."

Hearing a noise beside me, I turn to see Branx starting to wake. Great, chances are, he has been listening to this conversation. Time to act like a *Dark One* and search his mind. *Sorry Honey.*

With Doctor Brean looking on, wondering if he should continue speaking in front of Branx, I take this opportunity to search his mind. I need to know, how his mind is working. Especially if my husband starts to have any sudden urges or new tendencies to kill something, times like this, I need my mum.

Chapter Forty-Two

As I start to wake up hearing voices nearby, my first thoughts are — *Holy shit.*

Listening to my beautiful wife's voice, discussing my test results with the doctor.

What tests results?

By the tone of Alex's voice, even she was not aware tests had been performed. Well that makes two of us — I did not know the nursing staff had taken any samples for testing.

…Oh, boy, by the sounds of it, these tests results are not good, not good at all, especially what they are discussing about me and vampires.

Listening to Doctor Brean and my head

shaking internally. Really. The doctor has to be kidding me. There has to be some kind of freaking mistake...

I'm turning into a vampire, a vampire with *Dark One* abilities. *Holy ssshhhi...it.*

Why? How?

Come on, a vampire with *Dark One* abilities; this is complete BS; no way am I turning into a turned Vampire, just like my father.

What the...father?

Shit, this is some freaky stuff. I finally remembered the details of last tonight.

My birth father is a turned Vampire. He is the Head honcho, president, the king even — of one of the most powerful Vampires organisations here in the country.

Oh, my God. I'm related to a crime boss. A freakin mafia crime boss type — Vampire. Holy shit. I think I am in trouble.

My thoughts move to Brodlyne. Ha. What about my so-called mother, who as it turns out, is not my mother at all, no the woman has lied to me all my life.

My birth mother had died not long after I had been born and the woman, whom everyone had thought was my mother's sister, raised me. Only thing, Brodlyne, is not related to my mother.

My mother's shifter wolf family, had accepted Brodlyne as one of their own, after they discovered her as a teenager, beaten, abandoned and left to starve in the bush not far from their camp. I only found that part out, because Alex had searched Brodlyne's mind. This memory of Brodlyne's had been buried deep and hidden beneath her other memories.

Why do I have a niggling suspicion I am missing something important regarding Brodlyne? Something not just important, but extremely bad. For whatever it is, my mind keeps turning blank, and it is frustrating as hell.

With a groan of annoyance, I push my mind to keep trying to remember what the heck it is regarding Brodlyne.

"Honey. Hey, it's okay. Wake up, Branx. The doctor is here with some interesting news," Alex murmurs.

What, I am now placed in the *interesting basket!* My annoyance and anger are starting to grow. Well, that is just fanfuckingtastic.

Slowly opening my eyes, the first thing I

see is my beautiful wife's concerned eyes staring back at me.

With a croaky voice, I reply, "Hey, Baby." Shit, my throat is dry, "I have heard some of it. How in the hell am I turning into a vampire?"

Before I know it, Alex has a drinking straw propped up against my lips. Looking up into my beautiful wife eyes, witnessing her love for me, shining back at me. Okay, I am just a bastard, allowing my thoughts to run wild with these fucked thoughts about being a turned vampire. My sexy gorgeous wife loves me. And here she is providing me with sips of water, as she stands by my side caring for me.

"Oh, Branx. I don't know. It might have something to do with your father already being a turned vampire when your mother conceived you, this being a delayed reaction. Alternatively, maybe, because you have been consuming my blood that might have triggered off the reaction? Or maybe whatever Brodlyne had been doing to you over the years, might be the reason? Who kne—"

What the hell? What has Brodlyne been doing to me over the years? What in the hell has she been doing to me in the first place?

Cutting Alex off, I ask, "What has Brodlyne been doing to me, Alex?"

With a worried look, Alex looks down to her feet, then back over to the doctor who has been keeping quiet.

"Ah, Honey." I focus on Alex, biting her lower lip. What she must be going to say has to be bad, "Branx we found out, Brodlyne is not your real mother. First, we were told she was your aunt, your birth mother's sister, who had vowed a pledge to protect and raise you."

Biting her lip once more, I send her a message through our link. *'Come on baby just tell me.'*

With a nod of her head, Alex says, "Branx, we found out Brodlyne had been abusing you since you have been a teenager. You have been drugged, your body receptive to her ministrations."

Feeling as if someone just shattered my heart, my brain tries to work out exactly what Alex has just said.

"What the fuck do you mean receptive to her ministrations, Alex?" my voice loud enough to wake the dead.

With a slight shake of her head and a

single tear making its way down her cheek, Alex quietly says, "Branx, Honey. Brodlyne had been raping you."

Anger building within me. I start to shake my head in denial. No. Brodlyne would never… Just then bits of memory begin to form in my mind. Glimpses of a naked Brodlyne, sitting astride me. Me. Oh, fuck, no. No, no, my God no. Feeling sick to my stomach.

Hatred. Hatred and anger building and spreading within my body. I want to hit or smash something, and this is bullshit. This is not my life.

How can a woman I trust even contemplate such a shameful, despicable act towards someone whom she saw and treated as a son? No, my mind has to be playing tricks on me. Surely…

I yell, "That is bullshit, Alex."

Noticing Alex, keeping her distance from me — is she afraid or disgusted by me. "Branx, I only wish it was. We both had seen it buried in her memories when I had searched her mind last night."

Shaking my head in disgust, for all I know what Alex says is the truth, but I still do not want to believe it. No. Women do not go around raping men.

"Baby, what treatment you received had mainly been done since you were seventeen. Brodlyne was collecting your semen she wanted to impregnate herself. Brodlyne was using you to infiltrate your father's organisation. She wanted his power, his money and you."

Shaking my head, why would she. My mother's family loved Brodlyne like a daughter. I had seen the memories in Brodlyne's head.

Alex, hearing my thoughts, replied, "Branx, your mother's family are not responsible for Brodlyne's actions. She was planted as a spy, to infiltrate the pack. Her mission was to destroy your mother's pack and take over. When she found out your mother was going to marry your father, she thought all her Christmas' had come at once."

"But why?"

Hearing the doctor clear his voice, both Alex and I turn our heads and look at him. "If I may, I think I can answer the medical reason."

Battling to keep my anger under control, I ask, "Alright Doctor Brean, answer us. Why?"

"Well," Doctor Brean glanced back and forth between myself and Alex, "With his parents conceiving a child. Their child might grow to exhibit some extraordinary powers."

"Such as?" Alex asks.

"I believe, once Branx reached a certain age, he would have the ability and power of a vampire and shifter. Could you consider a super soldier of that nature? If Branx possessed these talents and powers, and then was able to successfully breed with other Entities, what his children would be, what they would be able to become?"

Hearing Alex, intake a sharp breath of air. I noticed her hand protectively covering her belly.

Our child.

My eyes lift to her face, watching the blood drain away from her features. Oh, no this is not good. Alex, turns her head towards the doctor, while her other hand reaches out and clutches my clammy one in a tight squeeze.

"Oh, my Gods. Are you saying this child I am carrying will also be able to turn into a

Shifter, a Vampire, with *Dark One* and Witch abilities?"

With a single nod of his head. Doctor Brean replies, "Yes."

Oh, shit.

Chapter Forty-Three

ALEX

OH, MY FUCKING GODDESS.

This is one big cluster fuck.

Where is Mum? She should have been here by now.

Reaching out with my mind, I soon contact her. *'Mum. Mum, I need to speak with you. It is urgent.'*

It does not take long for my mother to answer, *'Alex, baby girl. What is it, what is wrong?'*

It does not take me long to bring Mum up to speed on what Doctor Brean has said, reminding her of Brodlyne's actions over the years.

'Oh, crap on a stick. Alex, this is serious. We will have to have a meeting. Word cannot leak out regarding Branx.'

'No, shit, Mum. I am panicking here. Also what about my own baby, what is going to happen to her? She is going to have a target on her back.'

'Alex, watch your mouth. I know you are upset. Now, I have just contacted your father he is on his way to the hospital. I'm nearly at Branx room. Do not leave. You are going to require extra security. I'll bring Riley, with me.'

'Okay, Mum. I am staying here with my husband, right by his side.'

'See, you shortly, baby girl.'

Hearing Branx voice, I close the link to Mum. "Who were you just speaking with?"

With a small smile to Branx, I reply, "Sorry. My parents are on their way here to your room."

"Why, because of what Doctor Brean has said?"

My smile is fading, my face turning serious, "Yes. I am going to be the next Queen. This new situation is going to affect us more than either one of us realises. Our daughter will be Queen of Darshia one day, this has to be sorted, and a plan put in place."

"What are you getting at, Alex. What do you mean?"

Sensing my mother near the hospital door to Branx's room, I turn and face her, as she steps into the room.

The anxious look on my mother's face is a little overwhelming, hearing it her voice is another as she answers Branx's question, "Because Branx, my granddaughter is going to be powerful, that is what Alex means. The different *Dark One* communities and the Paranormal Entities are going to feel threatened. We have to organise a plan to protect her. Protect all of us."

Chapter Forty-Four

ALEX

"**Y**OU HAVE TO BE BLOODY KIDDING ME." With a shake of his head, I can see the frustration written on Branx's face. "Are you telling me, we might not be able to leave Darshia, because we might be attacked?"

My mother nods her head. "Yes, Branx. That will be the case."

Still shaking his head, Branx says, "Sorry Alexia, but no. I will not be staying in Darshia for the rest of my life hiding. My daughter will leave Darshia, to see her other Grandfather." With another shake of his head, he says with an adamant, "No. Just no."

With a sigh, my mother replies, "Branx, until we can determine who orchestrated the hit on Alex, Drake and I recommend for our daughter not to leave the safety of Darshia."

"What?" Spinning I face my parents. "Mother, I am not hiding. I am a trained agent and warrior. I do not hide."

A sad smile forms on my mum's face. "Alex, while you are pregnant, you will be taking every precaution there is."

Shaking my head, I look over to Branx before I turn and face my parents again and say, "Mum, Dad, I love you."

"Alex, why do I feel a *but* coming."

"Mum, because there is a very big *but*. I am not about to hide when someone wants to kill me. You never hid, so why should I have to?"

Looking at Branx, I say, "Honey I have to go back to our apartment for some of our belongings. I should not be long. I'll have a few of the security personnel travel with me."

With another shake of his head, Branx uses our mind link to speak to me, '*Alex. No, you are not going to the apartment. Chances are it will be a trap, if you go anywhere near there…*'

With a quick shake of my head, I say,

'Branx, I am not going to wait around for someone to track me down and kill anyone else. Anyway, I am going to pack some of our belongings into bags, just in case someone decides to trash our apartment.'

'I understand Alex, but not without me.'

Branx begins to move and I place my hand down on his shoulder to keep him from escaping the bed. *'Branx, until you're fully healed, no. This is something I need to do on my own. Look, I am only going to collect some of our belongings and photos, and I will be right back.'*

'Baby. Take Riley with you at least.'

Leaning forward, I place my lips on Branx forehead and then brush my lips against his.

'I love you.'

'Alex. Do not leave yet.'

I start walking towards the door.

'I'll be back soon, love you.'

"Alex," I hear Branx call out.

My father says, "Alex. Stop right there young lady."

I say over my shoulder, "Sorry Daddy, I have things to do, places to see."

"Alex. Wait," My mother demands.

Stopping in the hallway, I turn and face my mother. With all her Queen power, it is her mother voice, which gets me to stop and turn around. With my eyebrow lifting, I wait for Mum to say whatever she has to say.

"Baby girl. I know you are well trained. You are one of the best, especially with your magical powers when you use them. However, I do not want you to go off alone."

Giving my head a slight shake, I reply, "Oh. Mum." Walking back towards my mother and wrapping my arms around her in a loving embrace. "I really do have a few things I need to take care of. Look, I will take Riley and a few others with me, just in case I happen to run into any trouble."

With a firm hug back, Mum whispers in my ear, "Alex, please be careful. You have to remember; you are carrying a precious baby inside of you. You have to protect her."

Before I realise it, Mum connects our

minds. *'I have seen your thoughts, Alex. I know you are planning to confront Brodlyne. I understand, believe me, really I do. Make sure you wear one of the protection chest plates. Please do not pretend you do not have any magic, do not hide it, use it to your advantage. It will be the only way to protect yourself.'*

'Okay, Mum. I'll take extra precautions. I'll even bring my guns and sword. I'll be entirely suited up. Even though, Brodlyne will be long gone.'

'Alex. Don't. I am not stupid. I was young like you once. Make sure Riley and the others stick to you like glue.'

'Okay, Mum. I'll see you when I arrive back. I should not be long.'

'I love you, Alex. Both your father and I love you so much, it hurts. Do not get yourself killed.'

'I love you too, Mumma. Now look after my husband. I'll be back soon.'

With that, Mum and I release one another, and without looking behind me, I continued walking down the hallway with

Riley not far behind. No way, was I going to look back at Branx. I would have changed my mind and ran into his waiting arms. Plus, there is no hiding my facial expression from him. He would have been able to tell from my face; I am going to handle this bullshit and sort everything out with Brodlyne and Bravaile.

I have the feeling, I will be lucky to come back here alive, but I need to protect my husband.

With Brodlyne at the forefront of my mind — that woman is not touching my husband ever again.

Chapter Forty-Five

ALEX

AFTER SPEAKING WITH **R**ILEY AND EXPLAINING everything to him, we arranged to meet at my apartment.

As promised to Mum, I arrived at my apartment with three extra royal security personnel right by my side. I smile at the knowledge I am probably more dangerous than the three of them together. However, it is also good to know; I have someone at my back protecting me. With another three guards casually waiting around the building, keeping an eye out and dressed as if they live here in the building.

It does not take me long to change and suit up, in all my finery. I resembled more warrior than a Princess. I know, I am ready, feeling better now with all my weapons attached to my body.

With the last of my belongings thrown into another bag, and making sure to pack the wedding album with the packets of individual photos with a few of Branx's personal items I am not about to take any chances with our personal belongings, especially after being in a building as it had been blown up and destroyed.

Brodlyne must have had the apartment watched, because within thirty minutes after I arrived, I soon received a message on my phone from the *Biotch from Helz.*

> **B Helz:** It is time for
> the two of us to
> meet. Leave your
> puny guards
> behind, or I will
> make sure we kill
> each one before you
> leave the building.

> **Me:** What do you
> want?

B Helz: Your head on
a pike — would be
nice.

Me: Sorry. Not able to
fill your pathetic
request. Anything
else? I have places
to be, people to see.

B Helz: Don't piss me
off. I want your
pathetic arse in
your car. Then I
will forward you the
address. Make sure
you leave all the
guards behind.
Otherwise, I will
shoot you, now.

Shit, either they have cameras in my
apartment, or they can see me through the
windows. Not taking any chances, I had a
backup plan, with two other plain cars with
five guards waiting just up the road and out of
view. With another car, in the opposite
direction, just in case.

With my hand touching Riley, he can see and hear everything in my head, including the text messages, which he passes them to the other guards. Anyone looking in would think no one apart from me has seen my phone screen and the messages.

> **Me:** Tell me what you
> want and where.
> Branx is in the
> hospital, and I have
> left his side long
> enough.

> **B Helz:** What do you
> mean Branx is in
> the hospital. Which
> hospital?

> **Me:** Look, I do not
> have all day. Where
> are we going to
> meet?

I must have had Brodlyne off her game plan, because the stupid cow, replied with a text of the address. But then, I have the feeling; she will change the address when I am driving down the road.

Feeling Riley, in my head, he agrees with me. I know not to trust Brodlyne. I never have.

> **B Helz:** Go to Flinders
> Lane. Turn into
> Hay Pl and drive
> into the city
> building car
> parking. Once
> there, I will give you
> further instructions.

> **Me:** You better not be
> wasting my time,
> Brodlyne.

> **B Helz:** You have ten
> minutes to drive to
> Flinders Lane and
> into the multi-story
> car park in Hay Pl.

Shit.
With a few of our bags packed, with the

essential items, one of the guards start to take them downstairs to the waiting car. I give Riley a quick look before turning and heading for the door.

'Riley. Make sure you have the other two cars ready. Have one drive ahead of me and the other one follow at a distance. You can meet me there unless the bitch changes her plan and has me go to another address.'

'Princess Alex, I want you to be extra careful. I have spoken with Bravaile, and he now has a kill order on Brodlyne. After all, she failed in her protection of Branx. Her life is now forfeit. Once you leave the apartment, I will contact him and let him know, what is happening.'

'Riley, is the tracker still in my car?'

'Yes, Princess. It was still working until you stopped the car. It will also inform us if anyone has tampered with your car too.'

With a nod of my head, I take one more look around our apartment before walking out the door with my handbag another case of belongings. With another two suitcases full, the guards can carry them down to one of their cars. After all, I have to look like I am packing some things for Branx.

TURNING MY CAR, SLOWLY INTO FLINDERS Lane, it does not take me long to drive into Hay Pl. With my headlights on bright, I travel at a slow speed. Keeping a constant visual of everything around me, I do not require or need a bullet or weapon to the head or anything to jump out at me unexpectedly.

Feeling restless, I wonder how long it will take Brodlyne to send another message. The woman is a bitch, plain and simple. Playing games is her speciality.

Feeling the vibration of my phone against my leg, sensing by the tone I know it is Brodlyne sending another message.

B Helz: Drive to the
basement carpark.

The *Bitch from Hell* is definitely watching me, quickly notifying Riley, with our mind link. Glad to see my abilities are becoming stronger. Riley sends the message to one of the cars, which arrived before I did. Taking my time, I allow one of the vehicles to procede me to the basement car park level, as I collected my parking ticket at the boom-gated entrance.

My internal warning system is activating as I drive down two levels of the multi-storey car park, warning me, I am in danger. Geez, thanks for the warning buddy. I say to my internal self. I already know, I am in deep trouble. Pulling into an empty car spot, making sure to reverse the car up to the wall, in case I need to take off in a hurry. At least, no one will come at me from behind. I turn off the car engine and unplug my phone from its charging lead.

Hitting the record feature on my phone, if my phone rings or I receive any other messages, they will be recorded, and Riley will have an instant digital copy of all communications.

Just as I am about to place the phone back down on my leg, it starts to vibrate, and the ringtone of *Who let the dogs out* starts to fill my car.

Shit. Bloody phone. My body jumps with a start from the loud volume. With the silence of the carpark, any noise seems to increase in size.

Instantly glancing around the parked cars and my surroundings, I reach down for the ringing phone — mental note for myself — to remember to turn the ringer volume down.

Hitting the accept button, I answer the call, "As you can see, Brodlyne, I am here. Now what?"

"Glad to see you can follow instructions Alex. Your pet guard is still waiting for you at your apartment; I can see him standing there. Do you think, I will allow you to go anywhere, any place without my permission? That man is wasting his time remaining there, waiting for you. You are not going back to that apartment."

"Should I phone him, and fill him in, on your plans Brodlyne? He is a busy man; if he is no longer required, I might as well send him home."

"What games are you playing, Alex?"

"Me, playing games? You have to be kidding me, Brodlyne. No, I am not playing games. You are the one who is playing games. Look, I'll send my security team a message, to inform him he can now go home. Otherwise, he is going to wait there, until I return."

"Are you serious, he would wait?"

"Yes, Brodlyne. If he is given an order, he will obey. Now if you do not mind. I will phone him and let him know; he can leave."

"Okay, Alex. Remember, I am listening. If you try to tip him off, I will have you shot, where you sit."

Shit. Brodlyne is a bitch. Chances are I have about three shooters at this minute, aimed right at me.

Looking around, I start to concentrate on my surroundings, thank funk I increased my runes with a bit of extra power, nothing like increasing your magical powers to keep one alive. Within seconds, I can detect four separate men surrounding me from different positions here on this level all with their guns pointing right at me.

Ah, shit.

'Riley, have you managed to hear and listen to the phone call, with Brodlyne? Plus I have four. I repeat four separate snipers with their guns trained on me.'

'Roger that. My men are slowly moving in. We now have eyes on the targets.'

'Riley, I will be contacting you shortly and notifying you to go home, by phone. Brodlyne is somehow listening...'

'Roger that. I will send the decoy in my place, and he will travel out of town, and I will meet up with you shortly.'

'Roger that. See you soon, Riley.'

Returning to the phone call with Brodlyne, I say, "Brodlyne, how many men have their weapons trained on me, right now?"

Hearing a laugh come from the phone call. It soon becomes apparent; I might not make it out of the car alive.

"Alex, let me say, a couple of my men know to shoot when I give the word. Now. Contact your guard and send him home."

"Geez, Brodlyne, don't get your knickers in a twist. I have to end this call to do that. So I am hanging up right now. Bye."

And with that, I hit the end call button and cut the call.

Dialling Riley, I act as if I am following Brodlyne's instructions.

'Riley, did you get all that?'

'Roger that. The decoy is now standing in my spot ready for your call.'

I mentally reply, *'Roger that. Dialling now.'*

Tapping the screen on my phone, the sound of ringing soon starts, and within a few more seconds, I hear a male voice. Oh no. Thomasy is filling in for Riley. I hope the idiot has listened to Riley or this is going to be one very short phone call.

"Yes, Princess Alex. Do you require my services or should I remain here?"

"Riley, you can make your way back to Darshia. Everything is sorted, and I will be leaving in a few minutes. See you soon."

"Are you sure Princess, I can wait."

Feeling annoyed with the idiot. Thomasy might give the game away if he continues to push the issue.

"Riley. Do not question me. I said everything is sorted. Make your way back to Darshia."

"Yes, Princess. I will see you later."

"Goodbye."

Ending the call, before Thomasy has the

chance to say anything else. I say out loud as I turn the volume down of the ringer.

"Stupid Riley. He should just listen to me; I think I will be speaking with my mother about him."

Next thing, my mobile starts to vibrate, indicating it is now ringing once again. Noticing it says **B Helz** on the screen, I tap the screen and answer the call, "What do you want, Brodlyne?"

With an arrogant sneer to the tone of her voice, she says, "Alex, very good. I can see your guard is leaving the apartment building with a couple of others. Now, I want you out of the car and start to walk towards the exit sign to your right."

"Where am I going exactly, Brodlyne?" I ask. Making sure to delay the conversation long enough to allow Riley time to arrive here, "Are we staying here in the building or are you expecting me to walk to a different address?"

"Listen, Alex. I will notify you if and when you need to go to another location. Until then, get out of the car and walk slowly towards the exit door."

Casually looking back up noticing three different exit signs.

"The exit sign over there to the right." Knowing all too well, the door I am speaking of is not the one she had instructed.

"Get out of your car, Alex."

With a sigh and a shrug of my shoulders, I say, "Geez, Brodlyne. What is the rush? I have been on my feet for nearly thirty-five hours, and I am ready to sleep."

"Stop complaining, bitch." Hearing Brodlyne starts to lose her composure, "Get. Out. Of. Your. Car. Now."

'I'm here Princess.' Relief fills me, finally hearing Riley in my head.

'Roger that, Riley. Everyone ready? Has anyone had a visual on Brodlyne?'

Reaching for my handbag with one hand, reaching for the door handle with the other while I balance the phone with my shoulder and continue speaking with Brodlyne.

"Okay. Okay. I am getting out now."

"Stop delaying, Alex."

"Look Brodlyne; I am going to hang up now. You said to go to the exit door on the right, and that is where I am heading."

Feeling an irritated Riley in my mind, *'Princess, you are going to piss her off and end up shot. I know you are going to head for the other door. Don't do it.'*

'Riley. I am heading to the door she indicated — The exit door on the right.'

'Look, Princess Alex, we have not been able to locate Brodlyne. We found the hidden cameras, making sure we save footage of the four snipers we have discovered so far. My men are ready to take out the snipers. Oh, and we are about to begin the video loop of the snipers, so anyone watching will not be aware the snipers are no longer there.'

'Get ready, Riley.'

With my power, I reach down deep within me. Sensing my magic grow and swirl. Feeling my body become stronger, more alive and alert. Even my fingertips are starting to tingle, ready for the release of my power. Slowly allowing a little of my magic to come forth and out, I start the search once more. I need to find Brodlyne before it is too late.

Chapter Forty-Six

ALEX

'*What the hell are you doing Princess Alex? You are going to get yourself killed.*'

FEELING THE FULL FORCE OF HIS ANNOYANCE and agitation of the situation, sweep through my head.

'*Relax, Riley.*'

'*Do you have a death wish, Princess? We cannot protect you like this.*'

With a sigh, I reply, '*Riley, get ready to take the four men out.*'

With a grumble, Riley replies, '*Roger that.*'

Focusing back on my surroundings, with the thought of the four snipers preparing to shoot me. Oh shit. With my magic building up too fast, if I am not careful, my fingers are going to start to spark, warning anyone who is watching I have powerful magic and earn myself an instant bullet to the head.

Concentrating, I focus on finding Brodlyne. I know she has to be around here somewhere. The bitch will be sitting somewhere safe and out of harm's way. Well, not if I can help it. Feeling and sensing Riley and our men take out the four snipers at least that is one less thing to be concerned about.

Checking and scanning the next floor of parked vehicles. Sensing and feeling my way up to the following two levels of the building, I finally find the *Bitch from Helz*, sitting in the back of a parked van two levels up. Hmm. So authentic Brodlyne, sitting in the back of a van. With no windows, double doors at the back and one sliding door on the side. And it's a black van — really, how original — not.

'*Riley, I have found her.*'

Quickly sending the images to Riley through our mind link, and reminding him, I want a tracker placed on that vehicle. With my luck, the van will drive off, and I can guarantee, Brodlyne will try to escape.

This woman is going down today.

FEELING MY PHONE VIBRATE — ONE GUESS who is phoning me.

Reaching the exit, I place my hand on the exit door handle at the same time hitting the call button on my phone.

"What is it, Brodlyne?"

"Alex, can you explain to me, what you are doing?"

"Why, Brodlyne, I am following your instructions of course."

"Don't play games with me, Alex. You are walking to the wrong exit."

"What. No, I am not. I went to the exit to the right, just as per your instructions."

Hearing a frustrated sigh through the phone, followed by a growl. Oh-kaaaay. The animal side of Brodlyne is starting to show itself. Hmm. Interesting.

"Alex, turn around and walk to the other

exit and keep me on the phone or I will have the men shoot you where you stand."

"Oh, come now, Brodlyne. I am following your instructions. Maybe you need to explain yourself better."

"Don't push it, Alex."

"Brodlyne, why are you doing this?"

"What do you mean?"

I pause when I hear Riley in my head. *'The snipers are taken care of, you are clear.'*

'Roger that. Oh, and Riley. Thanks.'

'The rest of us are heading to Brodlyne's position now. We are nearly in place now.'

'Roger that,' I reply. Okay. Now to end this game, once and for all.

"Brodlyne. Why did you make that oath to both Bravaile and Xaiverly, knowing you were going to double-cross them?" Hearing a gasp, from Brodlyne, knowing I just hit a nerve.

"I do not know what you are speaking of. I never double-crossed anyone."

"Oh, Brodlyne. We all know, you double-crossed both Xaiverly and Bravaile. You broke the oath, and your life is now forfeited. I would not like to be in your shoes. Chances are you only have a matter of minutes to live. So the question is why did you do it?"

"You lie. Bravaile is not going to end my life; I mean far too much to him alive."

"Is that what you think? I know he is tracking you down as we speak. You are living on borrowed time."

"No. Never. I am carrying the next Prince of Darkness. He will never destroy the mother of his grandchild."

Now it is my turn to gasp. No. No. No. Brodlyne could not be. Just plain, no. She is lying to save her own neck. As my hand releases the door hand, I move it, protectively covering my belly.

Only one way for me to know the truth, I will have to confront the bitch and sense her body. Damn. Not what I had planned. Hang on, if Brodlyne is only just pregnant now. Either she is using old semen from before Branx, and I Joined together to become mated *soul mates*, or she is carrying someone else's child?

I wonder, if the Old Testament is true when two *soul mates* find one another and they complete the *Mating Ceremony*, they are no longer able to conceive with any other soul.

"What's wrong, Alex? You are not the only one who is pregnant," the Bitch says in her arrogant tone.

"Brodlyne, you do realise, Branx is unable to impregnate another female, he can only conceive with his *soul mate*. So the question is, whose child are you carrying?"

"No. You lie. I carry the next Prince of Darkness, and in minutes, you and that brat you are carrying will no longer matter."

Geez, is Brodlyne feeling cocky, either she had managed to use the old kept sperm of Branx, from before we met or someone else has been used to impregnate her? Whichever way it goes, Brodlyne is unaware her snipers have been taken out.

"Why do you say that? Are you going to have one of the snipers shoot me?"

"Why, yes. Yes, I am. I do not need you to ruin my plans."

"Um, Brodlyne, did you only have four snipers trained on me or have you got someone else hiding somewhere?"

"How do you know, there is four?"

Well, that is one question, Brodlyne

unknowing answered for me, now to see if she answer anything else.

"Just wanted to make sure, all four of them had been taken care of. I do not like to be unprepared."

"What do you mean all four of them have been taken care of. I can still see the snipers on the monitors."

Thank goodness, Riley's men had replaced Brodlyne's video feed with a continuous loop of her snipers.

'We have the vehicle surrounded. Moving in, now,' Riley murmurs.

'Roger that,' I mentally say with a straight face.

Knowing Brodlyne is watching everything I am doing. I start to turn, taking a step towards the other exit.

"Look, Brodlyne. They are your men," I start to say when something within me, warns me to stop and duck for cover.

Without further ado, I duck down low behind one of the building pillars. Instantly searching and scanning around me for danger, my senses on high alert doing the same. It only takes a matter of seconds to hear something hit the pillar and ground, where I had been standing just mere seconds before.

Oh, shit. There is another sniper, here. Scanning high and low, I need to find the person who is shooting at me. Not sensing any humans or Entities near my vicinity, I shake my head in question. Who had been shooting at me?

Maybe I am missing something, how else would one shoot? Hmm. Backtracking my steps, I must have missed something, I had not been expecting, but should have noticed, as I continue to search until I find it. Finding what I have annoyingly missed. With a roll of my eyes, I cannot believe it...

Oh, you have to be kidding me, surely not...why do I now have the feeling I have been led to a trap, and most likely triggered it when I turned... Looking down low and along the ground, my eyes barely make out a faint line along the ground. With my magic, I reach out to access it, and sure enough, I soon find it is part of a trip wire.

Alex, you idiot. How did you fall for a trip wire? Internally berating myself at my stupidity, my senses and eyes continue to scan the area for any more little trip wires and traps.

Sure enough, I discovered three more trip wires and four other type of traps hidden around the car park. Geez, if I had ventured too far towards one of the cars to my right, I would have fallen to pieces literally.

"Brodlyne do not get too cocky. I just found another one of your trip wires. A bit stupid really."

With her annoying bitch tone filling the silence over the phone line, "Ha. Why do you say that? Especially when you had just activated one of them."

"Why? Why you stupid woman," my annoyance building. If we are to remain hidden within the human realm, the stupidity Brodlyne is portraying is bound to attract humans here any minute. "Any human can come in here at any moment and activate the rest. You want the human authorities breathing down our backs."

"I do not see what the problem is. Fewer humans in this world are not going to bother anyone."

"A few. Are you mad, Brodlyne? You will be lucky if the human authorities are not on their way here right now."

"Alex. Move towards the exit. It is time we meet face to face. You are going to die. I am not sure who will be pulling the trigger though. I can still see my snipers waiting for my command. Now move it. We do not have all night."

"You are full of shit, Brodlyne."

Waiting for her to answer me with some snide remark, instead, I can hear her shouting and guns firing through the phone.

Uh-oh.

I take off at a fast pace. Keeping low and making sure not to set off any other traps or trip wires. I race towards Riley and his men. I have to know if what Brodlyne said is true. I need to know if she really is pregnant or not.

The sad truth is, if she is pregnant, there is a slim chance the babe she might be carrying may belong to my husband.

Using my powers, I protect myself from two traps and magically disarm the rest as I race towards the car parking level Brodlyne should be on.

'Riley, what is happening?'

'Princess Alex. We have Brodlyne in our custody; two of her goons are dead—'

Panic fills me, as I cut Riley off, *'Riley,*

Brodlyne is a shifter. Do not be fooled by her pliant behaviour. Chances are, she will try to rip out your throats.'

Next thing I hear coming from the commotion from the other end of the car park, is growling, and men are screaming in agony, guns firing and then silence.

Oh, no. No, no, no.

I bet Brodlyne just changed forms, turning herself into her animal half, attacking the men.

'Riley, are you safe? Have you been hurt?'

I wait for a reply... Nothing

'Riley, answer me damn it.'

The little hairs on the back of my neck start to rise.

This situation is not good. With this level of the parking area nearly dark, I soon find myself facing difficulties distinguishing between the shadows, which is not like me, not like me at all. Forcing my feet forward, I push my magic out around me. Making sure to concentrate and not allow the unknown and fear to overrule me.

Bloody hell. I do not know if it is Brodlyne or I am just, hearing things. However, every little noise seems to boom out, filling my ears and making me feel anxious, causing me to lose focus. Shit.

Come on Alex, don't be stupid. I tell myself. You are better than this. You are powerful. You are strong. You are your mother's daughter. You are pregnant.

What the hell, am I doing here, placing my precious unborn baby girl and myself in danger like this. Stupid move, Alex. I should be back at the hospital with my husband. But, no. I feel I am the one to sort everything out. Why do I do these things to myself?

Alrighty. With my heart racing, my ears pick up the small tell-tale signs a shifter is slowly moving towards me. Shit... I know I am freaking myself out because I can hear something dangerous slowly stalking me. A shifter, by the smell of things, including the taint of blood in the air, Brodlyne has killed some of Riley's men.

Oh, no. I hope Riley is still alive. Otherwise, my mother is going to kick my arse for this.

A fast-moving shadow catches my eye. I have two choices; One: I can run, allowing Brodlyne to win and kill me or Two: I can pull my big girl panties up and fight this war and succeed.

Okay. Without much thought to my plan, I decide to stay and fight. I have come this far. I might as well finish this and finish whatever Brodlyne has planned, only for me to still be alive at the end.

'Riley, can you hear me?' I ask through the mind link.

I need to know what I am up against. Feeling a faint familiar presence at my mind shields; relief hits me — *Riley.*

'Princess Alex. I am still alive. But I am hurt. I can see, five of my other men are down, three of them are dead. Another two are close to it. I have requested medical back up; they should be here soon.'

'Oh, geez, Riley. You make sure to stay alive, or Mum will never forgive me.'

'Princess Alex. It has been a pleasure knowing

you. I do not know, how much time I have left. I can feel my life slowly dying. Watch out for her claws; I think they are tipped with poison.'

'Oh, shit, Riley. Please do not die on me. I will be there to help you shortly. But first, I have to deal with Brodlyne. Any advice?'

With a groan, Riley replies, *'Yes, don't get yourself killed.'*

'Roger that.'

Focusing on my magic, I feel the rush of power travel through my system. Feeling my fingers tingle, knowing if I glance down, I am going to see the tips of my hands glow and spark.

Remembering the last spell, I performed with Aunt Lucy only hours ago; I hope it is strong enough to work. Enhancing my charmed necklace and increasing its protection, I am going to need all the assistance I can get.

Let the games begin!

Yelling out, I say, "Brodlyne, where did you go? There is something in here attacking everyone."

Okay, let's see if the *She-Bitch from Helz* is capable of understanding English.

I continue to scan everything with my senses on high alert. I start to feel the creature slowly creeping towards me. I know precisely where Brodlyne is, now. Preparing myself for the attack I know is coming. The stench of her foul breath makes it to my nostrils. Oh, goddess. I think it is time for Brodlyne to use a bottle of mouthwash.

"Aww shit, Brodlyne, is that your breath, floating towards me?" I say out loud, "Geez, woman you need to brush your teeth, ever heard of mouthwash?"

With my belly starting to roll from the foul odour and the acid is starting to rise up my throat. My hand covers my mouth and nose, instantly. Oh, goddess. I think I am going to be sick. No wonder, she was able to disable the Security Personnel, with breath like that, they most likely passed out.

Chapter Forty-Seven

ALEX

WITH MY HEART RACING AND MY ADRENALIN, pumping, if I don't get my arse jumping right now, the *She-Bitch from Helz* is going to pounce on me. I move quickly and as silent as my body will allow, especially squeezing between parked cars and concrete pillars. I glance around me, only to see shadows.

Crap this is not good. The She-bitch is close, I can sense her, the annoying part is my eyes are not able to spot her anywhere, but I do know she is near because my nose can smell her foul breath.

Just as I start to take a step forward, out of the corner of my eye, barely distinguishing the dark mass of shadow leaping out, aiming straight at me. Just in time I manage to duck and weave away from the large foul mass. Putrid wind whips by me including the horrid sound of her teeth snapping near my ear.

Holy crap. The She-bitch is bigger than I had anticipated. Wow, she is a large, butt ugly Bitch. Brodlyne resembles one of those dogs from hell, you see in the cartoons and movies. Big, ugly with reddish coloured eyes, hairless body and putrid, foul breath. I don't know what variety of shifter she is meant to be?

Whatever she is, it is not wolf or dog, she has several little tuffs of fur, over her body but nothing to cover her whole body just like a wolf or dog. She is something else, altogether. How in the world did she manage to fool an entire wolf pack? How did they not know, she is not a wolf?

With my magic at full force, I spin around, raising one hand creating a shield protecting my body, while the other I feel the power fly from the tips of my fingers. With a streak of a bright blue haze of light, I hit Brodlyne directly on her doggy creature chest, sending her sprawling backwards.

Hearing a yelp and the smell of burnt fur and flesh assaults the air, Brodlyne hits the ground hard with a thud. Taking the opportunity, I check behind me. I am not allowing the creature the chance to kill me for tripping over something.

Oh shit, leaving my back towards the creature, it soon becomes apparent how stupid a move that had been, especially removing my eyes from Brodlyne. I am dealing with a beast, not a human, and that creature is not dead.

One of my lessons comes to mind — 'Never remove your eyes from the danger' — my mother would repeat in my training. *Sorry, Mum*, I should have been listening to you more in my lessons.

Hearing a low, angry growl, from behind me my brain soon registers Brodlyne is getting back up. Oh shit. Shit. Bugger, I think I'm in trouble. What I had hit her with, should have killed her and yet, it had only stunned the creature. Oh, no this is not good. As best I as can, I try not to allow the panic to set in. My breathing and heart rate increases with each step I take. I know I need to place more distance between us, especially her potent foul breath.

Quickly moving away, I glance around for somewhere to go. A higher position is what I require. I have to move to higher ground, or I will be in trouble. Well more trouble than I already am.

With a plan forming I have to make sure to move the pair of us away from where the Darshia guards lay. Once the medical personnel arrive they will require unobstructed access to the injured — I need to keep these Darshia residents safe. If what Riley mentioned is true regarding her claws, anyone can die from a scratch from her poisonous claws, even *Dark Ones*.

The sound of clawed feet tapping against concrete lets me know, Brodlyne is on the move. Bugger. I think I am out of time. Now, what am I going to do? Keep walking and moving to the other end of the building...?

Re-evaluating the situation, at least I know, I have the creature away from the others, clearing the way for the medics. Well, I hope I have cleared the area enough. Making sure to keep several parked cars between us. It looks like I am back at the start of the car park entrance where I came rushing in.

Reaching out with my senses, I do not want to be continually looking over my shoulder, looking at the creature and find myself triggering another trap.

Speaking of traps, somehow my foot

barely misses triggering another one off. Carefully avoiding the trip wire with both my feet, and quickly move away from it. My eyes continually searching the ground focusing on the trip wire and what it is attached to? Not seeing anything and knowing it is dangerous is two different things.

Barely ten metres away from the trip wire, when I hear the tell-tale sound of the tripwire being triggered. Shit. Brodlyne set off her own trap.

With my heart racing against my ribs and my eyes scanning for danger, I barely had time to protect my body from the first explosion and a quick spray of bullets. Shit. Does Brodlyne have a death wish, or does she know, I am still close enough to be hurt? With all the commotion going on, the area is lit up exposing my position. Damn it.

With a magical shield protecting my body, I start to move, away from my hiding position when I sense something fast approaching from behind. Oh, shit no.

Rolling to my left, hitting the concrete hard with my body, with my gun in one hand, I manoeuvre enough to use a parked car as a shield. Instantly pointing the gun in the creature's direction, I start firing. I know for a fact, the bullets are hitting their target. I can hear them hitting flesh. Hearing the grunts of the creature with each shot hitting their target. Tearing through and lodging into fleshy sinew and muscle. The only thing is, the bullets do not seem to be slowing Brodlyne down.

I barely manage to move away from another parked vehicle as Brodlyne slams her bleeding body into the side of the car with a grunt. Whoa, an SUV I had been hiding behind, narrowly slides pass my body by three feet. Now that was close. Turning to face her once more at the same time carefully walking back towards another parked car.

I raise my other hand, as I start chanting a protection spell. Oh, goddess I am going to need all the protection I can get. As soon as I finish the first spell, I start to cast the next. Feeling my magic increase with each word, I know the spell I am casting; when it hits its target, the amount of damage it is intended to cause will increase tenfold.

I continue to keep my focus and continue different techniques and spells to stop Brodlyne, once and for all. It does not help when I do not know what type of shifter

Brodlyne is, one of these potent spells has to work?

Feeling my magic flow through me, heat begins to radiate through my arm and down to my hand as a burst of light is emitted through my fingers.

A beautiful and yet powerful blue haze of light arcs in the air until it hits Brodlyne in the chest once more at the same time I shoot as many silver bullets into the creature. With her blood seeping over the concrete flooring, I continue to cause as much damage as I can until the bullets run out with an empty clicking noise.

Placing the smoking gun back in its gun holster, I continue to chant and cast as many different spells as I can muster. Damn it, trying to keep calm and focused.

What variety of shifter is she?

The number of magical spells I have cast so far, surely something should work to take Brodlyne down, I think I have just about used all the powerful shifter spells I know.

The sound of an injured pained growl grows in volume, the painful cry being emitted from the creature, turns into a high pitch agonising screech — my magic is finally taking its toll on the beast.

Far too many minutes pass by and I begin to sense my magical powers starting to dim as the sweat drips down my body. If I want to live I have to finish Brodlyne off soon, or I will be too weak to protect myself. Chanting and calling on the Goddess for assistance, I start to dig deep from within myself, gathering as much magical power as I can muster.

Just one more powerful hit of magic should finish her off — I hope. With my fingers tingling and my hands glowing hot, I send another blast of magic, a brilliant blaze of light directly at the creatures head. Hitting her square in the forehead, causing its head to snap back against the vehicle before knocking Brodlyne over, from her creature like feet.

With the ugly creature falling unconscious sideways against a damaged car, her body starts to change back to human form right in front of my eyes. Oh, my goddess. Is all my brain can comprehend, what a shocking site for one to witness.

Just as Brodlyne's naked body hits the blood-soaked covered concrete, the sound I think I will never forget is the sickening sound of her skull splitting as it hit the dirty concrete floor hard.

Not knowing to move or not and with my

glowing and sparking hands ready for another attack, my breathing rushes out of my mouth as if I have been continuously running up a steep hill and my heart is racing, painfully galloping against my ribs as my wide, astonished eyes watch Brodlyne lay there unconscious, her body barely moving.

I force myself to snap out of the shock, I can feel my body starting to go into, I try and focus on my surroundings. I send my senses out and around me, to make sure there is no one else about to attack me. With relief, the only disturbance I can feel is the medics finally arriving at the entrance to the building, still another floor away. I send my senses towards Brodlyne. I need to know if she is pregnant or not.

Concentrating on her body, I detect her heartbeat is slowing down. At least I know she is still alive. Next, I focus on her lower belly, checking for any life forms.

With a hitch in my throat, I sense a weak fluttering heartbeat. A heartbeat, which should be beating faster. Oh, no. As I watch Brodlyne sprawled on the ground, the tiny little pulse finally stops its beating, and soon followed by Brodlyne's own dead heart.

Oh, my goddess. Brodlyne had been

telling the truth. She was pregnant. I wonder if the babe had belonged to Branx or someone else. Right now, is not the time to dwell on such atrocities.

Within seconds, I hear the medics arrive, looking up I soon discover security personnel right behind them, spreading out to secure the area.

Hearing my name, I slowly turn to face the person speaking, "Princess Alex. Are you hurt?"

I acknowledge my answer with a slight shake of my head before I say, "Riley is badly injured. He had said, he thought the claws of the creature had been tipped with poison."

The medics eyes dart in all directions of the car park looking for the monster, he cautiously asks, "Creature? What creature?"

As I turn my head, I focus on Brodlyne, as I say, "Creature... Don't worry. The creature is dead."

Chapter Forty-Eight

ALEX

Ten years later.

RELAXING IN THE SHALLOW WARM WATER, IN one of my childhood favourite places. My siblings and I would call this backyard our private tropical oases — a piece of paradise without being in paradise — the beautiful swimming pool at my parents' house, and next door to my grandparent's house, situated in the human realm.

Sensing Branx, before I can hear him, my husband slowly approaches the pool deck.

"Alex ...Baby." Hearing Branx, I

automatically turn my head towards him, "Talk to me." My eyes meet his, the first thing I see is the concern in his features. I try to give him a small smile but fail. Branx knows me all too well.

Watching each step, Branx takes, I drink in the vision of my lover, friend and husband. Even after all these years my heart still races and my body aches for his sensual touch, something only he can provide.

Breaking eye contact, I go back to watching the water cascade over the waterfall as my hand gently caresses my large protruding pregnant belly. Feeling the outline of a back raising beneath my hand. One of the twins I am carrying is awake and seeking love and comfort, my cheeky, son, by the feel of the mind link we share.

My little guy, Braxton, cocooned right beside his currently sleeping twin, Annabella. My cheeky boy is my only son amongst all my children; my two other daughters are spending some quality time with their Great-Grandmother, Mary. My dad's mother and her family, back in Darshia jumped at the chance to spend some quality time with Bellia and Breanna.

My husband joins me in the water and

lifts me into his strong muscled arms, taking us into deeper water. Leaning my back against his muscled chest, I rest my head on his shoulder and close my eyes. Enjoying the loving caress of his hands, as they glide over my sensitive flesh.

It is not long, before my loving husband has my body on fire, demanding his sensual loving caress, an enticement of erotic touches only he can wield.

With my nipples hard as diamonds, my nether lips are swollen with need, and weeping ready for his touch, I turn and face my husband, manoeuvring my body enough to wrap my legs around his naked waist. Feeling his hard solid length nudge then slide against the small piece of fabric separating us. My breathing is coming faster, and I start to lean back in the water as Branx keeps my upper body above the warm water allowing me to float on the surface.

'Branx, please stop with the sensual touches, I need you inside me. I need to feel you open me up and stretch me wide. To feel you pound away at my weeping flesh...'

Before I can say another word, Branx rips

away my bikini bottoms with one hand while holding me in place with the other before stealing my breath away as he thrust forward. Hard and fast, stretching me thoroughly, my weeping flesh allowing enough give from his welcoming intrusion with erotically enhance thrusts of his hips. After all, I had demanded Branx to fill me up with his solid hard silky length, and hitting all the right places in the process.

'Hmmm. Yes,' My mind screams.

We both let out a groan of pleasure, even though I am still struggling to fill my lungs with air, I don't care, who needs to breathe? As long as Branx can make me orgasm, my breathing does not matter.

With each thrust of his talented hips, the water swirls around me, moving harder and faster, just like my very own wave pool. It is not long until I notice my bikini top floating past me. How did that happen? Just as I am about to mention it to Branx, my exposed nipple is engulfed in the heated cavern of his mouth. Feeling his teeth scrap across my tender flesh, causing erotic tingles to travel down to my overheated core.

I feel my internal muscles tighten, and I know I am not far away from the orgasm I require, the one I hunger for, the one I need.

Switching nipples, Branx soon has his mouth full of my other breast, and my diamond tipped nipple in his talented heated mouth. Sucking and pulling hard against the hardened nipple, more and more erotic tingles and sensations flood through to my lower belly straight to my weeping pulsing core.

'Harder. More. Take more. Suck harder. More.'
Are the only words capable of leaving my mind right this second.

'Ah, baby, I love how you feel wrapped around me, your legs, your pussy, so tight and just right.'

'Branx, harder my lover. I need to feel you, all of you.'

Continuing the masterful swivel of his talented hips, Branx continues to pound into my needy body with every touch an overload of erotic pleasure flows through me.

'Ah, Baby, you are so tight. I don't know, how

much longer I will be able to hold on. You are squeezing my dick — like a vice. A beautiful fucking tight vice and all mine. Ah, fffuuuucckkkk.'

With Branx swelling in size just as his release erupts with a powerful thrust and shudder, feeling him filling me with is potent hot release while he continues pumping into my swollen weeping channel, in turn, sets off my own powerful orgasm. I know I screamed, I hope it was in my head and not out loud, or we will soon have poolside visitors.

With my eyes rolling back into my head, and my own New Year's fireworks going off behind my closed eyes. My legs tighten around Branx's waist as my channel constricts and refuses to let go of Branx's softening cock.

Ah yes. Now that is what I needed. Nothing like my husband to relieve me of the stress, I have been under. Now I feel like I can sleep for a week, feeling my body relax. Thank goodness for the man I love and his love for me.

Oh, goddess. How I love this man.

Hearing my thoughts, Branx replies, *'I love you too, Baby.'*

With a tilt of his head, Branx demands, *'Now drink.'*

AS MY TONGUE GLIDES OVER MY LIPS, SEEKING any stray drops of missed blood — I relish the time at my husbands vein.

With my hunger for my husband's blood sedated and my belly full, my hands make sure my bikini is back in place, as Branx asks, *'Baby, speak to me. Why are you here? As in here in the human realm?'*

Ah, my husband knows I should not be here. For I should be back in Darshia and being the Queen does not allow me enough free time.

My hand gently sweeps across the wet naked flesh of Branx's chest. My eyes zero in on his tattoo, the matching symbol to mine, a protection ward, with extra oomph. Especially when the ink used for the small tattoo of a leaf, contains the mixed blood from my family, to protect Branx, from outsiders from ever detecting his Wolf and Vampire sides. A tattoo inked upon Branx flesh within days of Brodlyne's death, all those years ago.

'Branx, I am here with my sister…'

'Sister… Is Alley here?' Surprise laced Branx's words. He was not expecting me to catch up with Alley here in the human realm.

Sensing my sister, I open my eyes towards the area of the guesthouse. Apart from a few of our most trusted security, no one knows we are here.

Being close sisters, somehow, we both managed to conceive just about at the same time and now due to give birth on the same day. Being pregnant together has strengthened our sisterly bond, and that same bond demanded we see each other.

In our family, when you have what we call our Spidey senses, and when they demand attention — something is about to happen. You listen. Alley knew something was wrong, and from there we had to meet.

Alley must have sensed Branx's arrival and coming out to see why he is here. I don't blame her, and my husband is a sexy panty melting looking man, one look, one touch and I become a puddle of goo at his feet.

Pushing my senses up and out, I sweep them out over the property, checking the security, not taking any chances with my family's safety. It does not take me long to notice another powerful *Dark One* arriving at the front gate.

Wow. It looks like our husbands knew where to find us.

Sending a message to Alley, via our mind link, I inform her, there is someone here to see her.

With a laugh through our link, Alley replies, *'Wow Sis. Your magical wards kept me from detecting my husband. I can barely feel him at my mind shields. He has not discovered me.'*

'Alley, when I say we need some alone time, I mean it. Don't worry though; I think our husbands need to be reassured we are safe.'

'Safe. Geez, Alex. With the amount of magic floating around the place, I am surprised we are not attracting other forms of Entities.'

The only reason why we are not is that of

the magical wards I have in place around the property. To anyone else, this is just another human house in the suburbs.

'Is it safe to come out to the pool, or is your husband expecting sex?'

With a laugh I say, *'Ha, my husband would always expect sex. What man wouldn't?'*

Sensing my sister sigh, I am sorry she has to go through this charade; her heart break of what might be the truth regarding her husband, Philip.

I check the property once again for any other beings and Entities my mind quickly evaluates Philip. Instantly not liking what I just found and the real reason why Alley and I are here together.

Feeling Philip progress closer, I send him a message. Being a powerful Queen has its benefits.

'Welcome, Philip. Are you looking for your wife?'

'Hello, Alex. You know, me being a King and all, you should not be able to penetrate my mind like this. And yes I am looking for my beautiful wife.'

'Oh, Philip. You knew you married into a powerful family. Plus I am my mother's daughter with powerful magic. Never underestimate me.'

'Alex. I never underestimate you. Just like your talented and beautiful sister. Now speaking of which, is Alley here?'

'Geez, Philip, Your wife comes and spends some quality time with her sister, are you saying she is not allowed to do such a thing?'

'Oh, no you don't, Alex. You are not going to trap me in one of those little sentences. If my wife is going to spend time with her sister, she needs to inform me, so I can make sure she is well protected. After all, she is carrying my son.'

With a sigh, I mentally shake my head to my brother-in-law's words. *'Philip, your wife is carrying your son and daughter.'*

'No. I think you are mistaken, Alex. Alley is having only one, not twins.'

'Really, Philip. Are you that daft?'

'Watch it, Alex. You might be the Queen of

Darshia—'

Cutting Philip him off before, he can complete his sentence, '*Watch it, Philip. Do you forget with whom you are speaking?'*

With my mind, I instantly freeze Philip where he stands, before he has a chance to speak. With only his mind he can listen, and that is all. Yes, I had learnt a few other tricks when I became the new Queen of Darshia. As soon as Alley spoke with me before, I allowed her into my head, so she was able to listen in on the conversation with her husband. She knew I would confront him.

The silly man has been spending more time away from his Queen. I, well, we need to know if he has been remaining faithful to Alley. It is well known in his family; the Kings take on courtesans, many different courtesans.

'Now, Philip. I would like to know, the truth. Why have you been spending so much time away from your wife? Also, you stupid man, you better have the right answer, because if you have been cheating on my sister, you're a dead man and no one will ever find your body. Do you understand me, Philip?'

Allowing his mind to answer me, '*Bloody hell, Alex. Is this the reason why I am here? Are you going to read my mind now? And tell your sister what I have done?*'

'*Philip, I do not have to tell her anything, for she is looking into your mind right now, as we speak. Also, by the feels of it, my sister is not a happy camper. I think it is time I had a look too, shall I?*'

Freezing Philip completely, making sure he does not have time to protect any of his thoughts or memories I plunge deep into his mind, looking and searching through all his memories and thoughts.

Oh, my fucking goddess. The scumbag has a mistress, which is who he has been with for the last week. Taking a deep breath in to calm me, I know better than to believe everything I see at face value. Knowing to always check deeper into one's mind, because I know memories can be altered. I continue searching until I came across when Philip met with this so-called Mistress.

You see, I know Philip and my sister are *soul mates*. Thus this mistress stuff has to be fabricated. Since their wedding and *Joining*

Ceremony, Philip can only drink from Alley and her from him. Lucky for Alley, she has secretly had Philip's blood bagged and kept safe. Even Philip did not know; she had been taking and storing his blood over three months ago without his knowledge. Let's just say it helps when you have friends in high places with strong magic.

When our mother found out from one of her associates, Philip had been meeting this woman regularly, and the rumours started he has a courtesan. Thus, mother had Philip followed secretly of course, and here we are. Because in our world, nothing is what it seems.

'Alley, have you seen this? That woman, whatever her name is…'

'How about we just call her Bitch-Face.'

'Yes, that sounds like a good name for now.'

'Yes, I thought so.'

'Well, Alley, I can tell straight away, Philip memories have been altered. Did you notice the differences, from the old memories with you and

your daughter to the ones of the last few months?'

Yes, I was hoping that is the case. Thank you, for clarifying it. So how do I tell what is real and what is fake?

'*When I work it out, I'll let you know.'*

Feeling and sensing Alley stay in Philip's mind for another few more minutes until she left, I continued my search. I was able to tell the difference sadly. Somehow, Philip has managed to have sex with Bitch-Face. Bad move for him — A very bad and deadly move for him.

Unfreezing Philip's mind enough to allow him to talk, I ask, '*How long have you known your mistress, Philip?'*

'*Why should I tell you?'*

Losing my patience, I demand, '*Look fuck knuckle. I know your thoughts and memories have been altered. All your memories well most of them with this woman are fake. So tell me, how long have you known her and why?'*

'Look, Alex, is Alley still looking in my mind?'

'No. Alley left. She had enough of the visions of you having sex with some slut.'

'Do not call her that.'

'Oh, Philip. Your memories are fake. This woman is fake and your—'

'Stop it, Alex, and let me go,' Philip mentally screams.

'Yeah. I don't think so, Philip.' My brother-in-law is stupid, and under the influence more than he or anyone has realised. 'Philip. Listen to yourself. Do you know your mind has been placed in jeopardy?'

Hearing a frustrated growl first, Philip says, 'My mind has never been touched by anyone, apart from you and my wife. So you tell me, what have you done to my mind?'

'Philip, this woman, whoever she really is, has tampered with your mind. Your life and the life of your wife and children are in danger. Your Kingdom is in danger.'

'*You are lying, Alex.*'

With a shake of my head, the stupidity coming from Philip is making me angry and disappointed. I am relieved Alley is not witnessing this conversation. It would break her heart.

'*You are an idiot, Philip. How can you not know, your pregnant wife is carrying twins. Your twins.*'

'*Alley is not carrying twins. I would know.*'

'*Oh yes, you would know. That slut has tampered with your mind Philip. You see, dickwod; you had been at the ultrasound. You had seen the twins. You even named your son. Your first born son to be and agreed with Alley on the name for your new daughter.*'

'*No, that is not right. I would remember that.*'

'*No, Philip. Whoever this strange woman is, she has altered your mind. Do you even remember the name you gave to your son?*'

'*No. I thought Alley came up with the name.*'

'Geez, Philip. Please go to the back of the house and wait for us there. I will continue to protect my sister. As right now, I do not trust you and when my husband learns of what you have done, he will beat the crap out of you. Do you understand me, Philip?'

With a side of smugness to his weariness, Philip replies, *'What, you would allow Branx, to touch a man who is being held against his will.'*

'Yep. You got it. However, then, I might allow Alley near you, and she will rip your dick off. You are a lying cock-sucking bastard. You fucked with the wrong family. How dare you show up here, looking for your wife, when you just came from your mistress's bed.'

'What. No, I have not.'

How am I remaining civil to this person, feeling disgusted, should I even bother with this man? My poor sister, seeing all those images of her husband, Alley must be so devastated, right now. I hope she remembers when I mentioned to her, the images we have been witnessing in Philip's mind are fabricated, I hope, Alley believes me.

'Yes, you have Philip. I was just in your head. Alley and I both saw your memories.'

'No. No that is not right. I was in my Kingdom, in the office. I had been busy with correspondence.'

'Philip that is a fabricated memory, you idiot. Your subconscious still holds your real memory. You had been fucking your slut. Plus, dickwod, you still have her fluids on your body — you filthy lowlife.'

'No. I have been in my office all morning.'

'Philip, you have been in the human realm since Monday. Today is Saturday afternoon.'

'No. That is wrong. Today is Sunday. You are playing with my mind.'

Shaking my head, at Philip's mislaid words. What does my sister see in this man?

Reaching out to my security, I request for them to go and escort Philip to the guest house. Once they have him, I cast a spell, and instantly Philip collapsed unconscious in the arms of my men.

Chapter Forty-Nine

ALEX

ALLOWING BRANX INTO MY MIND, HE SOON discovers the real reason why I am here with my sister. Listening to him speak, I wonder if I have done the right thing. "I am going to kill him — what a dickhead. He arrives at our family home, with the fluid from another woman on his body. Really..."

Shaking my head a little, I have to agree. However, something is not right. Sending another message to my security, requesting for Doctor Brean to arrive and perform several tests, on Philip.

Once my Security Personnel has taken Philip into the guesthouse, they will carefully strip him of all his clothing. First, we will require blood work and other tests performed on his body, and also I want his clothing kept for evidence and his phone checked by the IT department. I need to know where Philip has been all this time. Then the guys can hose him down, like the filthy dog he is.

'Queen Alex, we have confirmation. The woman who has been seen with King Philip is near the vicinity. I repeat. The woman is near our vicinity.'

I WONDERED HOW LONG THE BITCH-FACE would take to make an appearance here.

'How long do we have until the Bitch-Face is here, Riley?'

'An ETA of fifteen minutes if she keeps changing vehicles, maybe a little longer.'

'What…'

'Sorry, Queen Alex. The Bitch-Face has been changing vehicles and clothing. Thinking she has lost the people following her.'

'Glad to know, I can count on you, Riley. Now have security remained glued to her and increase the safety around the two properties. You know the drill. Make it look like we have no one here, protecting us.'

'Roger that, my Queen.'

Warning Alley, of our unexpected visitor, I make sure to keep Philip unconscious and enclosed in the secret room hidden in the guesthouse. Who knows what this woman and her people have done to Philip, for all we know, he might be mentally programmed to kill everyone here.

Once I know, my sister is laying down on one of the spare beds in an adjoining room to the one Philip is in. I increase my magic allowing Alley's body to relax as I clear her mind of all the turmoil of the day's events, sending Alley off into a well-deserved peaceful sleep. Somehow, I feel more comfortable knowing Alley is safe sleeping in a room beside Philip and away from the danger on its way.

With my mind, I recheck all my magical wards and increasing them where needed. Thankfully, Aunt Lucy taught me, to always have a trip wire placed in my security magic ward. If something crosses the boundary of one, I am instantly alerted. This little gem of knowledge has come in handy over the years — especially one for my own bedroom with the kids trying to sneak in and wanting to crawl into my bed, when Branx and I might be a bit busy and prefer privacy.

I have also included this magical ward to Darshia. It was a real revelation to find out, who was coming and going and the different portals created and used. At least now, Darshia is safe, and the residents of Darshia are well protected from outside threats and a few from within.

Moving back to my kitchen, I carefully waddle around the kitchen island bench to make a cup of tea. It seems I am going to be receiving visitors I might as well put the kettle on to boil. Shaking my head at my own joke, no way in hell would I allow this woman into my family house.

Sensing my old family doctor at the outside doorway, he would only be here, if he has an update for me. Just as he is about to knock, I yell out, "Come in, Doctor Brean."

With a quick turn of the door hand, the doctor soon enters the house.

"My Queen, I have some news for you. News, I think you will find interesting."

"Okay. Doctor Brean. What news do you have?"

"The young King has indeed been drugged. The tests, I was able to perform, the King has had his mind tampered with. From what I can gather, whoever performed the mind sweep, have also damaged his mind. There are parts of his memory he will never have back. Some of his body functions which rely on the brain have also been severely damaged."

"What are you getting at, Doctor Brean? How badly damaged is Philip?"

"Hmm. If you did not have Philip brought in for treatment, I would say, he would have become a living vegetable within two weeks. A walking and functioning *Dark One* puppet for someone to control."

Oh, my goddess no. Just, no.

Shock and disbelief, just a couple of the emotions surging through me. How can this be? Feeling the tips of my fingers heating up, I slowly take a breath in to calm down.

Giving my head a shake and releasing my breath, as I turn and face Doctor Brean. "Is there anyway, he can be repaired from the damage already caused?"

With a frown, Doctor Brean answers, "That is the main question; I would like to have an answer for. At the moment, only time will tell."

Shit. Now what I am going to tell, Alley? "Um, Doctor Brean, does my sister know of your findings?"

"No. Not yet. The last time I had seen Queen Alley, she was fast asleep and required the rest."

"Okay, that is wise; she has not been sleeping lately. Doctor Brean, what about Philip's blood, is it safe for Alley and the twins to consume?"

"At the moment, no. It is highly toxic. Maybe in another hour or so, I will have a better idea if King Philip's blood will be safe, as I have him attached to a blood cleaning machine. It is removing all the impurities from his blood. I will have to perform a few more tests, to make sure his blood is safe before I can be confident for her to consume any of it."

Shit, this is not good. What have these people done? How in the world did they corrupt Philip? Thank goodness, Alley had bagged Philip's blood all those weeks ago. The chances of Alley and the twins she is carrying might be dead by now if Alley had continued to consume Philip's blood straight from the vein.

"Thank you, Doctor Brean. We are about to receive some visitors. I think it might be in your best interest, to stay hidden with Philip."

"Yes, my Queen. I will do what I must, and your sister will be safe with us."

"For now, leave Alley to sleep in the room next door to Philip's, in the guesthouse."

"Yes. Queen Alex."

"Okay, take a couple of security with you. I want you to be well protected."

"Yes, my Queen."

With my cup of tea in hand, I make my way to the outdoor setting, just outside on our back entertainment area. In a shady spot, I sit down slowly and make myself comfortable. Well, as comfortable as anyone can be, pregnant with twins.

Sensing my husband, he appears from the doorway and joins me, sitting down in a seat beside me.

"Alex, what is going on?"

Taking another mouthful of tea, I casually

swallow it as my senses check the parameter once more.

Finding it is clear I look back towards Branx. "We are about to receive some visitors. Philip's little friend is due any minute now."

"Hmm. Okay. So are you safe out here?" Branx says as he casually looks around us.

"As safe as anyone. Plus I do not want that woman in our family home, tainting it with her presence."

"Okay. Okay, I will agree. But Baby, you are out in the open here. It is not safe."

My senses reach out, searching, around the property and just outside the boundaries. Sure enough, towards the front and rear of our property, I come across ten different individuals. Notifying Riley via our mind link, I keep a visual on these uninvited people until all six of them at the rear of the property have been apprehended. With the assistance of my magical wards and my magic, the six individuals instantly become unconscious.

With my people moving, these apprehended individuals into a unique vehicle, to prevent them from notifying, hurting or injuring anyone else. As for the four who casually approach the front of my family home, I warn Riley to have extra guards on standby.

It is not long until the four uninvited guests arrive at my front gate. With the first safety security wards triggered, glad to see, my safeguards are working. Followed by the second ward. With Riley and his men on high alert, they also feel and sense the wards being triggered. Hearing the front gate buzz, indicating someone is here.

Riley appeared from the side of my house. I think he needed to have a visual on me.

"Riley, do you know who is here?"

"The woman we have been following is not part of the group at the front gate."

Hmm. Okay. Who is here then?

Reaching out with my mind, it soon becomes clear; these four individuals are from Philip's Kingdom.

Lifting my hand, Riley soon realises I want one of the walkie-talkies, all my guards carry.

"Riley, make sure our guard on the gate remains on this side of the magical wards, and his walkie-talkie switched on and ready to go. I want to speak with these four visiting men. Something tells me, not to enter their minds though."

A shadow passes over Riley's face. "My Queen, what is it? What do you detect?"

Looking back at Riley, I say, "Something is very wrong, Riley. Do not allow these four to enter. Stun them if you have to. For I feel, we are being tested in some way."

Riley soon passes me the walkie-talkie.

Knowing one of the security guards awaits my command. I send a mind message out to him, *'Westlain, turn the volume up on the walkie-talkie. I want to speak with these four. Whatever you do, do not touch their minds, do not allow them through the gate either. Do you understand?'*

'Yes. My Queen. I am ready. The volume is set to its highest setting.'

'Very good. Thank you, Westlain.'

With my mind, I watch everything through the eyes of Westlain, while I listen through his ears and also through the walkie-talkie.

"Hello, Gentlemen. Who are you and what do you want?"

Seeing the four individuals all dressed in

military-style haircuts and clothing, as they give one another a strange look, before the one in the front replies, "We are here to see King Philip. We are to escort him back to the Kingdom with his wife."

"Hmm. Really. On, whose order?"

"On, his of course. Our King."

"Why do you think, your King is here?"

"His tracking device, ma'am."

Still does not answer my question. Okay, next one, "Apart from this so-called tracking device, what makes you think, your King is here? And what about the Queen?"

"We know Queen Alley is visiting her sister. Queen Alley has been here since yesterday. As for our king, we have had trouble with the tracking device. The stupid thing is finally working once again."

"What is your name?"

With another strange look between the four men again, the leading man finally answers me, "Ma'am. My name is Travis. I am here with Brench, Black and Southlyn."

"Hello, boys."

"Hello, ma'am," they say at the same time.

"Gentlemen, you do realise, I am not going to allow you on my property. If and when my sister and her husband decide to leave, they will when they are good and ready and not a minute before. Do I make myself clear."

"Queen Alex, no disrespect, but we are here to escort them both back to the Kingdom."

"Gentlemen, no — my sister is sleeping, and so is her husband. They both require their rest. I would suggest for the four of you to leave and come back tomorrow. Oh and if you know anything about the six other individuals who attempted to trespass onto my property, they have been taken into custody."

The four men, all look at one another with surprise on their faces. Noticing two of them shake their heads slightly. I know they are speaking via their own mind links and by the looks of it, they do not know who the six individuals are.

"What six individuals. We do not know of any others. Who are these people you speak of?"

"If I did not know any better, I would think you do not know who they are or of the woman who is approaching my house. The same woman, Philip has been having an affair with."

Sensing a strange car approaching and with Riley's comments, I soon have confirmation; the woman in the car is the Bitch-Face.

"What..?" Travis says, "That cannot be right. My King loves his Queen. He would not do anything to jeopardise his marriage."

"Well, Travis. This woman has damaged your king. So I would be polishing up your resume if I was you. Because you four will be out of a job, allowing this woman close enough to your king."

"What woman?" Brench asks.

"Turn around, gentlemen. The car, which approaches, has this woman within it. Oh, she is most likely dangerous."

All four men instantly turn and face the approaching vehicle, their hands automatically reaching for their guns.

Chapter Fifty

BEFORE THE FOUR MEN CAN SQUEEZE THEIR triggers, their bodies lift and fly through the air, as if a massive swirling wind picked them up and blew them high off the ground. If the men were innocent, I am sorry for their families, because I think all four of those men, has just been killed in my driveway.

Shit. *Not good.* I hope Darshia is not blamed for the four men's death.

With Westlain, safely behind my protection wards, he is protected, from whatever just attacked the four men.

Riley touches my arm, reminding me he is still beside me. With our skin to skin contact, I can hear him in my head, giving the warning signal to our people.

"Baby, what is going on? What was that noise?" Turning my head enough, I look into a concerned pair of sexy, bedroom eyes.

"Branx, I need you to go and stay with my sister. Can you protect her for me, please? I have a little job to take care of."

"Alex... What in the hell just happened? You have blocked me from your mind. What are you hiding from me?"

"Honey, remember I love you. I have to keep my focus on what is happening outside my magical wards. If you keep touching me and asking me questions, my concentration will break. I cannot allow that to happen. All our lives are at risk."

Oh, fuck. Feeling and sensing the strain against my protection wards, if I do not do something fast, these invaders will break through. I need to concentrate and protect my people from this so-called bitch of a woman. We are going to need more help, I just know it.

Hearing Branx in my head, I forgot to block his thoughts from our mind link. That is something I better rectify if I am going to keep concentrating. Hearing Branx speaks out loud, "Alex, should I call my father. He might be able to give us a hand. Whatever it might be?"

With a nod I agree with Branx. I think it is time; I brought Bravaile in. Seems, I have the strangest feeling whatever is happening today, also has something to do with him.

"Yes. Call Bravaile. Tell him, he owes me and to get his arse here right now with a lot of his men. Time to suit up." Looking back towards the front of the property, I say, "Oh, tell him, Monique is here."

"Who the hell is Monique?"

"Branx, let your father inform you. I am a bit busy right now. Oh and honey. Don't forget to look after my sister."

"Baby, who is going to look after you?"

Looking back at Branx, I could say my magic. But right now, I don't think that will be a very good answer. "Branx, my men are here. They will do until your father arrives. Now hurry and place that call."

My eyes turn back towards the front of the property, concentrating on my wards. My first two protection wards have now been broached.

Oh, shit. Not good.

"Riley, have the men ready. One and Two of the protections wards are down. Prepare for the next attack."

"Yes, my Queen."

Removing my shoes and sitting back down in my seat. Feeling the soft earth under my naked feet, as my toes dig into the dirt. Knowing my whole property is my casting circle, a ward surrounding the property for me to cast spells and replenish my magic safely.

Once my mind is clear, I start chanting one of my protection wards around us, calling to the Blessed Mother for guidance and extra protection. Within seconds, I start to feel earth magic rise up through the ground and up through my feet and into my body, feeling my strength and magic increase in volume. I remain sitting, while I concentrate on what I need to do next.

I start to focus and concentrate on the four element points of North, West, East and South, calling their elements of Earth, Fire, Air, and Water. It is not long before my magical strength increases, feeling rejuvenated before I focus on the fifth element — Spirit.

With warmth surrounding me and feeling tingling all the way down to my toes, I know my powers are ready to take on the dark forces approaching my defences and pushing against my protection wards. Thanking the Blessed Mother; my body and mind are prepared to take on the next task at hand.

Oh no. Within seconds, I realise my mistake, because I had stopped focusing on who had been at the front of the property. I am a little shocked to find I now have at least twenty Entities trying to break through my wards and front gate.

With fast efficiency I manage to re-enforce the main ward around the property to prevent these creatures from trespassing and breaking through my magical barriers. Once I am satisfied, I focus back on the group, surveying them all, until start to concentrate on the woman at the centre of all the commotion.

Protecting my mind, I warn Riley, of what I am about to do.

With his words of, discouragement, I continue anyway.

Within seconds, I easily slip into the mind of the woman at the front of all the trouble. I soon discover — Ms Monique Tantalone, is a practising witch using Black Dark Magic. Who also happens to be a turned vampire. Shit.

Searching a little further, I was right to mention to Branx the message for his father. This woman is mixed up with Bravaile, as she is one of his turned vampires. Until I search her mind a little more, most of the glimpses and memories are mixed. A few I can see are true images, others I soon realise are fake memories, just fanfuckingtastic, another paranormal with false memories today.

I soon realise Monique has planted these fabricated memories in her own mind to confuse anyone who manages to breach her mind shields. *Smart woman.*

This woman is good. However, I am better. With my hand and skin touching Riley, he too soon witnesses everything I see. Just as I am about to leave her mind, Monique discovers I am in her head.

Busted.

Quickly releasing Riley, I do not want him to suffer from my neglect of heaviness within someone's mind.

Instantly I start to pretend I have just

entered her mind and I say, '*Hello Monique. What do you think you are doing here?*'

With a smug look and a tone to match, Monique replies, '*Why hello, Queen Alex. Why are you in my head?*'

Protecting my mind shields, I reply, '*You are at my home, breaking onto my property and injuring men out in the open at my front gate. How else am I going to ask what you're doing here?*'

'*You could always invite me in.*'

'*Hmm. No. No, I don't think so.* *Maybe you should not have attacked those men. Why are you here?*'

With another smug laugh, I know it is time to exit her mind before she tries to attempt to keep me prisoner in her head. Bugger, I soon remember I need to keep her talking until Bravaile can arrive.

'*Queen Alex, I am here for Philip. I know he is here. Why is he not returning my calls?*'

Wow. Straight to the point, at least I know she is not able to make contact with Philip. I start to focus back on the conversation, *'Maybe, because the guy arrived here so exhausted, he decided to take his beloved wife to bed, and that is where they seem to be.'*

From within her mind, I feel Monique stiffen. Hmmm. I now know I definitely hit a nerve.

'What. Philip is not meant to be in bed with that slut.'

You have to be kidding me; this woman is a loose cannon.

What had Bravaile been thinking to change her?

'I think you better watch what you say, especially when Philip is married to my sister.'

'Oh, that is right. I forgot about that.' She sarcastically says, *'Anyway, look, I'll be out of your hair, as soon as Philip leaves with me.'*

Hmm. This female is a real Jekyll and Hyde with the attitude and behaviour.

'Oh, I'm sorry. What part did you not understand? My brother-in-law is asleep with my sister, and they are not to be disturbed.'

'Look, Queen Alex. Philip is my lover. He will be leaving here with me. Now you can go and wake him, or I will be breaking through your protection wards to retrieve him. Now, what is it going to be?'

'Monique. Monique, who is your Vampire Master?'

Feeling Monique stiffen to my words, her pause is enough to warn me she is here on her own accord.

'What do you mean, Vampire Master? I have no Vampire Master.'

'Hmm. Is that what you want to believe? You see, you are here at my home, in the human realm, where if I am not mistaken, my father-in-law is the Master of this side of the country. Well technically, he is the Master of the whole damn country. So that would make him the Master of Masters, I do not want to give him a big head or anything of his exorbitant status.'

Finally. My senses pick up Bravaile and his people. They should be here any minute. Okay, I can start to concentrate and deal with Monique's Entities.

'What do you mean, the Master of the country? You do not mean Bravaile, do you?'

'Why, yes. Didn't you know, Bravaile is my father-in-law. You see, he does not like having misbehaving little vampires near his grandchildren. And you Monique are misbehaving near his grandchildren.'

'Grandchildren?'

With Monique's thoughts elsewhere, I send out the first wave of my power, touching each Entity, causing them to collapse where they stand. Amongst the standing, I come across... Oh, great. Monique has human slaves; it seems I will have to enlist a different wave of my magical power to disable them all.

'Oh, yes, Monique. His grandchildren stay here. You heard me, Bravaile's grandchildren stay here

on this property. Plus I am also pregnant. Thus more grandchildren. Also, my sister is one of his favourite family members because he adores her and her daughter, my niece and the babies she is carrying. You know, Philip's twin babies.'

'No. Those brats are not his. They belong to someone else.'

'What bullshit, are you trying to speak? My sister and her husband, Philip are soul mates. Philip can only impregnate his soul mate. Didn't you know that? Of course, you didn't, and that is why you have been raping him. Yes, I have seen your memories and thoughts — the plans you have for my brother-in-law. That plan of yours to use Philip to become his new Queen — will not work. There are safety measures been put in place, by his family years ago.'

'What do you mean? My plans are foolproof.'

'Goodbye, Monique.'

'What do you mean?'

Sensing Bravaile standing just behind

Monique. I say to him only, '*About time you arrived, Bravaile. I am getting sick of handling your problems.*'

With Riley's assistance, he managed to update Bravaile of our little visitor and her now unconscious friends.

With his hands, Bravaile captures Monique in a tight hold.

Making sure they can both hear me, via our minds, I say, '*Bravaile, can you sort this little vampire out, please. I would warn you; she does play nasty by using Dark Black Magic.*'

'*No. No. No, nonono.*'

Quickly blocking Monique's screaming tantrum through the mind link, I turn to face Riley and say, "Do you have the screen to the front gate handy?"

With a smile, Riley lifts the small electronic device up for the both of us to see.

We watch the events unfold on the portable screen Riley is holding, I am glad we also have the different security cameras around the properties.

Within minutes, Bravaile and his people

surround and capture all of Monique's human and Entity slaves, placing them in their vehicles. Last but not least, Monique is quickly subdued and unconscious for transport.

Chapter Fifty-One

ALEX

"Queen Alex, it is always a pleasure to see you. How are my grandbabies doing?"

Bravaile reaches forward to touch my protruding belly, only for Branx to snatch his father's hand away from my body.

"Dad, how many times do I have to tell you? Do not touch my Mate. The next time, I will not interfere, and my wife will snap your wrist."

With a big smile, Bravaile turns back to me and says, "Oh Alex, I do love my woman capable..."

Lifting my hand, and wiggling my fingers with sparks emitted from the tips. Bravaile soon finds himself dodging my sparking fingers, stepping back away from me, his smile gone and concern written across his face. I have had enough of this man, he might be my father-in-law, but I do not have to take his crap.

"Bravaile, shut up. Do not attempt, to sweet talk me. It sounds disgusting." My body shudders at Bravaile's words and actions. "I am the Queen of Darshia. Do not ever forget it. Once again, I seem to be doing your job, Bravaile. Why is that the case?"

Standing tall. Bravaile soon realises we have skipped the family chit-chat and headed straight for the business end of his Vampire Empire. With one hand sliding through his hair while the other smooths down his dress pants. I have the feeling Bravaile is unconsciously moving his hands bettering his appearance. Bravaile starts to answer.

"Queen Alex. I had no idea Monique had been in this part of the country. If I had known, I would have been here sooner."

"Bravaile, I think you better take a closer look at all the vampires under your jurisdiction. Because for someone who is meant to be all-powerful. You have failed. Your grandchildren could have been killed today, and to me that is unforgivable."

"Queen Alex, with no disrespect, how should I manage the whole country?"

Is this man for real? Is he joking or is he asking for my opinion? Whichever way it goes, he is going to get it.

"Bravaile do you have each state covered by one of your lieutenants — a Master of State?"

"Yes."

"How often do you meet with these lieutenants?"

"Hmm. Once a month maybe?"

"What... No wonder your ruling function, is failing. You'd better start to shake up your lieutenants and meet once a week at the longest. You need to be on top of your ruling country, or you will be out on your arse."

No wonder, Monique managed to organise as much as she had and with so many human slaves and Entities.

"Once a week you say. Do you suggest meeting in person or via video link?"

Watching Bravaile, I can see his brain is thinking about what I am saying.

"Both. You need to make sure, you can feel and sense your people and if they are lying to you in person. You want to continue ruling; you had better smarten up. Otherwise, you are going to find a stake in your dead heart."

"Anything else, my daughter-in-law?"

"Bravaile, don't tempt me..."

With his strong, firm arms wrapped around me, Branx brushes his lips against my neck, just below my ear, sending erotic chills through my body.

My loving husband knows how to calm me. If we were alone, I might think of a couple of ways to loosen up.

"Baby, I think it is time for my father to leave. We have to check on your sister and her husband."

Damn. Now I am annoyed with myself, forgetting my unconscious sister and her disappointing husband. My husband sure is capable of making me forget my head.

Hearing Bravaile speak, brings my attention back to the present, "What about, Alley and her husband? Did Monique hurt them?"

Looking back at Bravaile, with a nod of my head, I say, "You might say that. Philip has sustained some serious injuries because of Monique."

"Let me check on him. I feel responsible for this."

With my senses deciding to allow Bravaile to see Philip, he might know of some form of treatment.

"Okay. Bravaile, I will allow it. However, if you try to hurt him in any way, you might just be starting a war between *Dark Ones* and Vampires — remember that."

❦❦❦

"I HAVE SEEN THIS BEFORE. PHILIP'S MIND AND memory are damaged, is that correct?"

"Yes."

"I can sense there is, other damage, also. Though the damage to his brain is the most extensive."

"Yes, that is correct."

"Alex, I might be able to help Philip, but he will require my blood. A lot of my blood."

I start to frown in thought. What is Bravaile thinking, which requires a lot of blood? "What do you have in mind, Bravaile?"

"I see, Philip has had his blood cleaned, by that machine over there. If we place a line from my vein with his clean blood, mix our blood and pump the mixed blood back into his body and wait for the chemical reaction.

426

My blood might be strong enough to repair the damage."

"Might? How sure do you think, your blood will work? But wait a minute. What about the vampire side effects?"

"Alex, Philip, might gain a few vampire traits. We will not know until he is conscious. The way I see it, my blood should repair the damage. It has in the past. I am probably Philip's best shot at a full recovery."

Looking back at Branx, I ask, *'What do you think? Can we trust your father? Do you think the crazy idea of his might work?'*

'Baby, from what I have heard over the years. My father usually does not offer his blood to anyone. Philip is a lucky man. With a powerful, strong vampire as my father is, Philip will host some potent blood, until his body processes it. Philip will gain some of my father's abilities for a short time. As for the healing abilities, I do not see why it should not work.'

'Okay. Let's get this moving. I want to try to fix, Philip, before Alley wakes up.'

'Baby, didn't you place Alley in a deep sleep?'

'*Yes, I did. I started the sleep process for her. Alley's body required complete rest; I made sure she stayed asleep, through the Monique saga. Plus with Philip's blood out of action, Alley will be hungry, and it would be better for her to sleep.*'

'Oh shit. *I forgot about that part of it. Can anyone else give Alley blood while she is pregnant?*'

With a shake of my head, I reply. '*No. They are soul mates, just like us. The blood can only come from Philip. When I went in to check on Alley earlier, I came across the empty bag, the last of her bagged blood, she consumed before laying down to rest.*'

'*Okay. Let's get my father comfortable.*'

'*Branx, I'll call the doctor to come in, and he can start the procedure.*'

'*Okay, Baby. I will speak with my father until then.*'

Chapter Fifty-Two
ALEX

Forty-eight hours later.

"ALEX, THANK YOU FOR EVERYTHING. Without your assistance, I would have lost Philip to that crazy woman," an emotional Alley says.

With our arms wrapped around one another and our big bellies side by side, Alley and I manage to give one another a much needed big hug.

"Alley, what are sisters for, I am always here for you, okay. You knew there was something extremely wrong with Philip. No one would listen to you back in the Kingdom. I am just relieved we were able to help Philip and capture that crazy woman."

Not wanting to go into detail, I only filled Alley in on the brief points of what happened. Alley does not need to know; her husband had been on death's door with major brain damage. His body being used as a human puppet, while the poor guy had repeatedly been raped.

Silly Monique thinks she would be able to fall pregnant and conceive with a *Dark One* and become his Queen. Talk about living in a fantasy land of grandeur.

While Alley had taken another nap, I thought it would be wise to speak with Philip and explain what really happened to him. Over cups of tea and coffee, Philip and I sat around the kitchen table with two of Philip's trusted advisers and security personnel.

Philip had recommended for our discussions to be recorded, two copies to be kept separately for future reference, especially when the truth started to surface. The men had been shocked to learn what had been happening right under their very noses — the lack of his security and how they need to improve their technique of protecting their King.

They soon realised with a sinking heart; the Kingdom had failed to prevent and protect their king. If I had been Philip, I would be debating whom I can trust, seems they all had failed their King — especially the men sitting around my table.

The decision had been agreed upon, especially the changes for the safety protocol of the King and the Kingdom, including a significant shake-up of Philip's council. Someone on the inside had to have known what had been happening; there had to have been a cover-up.

Once the discussions were completed, Philip urged me to wipe his mind of most of the gory details. He had said it would be safer for him not to remember, thus Alley would never truly find out what had taken place with her husband — the atrocious acts performed to him over the last couple of months.

He agreed he did need to know what had been happening to him. Therefore, something like this will never again occur. He had been extremely disgusted with himself finding out; he had been having sex with another woman. All Alley knows, is the memories she had initially seen in Philip's mind were fake and entirely fabricated. Alley does not need to know the truth. Philip would never have sex, with any other woman intentionally. Not if he values his life.

The sad truth is, it is nearly history repeating itself again — the year Alley and Philip were married. With Aunty Lucy's assistance, all those years ago, we both managed to remove memories from both Alley and Philip's minds, so the pair were able to make a fresh start of their lives together.

Once again the evils of this world came close to controlling Philip and taking over the throne. Alley managed to save her husband, only to lose her newly discovered second *soul mate* in the process. With a broken heart, she made the hard decision and begged me to remove all her fond, and horrendous memories of her old lover, from her mind.

At least, Philip is now fully healed, with his health fully boosted, and his brain function and the rest of his body back to normal. The thought of Alley, also consuming the rich potent vampire blood via Philip, is a little nerve-wracking, knowing it will be passed on to her twins.

Doctor Brean had mentioned to me

regarding Philip, if the vampire blood did not work, Philip would have died within twenty-four hours. The amount of damage Philip sustained had been worse than the first set of tests indicated.

It remains a mystery how Monique managed to create her spells. These spells were causing such devastating damage to the unwilling victim — her puppet — would eventually die sooner rather than later.

As for Bravaile, arrangements have been made by a secret vampire firm to extract what information is left in Monique's mind, followed by being dusted within forty-eight hours, an execution fit for a traitor.

Bravaile had been adamant he would take on my advice, even though I had initially thought he was joking when he asked me what he should do regarding his Vampire Empire.

He will hold his first lieutenant meeting in a couple of days. All lieutenants and their next in command are required to attend. Any of the lieutenants who fail to be present at the meeting will be dismissed.

More likely they will find a stake to the heart once they have been caught. Bravaile's people do not know they are about to be tested. Especially after what Monique tried to accomplish, Bravaile realises, he has let his hold slip on his vampires throughout the country. Time for him to regain control is way past due before someone kills him and takes over his reign.

I have the feeling; Bravaile would prefer his son to take over his ruling of the Vampire Realm. No one knows what Branx is willing to do. At the moment he is still happy standing by my side while I rule Darshia. With any luck, it will only be another fifteen to twenty years before I can officially retire, from being the Queen of Darshia and by then Branx will no longer have to hide the fact he is born to a vampire and a werewolf.

Seeing Branx with his vampire side had taken some time to adjust at first, especially now he drinks my blood as much as I drink his. However, seeing Branx shift and transform to his massive black wolf is something else altogether. Nothing like waking up during the night overheating and surrounded by a massive fur rug with a pulse — talk about a protective watchdog.

Taking a step to the side of Alley, my eyes catch a glint of shine, coming from one of the newly installed security camera's, reminding me of our little, well our over six foot plus and solid muscle, younger brother, Dane. Luckily I managed to arrange for Dane to arrive last night with his security company on short notice. After everything, I wanted to make sure all our video surveillance and motion sensors, well basically all security is up to date.

I had Dane check over the security and surveillance in and around both our grandparents' home and our family home, here in the human realm and resetting all security. No way, am I going to take any risks when it comes to our family. With Dane's assistance, I managed to increase all the wards and magical protection to both properties. I would never allow anything to happen to our grandparents if I can help it.

Dane mentioned he has been working with a *Dark One* and vampire business interstate. Sounds interesting, but then, why do I have the feeling the way Dane speaks about his young female boss, I think he likes her more than is willing to admit. I have the impression, there is going to be some significant shake-up happen, and Dane is going to get caught up in the middle of it. The more I think about it, the more my mind agrees, I will have Riley check into this woman, especially if she might become more than just a client to my little brother.

Since the death of Brodlyne, and finding out the truth about Branx's birth parents; and where he really comes from. Branx had soon discovered he has more vampire in his system than he ever realised and enough shifter, to change forms.

With all the medical testing, we now know, our children will also be able to shift into a wolf, just like their father. At least, the change does not happen on full moons. I had been concerned for our children, with what I have discovered, our kids will not turn into their animal half, until well after they hit puberty. Maybe not until they are in their early twenties, just as Branx found out the hard way.

Brodlyne had drugged Branx on those occasions when he was ready to shift. Somehow, with the use of dark magic, Brodlyne managed to control Branx's animal side. With her death, it also broke the spell, which she had cast over Branx, several years beforehand.

Now, my children are part, witch, shifter, vampire and *Dark One*; all rolled into one. Time will tell just how powerful they will turn out. As for Alley and Philip's twins, they will be a full *Dark One* with dominant vampire traits. A scary mix, if you ask me, which will mark both our twins' lives in more danger because of their heritage.

"Alley, what is it. I am sensing... Is Damien okay?" With a worried look form over Alley's face, I know when she is communicating with her twin.

Oh, goddess. My poor brother, my heart breaks when I think about what he has been through these last few months. Finding out his wife had been expecting their first child, only for his wife, Eliza to lose the baby in unexplained circumstances and shortly followed by the tragic car accident, resulting in a massive fireball.

There had not been much left of her car and only a few items to distinguish a mutilated burnt body from being that of Eliza. Ever since, Damien has been beside himself with grief, with the loss of Eliza, wondering what he could have done differently to prevent her death.

"Alex, I am worried for Damien, I can feel his grief, his sadness. His heart is breaking. If we cannot break through to him soon, I fear for his life. He will not listen to me."

Reaching for and entwining our fingers together, I give Alley's hand a slight squeeze. How do I say, 'Eliza had found her *soul mate*, and the woman who was once our sister-in-law had been leaving our brother to be with her new found *soul mate*, the night of the accident.' Chances are, the child she had been carrying might not have been Damien's at all.

"Alley, if Dane is still around, I think it might be wise for our little brother to take Damien back with him. A change of scenery is what Damien needs. Not to be reminded of what he has lost."

With a nod of her head, and a silent tear making its way down her cheek, Alley whispers, "I think you are right. Damien needs to get away and enjoy different scenery. I hope Damien can fill the hole in his heart with a new adventure."

With a small smile, I reply, "Okay, I'll contact Dane. I think it is time for our little brother to show Damien exactly what he does for a living. Also, a few of Dane's female friends might be able to keep Damien company during the night."

"Alex, I think you are right and on that note, even though I do not want to know anything regarding our brothers' and their sex lives." Alley screws her face up with disgust including a body shudder, to her own comment.

We have seen enough of our brothers' and their sexual escapades to last us a lifetime. Alley will completely agree with me on that score, and we do not need to be reminded.

"But, alas, it is time to take my husband home, Alex. Now Philip is on the mend; I think there will be some shakeup regarding his people listening to his wife. If they had only listened to me in the first place, this whole situation would never have reached the point it had." Moving from foot to foot, Alley starts to turn her head away from me, "I know, you are not informing me of everything Alex, I know you are protecting both Philip and me. With the way you have been behaving and protecting your mind from me, I do not want to know what really happened to my husband do I?"

I shake my head as a lone tear, slowly makes it way down my cheek. I try to stand a little taller with everything I know, weighing heavily on my shoulders, what can I say without hurting my sister. "Alley, I have agonised over the facts. In reality, for you to know the whole truth right now, would not be healthy for you or the twins. One day, I will speak to you about it. But not today, okay. Just remember to *never, never give up*. I want you to live and be happy with a healthy pregnancy. I do not want you to go into early labour."

How do you tell your sister, this is not the first time this has happened to her husband. Only many years before, Alley had agreed to have their memories altered, it was the only way she would have been able to live with Philip. Never again will I be responsible for their memory alteration.

"Shit, Alex. Is it really that bad?"

"Yes. It is worse than you can ever imagine. One day when we are both ready, I will inform you, and we will decide what we will do about it then. But not before."

"Geez, all this Queen of Darshia stuff must be going to your head."

With a soft slap on her upper arm, I say, "Watch it, Alley. It was meant to be your job remember."

Noticing a couple of tears make their way down Alley's cheeks, I give her another big hug.

"Come here," I say as I manoeuvre my big belly beside her baby belly and feeling my twins move against Alley. "I love you, Sis. You make sure to look after yourself."

"You too. No going into labour before me. You got it," Alley mumbles near my ear.

"Ha. These four will be born, when they're ready," I say, as we slowly pull apart as we both rub our own baby bulge. "I have the feeling we are asking for trouble with this foursome. They are going to be a force to be reckoned with."

With a big smile on her face, Alley cheekily says, "Yeah, you're right about that, but — you never know, especially with us as their parents. Thank goodness for nannies…"

"Yes. After the four of us, I think, Mum and Dad, appreciated having nannies over the years. Look at how we turned out." With a smile on my face, I start to rub my rounding belly thinking back to our childhood and what we used to get up to. On second thoughts, oh, boy I think we will be in trouble, "You never know, these four might be what the Vampires, *Dark Ones* and other Entities are looking for to lead us into the future as one."

With a nod and a smile, Alley replies, "You Never Know."

Thank you so much for reading

You Never Know.

I am honoured you have selected this book.

I hope you enjoyed being submerged in the world of You Never Know - The third instalment of Sex, Lies And Family Secrets, as much as I enjoyed creating the world of Alex and Branx, along with Alley, Alexia and Drake.

Without you, my writing would have no meaning. Thank you, make sure you grab the fourth book and continue to enjoy the characters in the world of Darshia.

Make sure to grab a copy of the next book - It's You. Follow Alley and her journey with her wolf and beloved.

If you enjoyed reading this book, please consider leaving a review where you purchased it. This will help other readers make a choice to select this book.

The best way to say thank you to your favourite author, is by leaving a review. Even if it is only three little words 'I like it' - 'I enjoyed it'

Please visit me at:
http://www.mltompsett.com to sign up and receive the latest news and updates and competitions - giveaways.
I would love to connect with you on Facebook:
https://www.facebook.com/M.L.TompsettAuthor

You can also find me on
My Website I Facebook I Instagram I Twitter
I MeWe I Goodreads

Acknowledgments

To my boys, thank you for allowing me to type and create, design, and hover over my trusty laptop, including driving you all mad with the world of Alexia and Drake, Alex and Branx and all the other characters, all things in the world of romance – love you guys, don't ever forget it. Big hugs and kisses.

To my beta readers, I am sorry for your headaches and apologise for my annoyance and interrupting your lives with my constant onslaught of material to read. Stand outs - - Anthony, Michele, Alli, Kylie, Emma, Rashelle, Sally, Amy and Gwen, thank you, for your input is always welcome.

To my special people, for your appreciation of our friendship and my ability to drive you mad with my writing talk - Anthony, Sharon and Robyn, thank you. One day soon we shall meet up and enjoy a cold glass or three, of something special - Thank you.

To Reece with your assistance, I can continue to create fantastic book covers - **Thank you**. Big hugs and kisses, and to Jay also - for your valuable input and assistance.

To you, all my beautiful readers, thank you, for taking the time to pick my book up and read the pages of Alex and Branx. I hope you enjoyed the story and the drama of Alex. If you enjoyed it, won't you please take a moment to leave me a review at your favourite retailer? I look forward to your comments; make sure to keep an eye out for the next competition to win a copy of the necklace Alexia was given by Lucy, or one of the other competitions.

Make sure to look out for the next book in the series - It's You.

Once again, your little typist with a wicked imagination of fiction fantasy romance…

Note to self – *must walk more*! Look at the clock, it must be cuppa time!

— M. L. Tompsett

www.ingramcontent.com/pod-product-compliance
Lightning Source LLC
Chambersburg PA
CBHW020649110726
47901CB00001B/105